The Sedgemoor Strangler
and other stories of crime

a&b

The Sedgemoor Strangler

PETER LOVESEY

First published in Great Britain in 2002 by
Allison & Busby Limited
Bon Marche Centre
241-251 Ferndale Road
London SW9 8BJ
http://www.allisonandbusby.com

Copyright (2001 by Peter Lovesey
'The Sedgemoor Strangler' was first published in Criminal Records (Orion) 2000;
The Perfectionist' in The Strand Magazine, 2000;
'Interior, With Corpse' in Scenes of the Crime (Severn House) 2000;
'Dr Death' in Crime Through Time III (Berkley) 2000;
'The Four Wise Men' in More Holmes for the Holidays (Berkley) 1999;
'Away with the Fairies' in Malice Domestic 10 (Avon) 2001;
'Showmen' in Past Poisons (Headline) 1998;
'The Word of a Lady' in Ellery Queen's Mystery Magazine, 2000;
'Star Struck' in Death by Horoscope (Carroll & Graf) 2001;
'The Amorous Corpse' in The Mammoth Book of Locked Room Mysteries and Impossible
Crimes (Robinson) 2000;
'The Kiss of Death' in The Kiss of Death (Crippen & Landru) 2000;
'The Stalker' in this collection;
'Ape' in Mary Higgins Clark Mystery Magazine, 1998;
'The Usual Table' in The Mysterious Press Anniversary Anthology (Mysterious Press) 2001;
'The Problem of Stateroom 10' in Murder Through the Ages (Headline) 2000;
'Murdering Max' in Ellery Queen's Mystery Magazine, 2001.
The moral right of the author has been asserted.

A catalogue record for this book is available from
the British Library.
ISBN 0 7490 0523 8
Printed and bound by Creative Print & Design,
Ebbw Vale, Wales

Peter Lovesey is the author of more than 20 full-length crime novels and various short stories. He was recently awarded the Crime Writer's Association Cartier Diamond Dagger in recognition for his thirty-year career as a mystery writer. The creator of Sergeant Cribb, Peter Diamond and the Victorian sleuth Bertie, his work has been translated into 22 languages and has won him acclaim across the globe. He and his wife Jax live in Chichester.

Contents

Foreword

If there is a theme to this collection it is the idea of the perfect murder. As Jacques Futrelle, the creator of The Thinking Machine, explains in *The Problem of Stateroom 10*, crime writers deal in murders that are imperfect. Ingenious, maybe, but imperfect. The pleasure comes from setting up a mystery, or a challenge, that almost succeeds. Presumably in real life perfect murders are committed and we never hear about them.

This is not quite the same as unsolved murders, such as the Jack the Ripper crimes. The incompetence of the police ensured that Jack went unpunished, rather than any ingenuity on his part. His awe-inspiring name became a by-word and showed a touch of genius, but may have been invented by one of the scores of attention-seekers who wrote letters at the time.

So a satisfying story will intrigue the reader with a crime that aspires to perfection and almost succeeds. It may be the sort of challenge issued to The Perfectionist, or young Finch, in *The Problem of Stateroom 10*. Or it can take the form of an "impossible" event, like *The Amorous Corpse*. Or maybe a serial murderer must be unmasked before he strikes again, as in *Dr Death*, and *The Sedgemoor Strangler*.

Prepare to meet some famous and infamous figures from the world of crime. Sherlock Holmes and Dr Watson investigate *The Four Wise Men*; and, in *Showmen*, William Hare, the body-snatcher, explains what it means to get away with murder.

In almost all of the stories there are decent, law-abiding people plunged into events outside their normal experience. It is my hope that you, my reader, will want to share in the shocks and surprises. You never know when it may come in useful.

The Sedgemoor Strangler

"Listen."

"What is it?"

If there was a sound, it was not obvious. All Emma could catch was a scent, the mock orange drifting across the lane from one of the cottage gardens. On this warm June night, hidden among the withies with her dreamboat of a man, she was thinking only of romance.

"Kiss me."

"No. Listen. Can you hear a rustling sound?"

Emma was not minded to listen. She curved her hand around his neck to draw his face closer to hers.

He resisted, bracing his shoulders. "It's all around us. What is it - insects?"

With a wriggle of her hips, she let him know she wasn't lying naked on the ground to discuss the wildlife of Somerset.

"Just listen."

"There's nothing," she murmured. "It's only the wind, I expect. Come on, lover."

He was not her lover yet, and he would not relax. "Wind? There's no wind."

She hesitated. Until this minute, he had seemed so confident, so appreciative of her. She really wanted him. Their first passionate coupling would be ruined if she lost her patience.

He insisted, "There isn't a breath of wind tonight."

"Then it must be the withies growing."

"The what?"

"All around us."

This was true. On a hot day on Sedgemoor, a crop of these fine willow wands may get taller by two or three inches. After dark the process continues, more slowly, yet, in the still of the night, it is audible. The rustle he had heard was the sound of growth itself. Months back, in winter, the withies had been pruned to the stump. Now taller than a man's reach, with graceful foliage, they testified to the richness of the earth that nourished them. This mud that Emma was lying in - call it earth, silt or topsoil - was the lifegiver. All you had to do was push a willow-cutting into the ground and it would sprout roots and grow.

The crop screened the couple from the row of stone cottages across the lane. A withy bed is not the ideal place to lie down and make love, but you have to take what you can find in the flat landscape of the moor. These two had gone to some trouble to avoid being seen. His car was parked outside the village, up a track leading to a field. They had approached from around the back of the crop, away from prying eyes, regardless that the fading light would shortly bring them privacy anyway. But there: lovers are not good planners. Persevering, stepping with care to avoid the nettles, eventually they had found this space between the tall willow wands.

The secretiveness was more at his insistence than Emma's. Nobody would recognise her. She was not from withy-growing people. Her parents were middle-aged hippies who ran one of the many "alternative" shops in Glastonbury, selling trinkets and jewellery with so-called occult properties. Emma had rebelled against all that in her early teens, found work pulling pints in a pub for better money per week than her parents made in a month. She made new friends there. It was such a treat to mix with people who earned enough to take you out for a meal and buy you the occasional present.

By now she was becoming just a little impatient with her partner. "Is there a problem?" she asked, but trying to put some concern into her voice. "Haven't you done it outdoors before?"

"Keep your voice down."

"Nobody's about, and if they were, it wouldn't matter. They don't know who we are."

Reassured, or goaded into action, he turned on his side and drew her towards him, slid his hand down her back and over the rise of her hip and announced, "Your backside is covered in muck."

She giggled. He was no better at sweet-talk than she was. She squirmed closer, presenting all of her bottom for him to pass his hand over, supposedly to brush off the specks of earth. The undressing had been one-sided up to now. His own rump was still enclosed in denim and whatever he wore underneath. Still, Emma didn't mind - if it led to a result. All blokes were different. This one definitely needed coaxing.

She located his belt and unfastened it. He tensed. She freed the top button of his jeans.

This man was not much of a stud. He came prematurely, when Emma was thinking of other things. Asking herself "Is that it?" she lay in the mud and looked at the stars.

No, that was not it. Presently she felt his hands around her throat.

The tourist board calls this place the Wetlands or the Levels; to the inhabitants it was, is now and ever shall be Sedgemoor. It needs no glamorizing. It has more of legend, mystery and tragedy than anywhere else in England. If you have heard of Sedgemoor, you probably connect it with the bloody battle that was fought there in 1685, when the Duke of Monmouth's pitchfork rebellion was crushed by the King's Army. Sedgemoor as the locals speak of it ranges far more widely than the battlefield. It is the entire tract of marshland bounded by Bridgwater Bay in the west and the Mendip and Quantock Hills inland. When the Ice Age ended and the waters rose, the region became a stretch of sea, with a few tiny islands. Ultimately the sea receded, drew with it a mass of clay and left a ridge that formed a natural dyke. Sedgemoor was enclosed, a vast floodplain waterlogged each winter by rivers that overflowed. Flooding may devastate, but it also spreads deposits of fertile silt across the earth.

In times relatively modern, drainage systems were introduced, and with them cattle, cider-orchards and withy beds.

The talk in the public bar at the Jellied Eel in Bridgwater was the usual: who was laid off work and who was about to be. The modern economy had punished the people of Sedgemoor worse than most. Few of those in the pub had full-time work. Farming, the main employer, had shed thousands of workers as a result of automation, quotas and food scares. Beef, dairy products, cider, all were in decline. The demand for withies was negligible. The only viable industry was the peat, and that was not a major employer. Peat-cutting machines were job-cutting machines.

The young woman behind the bar, washing glasses, was not thinking about employment. Unemployment was Alison Harker's dream, lifelong unemployment, sunning herself on a yacht in a Mediterranean bay. She had met a man across this bar two weeks ago who was capable of turning the dream into reality. Her pale, Pre-Raphaelite looks, the oval face and the long, red hair, had appealed to him at once. She knew. Some fellows practically drooled at the first sight of her. Tony was one of these, a pushover. He had only dropped in for a quick pint after doing some business in the town, and she wouldn't normally have expected to see him again, but he returned in a couple of days, his eyes shining like chestnuts fresh from their husks. She knew she could have him whenever she wanted, if she wanted - so cool was she about the prospect until someone told her his Mercedes was outside, with the chauffeur sitting in the front listening to the cricket on the radio. Then her knees wobbled.

Their first date was a Saturday lunch at the best hotel in town. She thought about adjourning to one of the rooms upstairs for the afternoon, but she didn't want him to get the impression she was easy, so she kept him (and herself) in suspense.

The next time he offered her an evening meal at a restaurant up near the coast, in the village of Stockland Bristol. She'd heard that it was highly regarded for its cooking, a place that catered mainly for tourists and people from "up out" who could afford the prices.

Somewhere along the route they were forced to stop because the narrow lane was blocked by cars. There was an emergency in the field on their left. Rather than sitting in the car to wait, they got out to look. It was a situation familiar to anyone from the moors. A cow had stumbled into the ditch and was up to its shoulders in mud and water. A Sedgemoor ditch is more than just a furrow at the edge of a field. It is more than a stream. It is broad, deep and dangerous, kept filled in summer to act as a barrier between fields and provide drinking water for the animals.

A lad scarcely old enough to be in charge of a tractor had tied a rope around the cow's neck and was giving full throttle to this old Massey-Ferguson in the hope of hauling the beast out. The mud was doubly defeating him. The wheels were spinning and the cow was held fast. Alison saw that the poor animal was in danger of strangulation. It was making no sound, yet the distress in its eyes was obvious. The taut rope was around the throat in a knot that could only tighten as force was applied. Reacting as a farmgirl, she ran across to the kid on the tractor. She had rescued cattle from ditches herself and there was a right way to secure the rope. The boy didn't like being told this by a woman dressed as if she had never been near a farm, but it was obvious from the way she spoke that she was experienced. At her bidding the lad backed the tractor far enough to slacken the tension. She took off her shoes and tights and handed them to Tony. After hitching the skirt of her new midi dress under her knickers, she let herself some way down the side of the ditch. Up to her thighs in the murky water, she strained to loosen the rope. It took all her strength. Twice the cow sheered away, almost dragging her into the ditch. At the cost of some torn fingernails, she finally untied the knot and attached the rope properly behind the cow's horns. She scrambled up the bank and told the boy to try again, pointing out where the tyres would find a better purchase.

The tractor took up the strain and the rope tightened. With a tremendous squelching sound and much splashing the cow was plucked out of the mire and enabled to scramble up the bank, where it stood shocked, silent, dripping mud.

On the way back to the car, Tony said, "So you're not just a pretty barmaid."

Alison grinned. "Pretty muddy. I'm going to make a mess of your car."

"Blow the car. I'm more worried about your dress. Keep it hitched up until your legs dry."

"I can't go to a restaurant in this state."

"Leave it to me."

"I mean I wouldn't want to. I look disgusting like this."

"You don't." And he meant it. He might have been looking at the treasure of Troy. "But I understand how you feel. Don't worry. The people who own the restaurant live upstairs. They're sure to have a shower."

Typical of a man to dismiss the problem so lightly, as if it didn't exist. "I can't march in and ask to use their shower."

"I can. They know me."

The chauffeur produced some clean paper tissues from the glove compartment and Alison wiped off the worst of the mud. If she had known Tony better, she might have asked him to help, but this was only their second date and they had made minimal body contact on the first, so she coped while he acted the gent and stared fixedly across the fields like a birdwatcher. As it happened, this saved an awkward explanation, for when she opened one of the tissues she found a lipstick imprint, obviously made by some previous passenger. Amused, she folded the tissue again and tucked it into her handbag thinking she might tease him when she knew him better.

You can only do so much with a few paper tissues. She sat self-consciously next to Tony in the rear seat of the elegant car with her smeared legs exposed while they were driven six miles to their destination, an old stone house converted into a restaurant. Tony explained the problem and the woman owner took Alison upstairs as if a shower for the guests was the usual pre-dinner appetizer. The private bathroom was immaculate, with fluffy white towels and everything gleaming. After showering, Alison trimmed her damaged fingernails. Then she looked at her clothes. She was relieved to find that the specks of mud on her dress had already dried, and they rubbed off, leaving no mark anyone else would notice.

Sipping red wine at the candlelit table, she admitted she had been brought up on a farm and was used to dealing with cows. "My people are dairy farmers. Generations of them."

"Locally, you mean?"

She nodded. "We know the moors. Grandfather used to keep a boat tied to the back door because the winter floods were so bad years ago. They regularly got several feet of water. The fields still get flooded to get a nice, rich covering of silt, but it's under control these days."

"So why did you leave? What brought you to Bridgwater?"

"My pig-headed attitude. Women are supposed to do the same work the men do, or near enough, up to your knees in dung and silage. I wouldn't have minded, but they told me my brother Henry, who is seven years younger than I am, was going to inherit the farm and everything father owned. Blow that. I left."

Tony's face creased in concern. "Do you mean they would have left you penniless?"

She smiled. "It's not quite so melodramatic. I was expected to work for my brother when the time came. He would have given me a wage."

"But there was no question of you sharing the farm?"

"No chance." To shift the attention from her family, she asked Tony about his work. She already knew a certain

16

amount. He was the new money, a marshland millionaire, the owner of a fleet of digging machines that stacked sliced blocks of peat in tidy walls. He lived in an architect-designed villa in the Brue Valley and he had a bigger house in Gloucestershire. He was thirty-four, not bad-looking, curly-haired, dark and as tall as she would have wished.

"Here's a confession. I got my start through inheritance," he told her with a flicker of amusement, "but I didn't cut out any sisters. I don't have sisters. My Dad saw the potential of peat years ago, before the price jumped, in the days when they called it turf-cutting. He was in there before Fisons, or any of them."

The peat that was Tony's fortune is the principal asset of the moors. Where there is shallow water, there are reeds, and the reeds of five thousand years ago fell into the swamps, rotted down and were compressed. Many generations later, mankind discovered that the soggy brown fibrous stuff had a use. It was cut from the ground, stacked, dried and used mainly for fuel. Some clever entrepreneur even shipped it to Japan to be used in distilling whisky. But what transformed peat-cutting into an industry was the nineteen-sixties' boom in natural fertilizers. Millions of people living in tidy suburban homes with patches of garden at front and back wanted the peat to nourish their soil. In the new wood-and-glass garden centres all over the country it was stacked high in bright plastic sacks, and the profits were high as well. An acre of Sedgemoor that you could have bought for five pounds in 1939 was worth at least ten thousand now.

And no one had ever seen Tony with a wife.

After the meal they drove through the lanes to a village at the west end of Bridgwater Bay that smelt of the sea. A bulwark of enormous quarried stones had been heaped along the front to keep back the highest tides. They clambered up and found a place to sit among the stones and watch the sunset. It would lead to some kissing, at the least, Alison assumed. First, there were things she wanted to know. "Have you brought anyone here before?"

He shook his head. "Never been here."

"How did you know it was here, then?"

"I didn't. The lane had to lead somewhere."

They listened to the mournful, piping cry of a curlew and stared at the sunset reddening the shallow channels that lay on the vast expanse of mud. Down by the water, the tiny figure of a fisherman was manoeuvring a sledgelike structure across the mudflats, bringing in his catch of shellfish from the nets further out. Soon the tide would turn. Along this coast the Bristol Channel has a rise of nearly forty feet and the water rushes in at the rate of a galloping horse, so timing is crucial for the fishermen.

Alison picked up the conversation again. She had not forgotten the lipstick mark on the paper tissue. "Where do you take your girls, then?"

"What do you mean - 'take my girls'?"

"Women, if you like. Birds, or whatever you call us. Where do you take them after dinner in that restaurant?"

Tony turned to face her. A hurt look clouded his features. "I'm not the playboy you seem to think I am."

She asked the big question, trying to sound casual. "Married?"

"Do you think I would be here with you if I was?"

It was as good an answer as she was likely to get without spoiling the evening. She guessed there was something he didn't want to discuss at this minute, like a recent divorce, or a failed relationship. She didn't mind if he had a past, as long as it was over for good. You expected a man to have experience. She had a certain amount herself, come to that.

As if that cleared the way, he kissed her for the first time. He held her bare shoulders and traced the line of her neck. She could feel the links of his gold bracelet heavy and cool against her flesh. She pressed close and rested her head in the curve of his neck and shoulder. But they did not have sex, there in the setting sun, or later. She was not ready to suggest it, and nor, apparently, was Tony. They returned to the car and Hugh the chauffeur drove them back to Bridgwater. After being so direct with her questions Alison half-wondered if she would be invited out again, but Tony suggested another meal the next week.

Over the next days she gave sober thought to her needs, sexual and material. No amount of wishful thinking was going to transform this man into a great lover. He seemed content with kisses and cuddles so toe-curling that she was reminded of her pre-teens. So she considered the trade-off. Whoever got hitched to Tony need never work again. She pictured herself in the designer clothes she had seen in expensive magazines at the hairdresser's. With her looks and figure it would be an injustice if she never got to wear such things. She thought of the holidays advertised in the travel agent's window. She weighed the other advantages: being driven about in the car; the choice of two houses; a swimming pool; meals in posh restaurants.

I wouldn't be ashamed of him, she reflected. His looks are all right, quite dishy, in fact. He must be intelligent, to be running the business. He treats me with respect. I haven't noticed an aggressive side to him. And his work keeps him busy. Wicked thought: if I felt the urge to go out with blokes who appealed to me more, I could probably get away with it.

At the pub where she worked was a man Alison knew from experience would make a more passionate partner than Tony. She had slept with Matt Magellan more times than she cared to admit. Matt understood her needs. He was a tease and an out-and-out chauvinist, but when it came to sex he treated her right. He seemed to know instinctively the fine mix of flattery and passion that inflamed her. His touch was magic. She'd known him since childhood, which was a pity, because she could remember him at fourteen when he didn't come up to her shoulder and she'd refused to go out with him for fear of making an exhibition of herself. He had put on some inches since then, but he was still below average height. A lovely mover, though, comfortable with his physique, beautifully co-ordinated on the dance-floor, regardless of what sort of dancing it was. More than once, she had caught herself wondering if she loved him. But how can you love a slaughterman who drinks in the pub each night and has about as much ambition as the cattle he kills?

"Fill them up, Ally," he called over to her. His round.

She went to his table to collect the glasses.

"Have one thyself?" he offered.

"No thanks."

"A half, then?"

"Not even a half."

"Saving thyself?"

She reddened. "What do you mean?"

"Isn't that obvious? Who were treated to a tasty supper out Stockland Bristol way the other evening?"

One of Matt's drinking friends, John Colwell, a particular enemy of Alison's, said, "Tasty supper and tasty afters, I reckon."

Her contempt came as a hiss. She could neither confirm nor deny that kind of remark with any dignity. After filling the glasses she carried them to the table and made sure she slopped Colwell's cider when she placed it in front of him.

Matt said, apparently for the amusement of his fellow-drinkers, but not without bitterness, "She'm given up cider for champagne."

Every barmaid is used to suggestive remarks from the customers and Alison generally laughed them off. This was not like that. It was edged with malice. She said witheringly, "It isn't the cider I'm sick of."

Back behind the bar, she turned up the music to drown the crude remarks they were sure to be making about her, thinking how unjust it is that nobody remarks on the company a man keeps. Why shouldn't she go out with a stranger? What a dreary prospect only ever spending time with clodhopping yobs like that lot.

With no other customers to serve, she picked up the local paper and read once again about the murdered girl they had found at Meare Green a week ago. Only seventeen, poor soul, naked as a cuckoo, and strangled. They reckoned she must have been lying among the withies three weeks before she was found, her clothes beside her. She came from Glastonbury, fifteen miles away, so the police had worked out that she was taken there in a car. It was about the only thing they had worked out. They were still appealing for witnesses. Some hopes, Alison thought. Meare Green always looked empty of inhabitants.

The girl's name was Emma Charles and she had worked as a barmaid. From the picture, one of those brightly lit studio shots with a pale blue background obviously taken when she was still at school, she was dark-haired and pretty, with thick eyebrows, a wide, sensuous mouth and dimples. There was a lot of speculation that she may have met her killer in the pub. Glastonbury, with its legends and ley-lines, has more than its share of freaks and weirdos passing through or camping there in the summer. The girl's parents owned an "alternative" shop that went in for incense-burning and astrology, mandalas and mysticism. They were pictured in their tie-dye shirts, the father with a blond ponytail, the mother with cropped hair and a large Celtic cross hanging from her neck. But it seemed that Emma had left home and had not spoken to either of them for weeks.

It was easy to identify with her.

The report went on to state euphemistically that Emma was known to have had several close friends. Detectives were questioning a number of men believed to have associated with her.

"So when are you going out with him again?"

Startled, she looked up from the paper. Matt was by the counter. She had not noticed him, assuming that he and the others would be busy with their drinks for some time. His question was best ignored.

He said, "I want three packets of crisps, vinegar-flavoured."

Alison reached behind her and put them in front of him without a word. He dropped a couple of coins on the counter and said, "Keep the change. You never know when you might need to catch a bus home."

The next Saturday she went with Tony to see a film called Seven, about a serial killer. She'd have preferred a Woody Allen film which was showing in Glastonbury, but Tony wasn't keen. He seemed to dislike Glastonbury as much as she found Bridgwater a bore. Seven shocked her with its violent scenes, well-made as it undoubtedly was, but she didn't admit this. "I couldn't believe in the story," she said when they had their drinks later. "Murder isn't so complicated."

"What do you mean?"

"Real serial killers aren't like that. They simply repeat the same method several times over. They're not inventing wild new ways of killing people."

"I wouldn't know," said Tony.

"They're not that intelligent," she went on. "They can't be. Take the case of that girl who was found at Meare Green."

"That's not a serial murder."

"You can't say," she pointed out. "It could turn out to be."

His eyes slid downwards, staring into his drink. "All right," he conceded. "What were you going to say about the woman at Meare Green?"

"Just this. She was strangled. Manually strangled, the paper said. That means with his bare hands instead of using her tights or something, doesn't it? Now, if that bloke did a second murder, you can bet he'd do exactly the same thing, with his hands around the woman's throat. That's how the police catch these people. They call it their m.o. It's Latin, isn't it?"

"You seem to know a lot about it."

"If you're a woman, you need to know." She had a sense that he wanted to end the conversation, but something was spurring him on.

"You're saying this man, whoever he may be, isn't capable of thinking of some other way of killing the next one?"

"Yes."

"But you don't know anything about him."

"I know he's thick."

"You can't say that. He might have a degree in astro-physics."

"Intelligent men don't murder people just at random. Serial killers are thick, so they do the same thing and get caught."

"The guy in the film wasn't thick. He changed his m.o."

Alison smiled. "And still got caught. Serve him right."

It was still warm when they left the pub, so she suggested they walked back to her flat. He told Hugh to drive the Mercedes round to her street and wait there. Having a chauffeur constantly on call was not always such a useful arrangement. It was not unlike having a chaperon.

"Do you ever go anywhere without Hugh?" she asked as they strolled through the silent streets, his arm around her waist.

He laughed. "Does he cramp my style, do you mean? I give him days off sometimes."

"Then do you drive the car yourself?"

"I use taxis."

The Mercedes was waiting in her street when they reached it, on the opposite side from her flat, the lights off.

She looked up at him. "Coffee?"

"Another time."

"I have a phone, you know. You could call a taxi." As she spoke, she thought this is wrong. I shouldn't be rushing him.

He took her hand and squeezed it gently. "I appreciate the offer. I'm due back in Gloucester tonight. An early appointment tomorrow. Shall I see you next week? When's your night off? Saturday again?"

"Saturday."

They kissed. Then he walked across to the waiting car.

A man with an old-fashioned haircut with sideburns and a parting at the side came into the pub a couple of evenings later and didn't buy a drink. He went straight to Matt's table and started talking to the group. After a while he took a notebook from his pocket and wrote things down. Then he moved to another table. Matt and his friends stared after him and talked in lowered voices among themselves.

Alison was uneasy about this stranger disturbing the customers. She went across to Matt's table and asked who he was.

"Fuzz," said Matt. "Wants to know if anyone here knew that girl who was strangled. We told 'un there's no sense in coming to Bridgwater asking about a girl from Glastonbury."

"Why is he here, then?" said Alison.

"He says they've been to all the pubs in Glastonbury, including the one she worked in, and now they're extending their enquiries."

"She's never set foot in here."

"That's what we told 'un."

"He's wasting his time, then," said Alison. She returned to the bar counter and continued to watch with disfavour the detective go from table to table.

Finally, he walked across to her. His blue eyes assessed her keenly. The voice had a note of Bristol in it, that soft, unhurried way with words that can be so disarming. "Detective Sergeant Mayhew, Somerset and Avon CID. You don't mind if I ask you a couple of questions, do you, my dear?"

"What about?"

"I'm sure you know by now," he said, bringing colour to her cheeks. "I watched you go to the table under the window and ask the lads what I was up to. Fair enough. You have a job to do. I could be dealing in drugs for all you know. But I'm not, am I? What's your name, love?"

She told him, adding, "That dead girl has never been in here to my knowledge."

"Maybe her killer has, though."

Shocked by the suggestion, Alison retained enough of her composure to say, "We've no way of knowing."

"I don't expect you to know, miss. How could you?" He took a leisurely glance around the room. "But you want to be on your guard." While Alison tried to look unimpressed, the sergeant went on, "It was a barmaid who was murdered. We've questioned a number of local men she knew, and they seem to be in the clear. The chances are that he isn't a Glastonbury man. More likely he's the sort of fellow who comes into the pub once or twice and chats up the pretty girl who serves him. You've met a few of them I dare say?"

"Hundreds."

"A certain amount of charm, good looks, gift of the gab. Pushing their luck, trying for a date?"

"Some do."

"Anyone lately?"

She shook her head. Strictly speaking, Tony fitted the profile, but she excluded him. A man too timid to come in for a cup of coffee at the end of an evening was hardly likely to strangle you. "No one I can recall. What makes you think he'd come to Bridgwater?"

"He wouldn't want to show his face in Glastonbury, would he?"

"I suppose not."

"Could be Burnham he tries next, or Langport. Burnham and Langport aren't my patch. Bridgwater is, and that's why I'm here, giving you advice."

Alison said nothing. Let him give his damned advice. She didn't have to thank him for it.

He asked, "Are there any other girls employed here?"

"Two others help at the weekends. Sally and Karen. It's lads, apart from them."

"I may look in again, then, Miss Harker, but you'll do me a favour and pass on my advice, won't you?"

After he had gone, business at the bar was brisk and the level of noise rapidly returned to normal. Alison was too busy serving to give any more thought to the murdered woman until near closing time, when she went to Matt's table to collect empties.

Matt grasped her by the wrist. He had a powerful grip. "I hope you told the copper about your fancy man, him you spent last Saturday night with. Seems to me, he's got to be a suspect, going out with barmaids."

"Don't be ridiculous, Matt."

"Ridiculous, is it? I'd have said he's just the sort of bloke they're after, the kind that moves from town to town looking for a woman foolish enough to go out with him."

"Let go of my arm."

"We all know he's got wheels. With that great car of his, he could have driven the poor lass from Glastonbury out to Meare Green and strangled her. I'd say you have a duty to mention him to the police - if you haven't already."

"I bet she hasn't," said John Colwell.

"Don't you have any brains in your head?" said Alison, wrenching away her arm, which had become quite numb where Matt had gripped it. "Tony's car is driven by a chauffeur. If he wanted to murder anyone - which I'm sure he doesn't - do you think he'd have the chauffeur drive them to the spot and wait in the car while he did it? What's the chauffeur going to think when he comes out of the withy-bed without the girl? Oh, get with it."

"Happen he gives the chauffeur an evening off," said Matt.

"When he does, he uses a taxi."

"Who told you that?"

"He did."

"He would, wouldn't he?"

She rubbed her arm. It was turning red. She wouldn't be surprised to find a bruise there. "You're so puerile, you lot.

26

As a matter of fact, Matt, if I wanted to report anyone to the police, it ought to be you. See this mark coming up? If they're looking for someone violent to women, I can give them a name."

"They'd laugh at you," he told her.

"And I could tell them you have a rusty old Cortina you drive around in."

John Colwell grinned. "He does, and all."

Alison had neatly turned the fire on Matt. He could squirm, for a change. "Talk about suspects. What's to stop you from driving over to Glastonbury and picking up some unfortunate girl and killing her?"

Matt tried to laugh it off. "Little old me, the Meare Green strangler?"

"Killing's your job, isn't it?"

His friend Colwell grinned. "She's got you there. You've got to admit she's got you there, Matt."

The seed of anxiety was sown, not about Matt, whom she'd known all her life, almost, and not about Tony either. The worry was over her personal position. She could get into trouble for failing to mention Tony to the police. He fitted the profile Detective Sergeant Mayhew had given her: not a local man, but with charm, good looks and the gift of the gab, the sort who visits the pub only once or twice and gets friendly with the barmaid. She knew Tony was harmless. Well, she felt certain he was harmless, which is almost the same. A guy who passed up the chance to make love after buying her expensive meals was hardly likely to strip the clothes off her and strangle her. Unfortunately Matt or his cronies were liable to make mischief and tell the detective about Tony's visits to the pub and his evenings out with her. She knew that crowd and their so-called sense of humour. They would think it hilarious to embarrass her, forcing her to answer questions from the police about her dates with Tony. For Matt, who was jealous, it would be a kind of revenge.

Sergeant Mayhew had said he would probably be back at the weekend, to talk to the other barmaids. Alison decided it was in her interest to be on duty on Saturday after all, in case anything was said. If she handled this right, she could get to Sergeant Mayhew before Matt did. She and the other girls could monopolise him.

She spoke to the manager next day and fixed it. She would take Thursday off and come into work Saturday. Then she called Tony on his mobile and said unfortunately she couldn't go out with him on Saturday as she'd been compelled to change her shift. He was relaxed about it and good enough to suggest they met the following week.

Thursday was an opportunity of doing some detective work of her own. She had thought of a way of finding out more about Tony's recent past. In brilliant morning sunshine that brought extraordinary clarity to the scene she cycled six miles though the lanes, past fields where sheep and cattle grazed and the wild iris, kingcup and sweet gale abounded. At the edge of the lane, baby rabbits crouched and butterflies swooped up. Her destination was Stockland Bristol, the restaurant she and Tony had visited the previous Saturday.

The woman owner remembered her, of course, as the customer who had showered in her bathroom. "Did you leave something behind, my dear?"

"No. It's just ..." Alison hesitated, uncertain how to phrase this. "The gentleman I was with - Tony - Mr Pawson - he's a regular customer of yours, I gather."

"I wouldn't say regular. Occasional describes it better. We're always glad to see him, though. Is anything wrong?"

"Oh, no. Well, to tell you the truth, I've become rather attached to him."

"I'm pleased for you, my dear. He's a charming gentleman."

She fingered her the ends of her hair. "I don't know how to ask this. It's a terrible cheek. I thought, being a woman, you might understand."

"What on earth is the matter, my dear?"

Alison blinked hard, and succeeded in getting a tear to roll down her cheek. "I keep thinking about the times he came here before. Is there anyone else - I mean is there another woman - he brought here recently, say in the past six weeks?"

Eyebrows raised, the woman said, "It wouldn't be very discreet of me to say so, would it? We owe our patrons some confidentiality over such matters."

Alison's hopes plummeted.

"However," the woman went on, "since he has only ever brought gentlemen before who were obviously business-men, I can set your mind at rest without seriously breaking any confidence. Is that what you wanted to know?"

Alison sang as she pedalled home through the lanes.

Detective Sergeant Mayhew's second appearance in the Jellied Eel couldn't have been more convenient for Alison. He came in about six on Saturday evening, well before Matt usually arrived. John Colwell was already there, but he did-n't matter, because he wasn't the sort to start a conversation. He wouldn't make trouble.

Just to be certain, Alison came from behind the bar to greet the policeman and escort him across the room to meet the other barmaids. He made his pious little speech about the wis-dom of rejecting invitations from customers they didn't know.

Karen, blonde and with more brass than a cathedral, was moved to say, "Why?"

"Why what?"

"Why should we be careful? Only one girl is dead, and she was in Glastonbury."

Sergeant Mayhew shook his head slowly at Karen's naivety. "This isn't your run-of-the-mill murder. Men who kill girls they go out with can easily get a liking for it. And if they do, it's a pound to a penny they move on to another town."

"What is he - some kind of sex-maniac?"

"I can't answer that, miss."

"The Glastonbury girl was stripped and raped, wasn't she?"

He pondered the matter. "Difficult to tell. She wasn't wearing anything, it's true. But the body had been lying there some time in hot weather when it was found. Even the best pathologist can't tell much from a decomposing corpse."

Karen screwed up her face at the thought, and Sally steered the conversation back to the living end of the investigation. "I expect you've got the names of all the local weirdos and rapists. I hope they all get questioned."

"That's been done, miss. The trouble with this case is that we don't know which day the girl was murdered, so it's no use asking people like that where they were at a particular time."

"How will you find him, then?"

Karen said cuttingly, "The way they always find them. Through a tip-off."

The sergeant didn't seem put out by the comment. "Young ladies like yourselves can certainly help. Be alert. Get on the phone to us if anyone you don't know tries to ask you out."

"Will you be calling at all the pubs in Bridgwater?" Sally asked.

"That's a question I'm not at liberty to answer, miss."

Karen quickly followed up, "We've been picked out. Why?"

"I just made myself clear, miss. There's nothing I can add. Just be on your guard - here, and specially on your way home."

Alison decided this was the cue to usher him out. "Would you like a drink before you go?" She knew he was likely to refuse. To her profound relief, he looked at his watch and agreed he ought to be on his way.

"I can tell you why this pub is being targeted," said Karen after the sergeant had left, her eyes as wide as beermats.

"One of those perverts on their list has been seen drinking here. They can't arrest him without proof."

"Keep your voice down, Karen. You'll upset the customers."

"Sod the customers," said Karen. "We're the ones at risk."

For all her bluster, Karen was only a relief barmaid. When Alison told her firmly to drop the subject, she obeyed. For more than an hour, the public bar returned to normal. Then Matt came in and joined John Colwell and the rest of their crowd. When Alison next looked across, Karen was at their table in earnest conversation, undoubtedly passing on her version of what Sergeant Mayhew suspected.

Later, in a quiet moment behind the bar, Alison told Karen, "If you say one more word about that murder, I'm going to report you for upsetting the customers."

"Upsetting that lot? You must be joking."

But the damage was done. Matt came over to order another round and leered at Alison. "Police were in again, I hear, still looking for the barmaid strangler. They'm watching some pervert, that's for sure. Must be frustrating for 'em, knowing the bastard who did it and not being able to nail him. People have a public duty to report things, I say."

She busied herself with the order, trying to ignore him. In topping up the first of the five beer glasses, she spilt some.

"Losing your touch?" said Matt.

She said nothing.

"Don't suppose you told 'un about your evening out with the peat millionaire."

She stood the fifth of the glasses on the counter and said the price.

He held out a ten-pound note. "You know the old saying? 'Gold-dust blinds all eyes'."

She said through her teeth, "Get lost, Matt."

"Think about that."

"One more word, Matt, and I'll spit in your glass, I swear I will."

He grinned. "Go ahead. But I'll have my change first, if you don't mind, not being a millionaire myself."

She turned to the till and took out her anger on the keys. Then she slammed his money on the counter, avoiding his open hand, and went to the next customer.

Matt's words stayed with her. She went to bed with her thoughts too turbulent for sleep. She hated admitting it to herself, but there was some truth in what he had said. Tony's money was an attraction. Her romantic notions had focused on the life he could so easily provide for her. Persuaded that he was generous and inoffensive, tall and good-looking, she could grow to love him, she had told herself. He seemed attracted to her, else why would he have invited her out? She had these looks that turned men's heads, not always men she wanted, so she was fortunate when it happened to be someone she could kiss without flinching. More than that, she had yet to discover. But it was the high life that beckoned.

I feel safe with him, she reasoned. He's a pussy-cat to be with. If I had the slightest doubt of his conduct, I'd talk to the police. Is that a delusion? After all, when I go out with him, I'm backing my own judgement with my life.

About four in the morning, aroused from a short, disturbing dream, she needed a cigarette. She reached for her handbag and felt inside for the pack she knew was there. She didn't often smoke these days. Delving deep into the bag, she withdrew the pack and with it came a paper tissue, neatly folded, unlike the others she stuffed into the bag. Remembering where she had got this one, she switched on the light, opened out the tissue and spread it in front of her. The lipstick print looked unusually vivid, and in her heightened state she felt that those slightly-parted lips were about to say something to her. She folded it quickly and returned it to the bag.

When she woke, it was almost ten. Sunday. She was not on duty until twelve. She shuffled into her small kitchen and switched on the kettle and the radio and started performing those automatic actions that would shortly provide her with the coffee she needed to clear her brain.

The radio was tuned to the local station and the newsreader was going on about some incident in the Iron Age Village reconstruction at Westhay, near Glastonbury. Alison continued to potter about without paying much attention. He was saying, "... was found in the largest of the roundhouses by one of the staff when he came on duty this morning. The woman has not yet been identified. A press statement is expected from the police later this morning. Last month, the body of Emma Charles, aged seventeen, from Glastonbury, was found at Meare Green, some twelve miles away. No one has been arrested for the crime."

Roused from her stupor, she reached for the volume switch. Too late. They were talking about the weather. She stood by the radio clutching the front of her nightdress in frustration.

This had to be another victim. They wouldn't have mentioned the first girl unless there were similarities. Sergeant Mayhew's warnings about a possible serial killer were justified.

Alison knew the Iron Age village from being taken there as a schoolgirl. She had squatted with her classmates inside one of the reconstructed dome-shaped huts of wattle and daub, smelling the peat-fire that smouldered in the centre, not really listening to their teacher twittering on about the people who lived on the moors oodles of years ago in huts like that. The history lesson had made less impression than the cosy atmosphere in the building itself. The snug interior had appealed. She had imagined herself sleeping there contentedly under thick furs, her feet warmed by the fire. In no way could she picture it as a murder scene.

The next bulletin would be on the half-hour. She drank her coffee, showered and dressed.

Part of the main statement at the press conference was broadcast live at ten-thirty. "The Peat Moor Visitor Centre, where the victim was found, has been closed to visitors while the scene is examined by forensic experts. The dead woman, who is believed to be in her early twenties, was white, with dark, shoulder-length hair, slimly built and about five foot six in height. She was unclothed. Her clothes were found beside the body inside the reconstruction of a prehistoric Iron Age hut. She appears to have been strangled. We appeal to anyone who saw a woman of this description, in a black sleeveless dress with shoulderstraps, black stol and black shoes with silver buckles, in the area yesterday evening, either alone or in company, to get in touch with Glastonbury Police. We also wish to hear from anyone who knows of a woman of this description who did not return home last night."

No reference this time to a possible connection with Emma Charles's death. Possibly the police were more cautious than the radio station. But if strangulation was the cause of death and the victim was unclothed, the chances were high that Emma's killer had committed a second murder.

By lunchtime, when Alison came into work, still shaky with the news, the pub was buzzing and there was a rumour that a barmaid at the King's Arms in Langport was missing from home.

Another barmaid in another town. Just as Sergeant Mayhew had warned.

On the one o'clock television news the story was confirmed. An unmarried woman of twenty-two called Angie Singleton had been identified. Saturday was her day off. She was last seen leaving her parents' house at six-thirty that evening. They had assumed she was meeting two of her girlfriends at the pub where she worked and going on to a disco in Glastonbury.

"My God," said Karen to the pub in general. "I'm chucking up this job. He's done Glastonbury and Langport. He's got to come to Bridgwater next."

"Don't panic, love," one of the older men called across. "They'll catch the bloke this time. That poor lass who was found over at Meare Green had been dead three weeks. This one is fresh. They pick up all kinds of clues at the scene of a murder. By now they know exactly who they're looking for. They'll have the colour of his hair, the shoes he wears, the make of his car and the size of his John Thomas, I wouldn't be surprised."

"You watch too much television," Karen said with scorn. "Real cases aren't solved that easily. How do you think serial killers manage to do in seven or eight women without getting pulled in?"

Alison kept out of the argument. She, too, was frightened. In truth, she was also relieved that she wasn't the focus of attention she had expected to be.

But later in the day the spotlight turned on her again. A man she had never seen before came into the bar and asked for her by name. He spoke first to Karen, whose silly reaction was to give Alison a boggle-eyed look that meant this could easily be the strangler. The stranger was in his thirties, in a leather jacket, red tee-shirt and jeans. His dark eyes assessed Alison with alarming intensity. He approached, leaned over the bar, beckoned to her to come closer and said in a tone nobody else could possibly overhear. "I'm DI Briggs, Glastonbury Police. I have some questions. Would you step outside to my car for a few minutes?"

She was about to say, "How do I know?" when she realized she was looking at a police ID card masked from the rest of the room by his jacket. She asked Karen to take care of things for a few minutes.

In the car, he came quickly to the point. "This man you've been going out with. Tony Pawson. You know who I mean?"

Her skin prickled. She was in trouble now, and so was Tony.

"How did you meet him?"

"He's a customer."

"A regular?"

"I wouldn't call him a regular, no."

"Chatted you up and made a date, did he?"

"Something like that."

"When did this start?"

"About three weeks ago. We've only been out three times altogether."

"Where did he take you?"

"Twice for a meal. And once to a film." Her voice trailed off revealingly. Until this moment it had not occurred to her that Tony's choice of film was going to interest the police.

"Where?"

"The film? Here in Bridgwater."

"The meals."

She was mightily relieved to pass over the film and discuss the meals. "The first was just up the road, at the Admiral Blake. And he also took me to the Levels Restaurant at Stockland Bristol."

He asked for dates and times. She told him each outing had been on a Saturday, her day off.

"Have you slept with him?" Responding to the look he got from Alison, he added, "I wouldn't ask unless -"

"No," she cut in. "I haven't."

"When I say 'slept' -"

"You can put down 'no'. We had a few evenings out together, that's all. Ask his driver if you don't believe me."

"The driver came too?"

"He waited in the car. If anything happened, he would know. His name is Hugh, and he drives Tony everywhere."

"You're saying Pawson doesn't drive? Is he banned?"

"I've no idea. I can only tell you what he said to me. Sometimes he uses a taxi."

He was frowning. "Let's have this totally clear. On three dates with Pawson, there was no sex."

"I've said so."

"It wasn't suggested, even?"

"I don't know why you're pursuing this. I felt perfectly safe with him."

"Maybe the others did." He shook his head, chiding himself. "Disregard that. I'm thinking aloud."

She felt her skin prickle. "Those girls were raped. It said in the paper they were raped."

DI Briggs hesitated. "If I tell you something confidential, can I trust you?"

She shrugged, guessing that he wasn't doing her a favour. Why tell her anything in confidence unless it was to undermine her? "I suppose so."

"In a case like this, we don't release all the details. Some things are known only to the killer and ourselves. Then, you see, we can tell if we've got the right bloke. The signs are that there was sex in both these cases, but it wasn't forced. It was consensual. Do you follow me?"

She stared at him in disbelief. "You mean they let him make love to them?"

"And then he killed them. Were you with Tony Pawson yesterday?"

She shook her head.

"Why not? It was your day off."

"I changed my day. I took Thursday instead."

"Did you go out with him Thursday?"

"No. I expect he was at work." She didn't volunteer the fact that she had spent Thursday checking on Tony's previous visits to the restaurant at Stockland Bristol.

"Any reason why you changed your day off? Was he due to go out with you last night?"

"Those are two different questions."

"Answer the first one, then."

"I changed over because Sergeant Mayhew said he was coming back to the pub at the weekend. Some stupid rumours were being put about and I didn't want people discussing me behind my back."

"Rumours about you and Tony Pawson?"

"Yes, and there was no foundation for them. I've told you the truth about my evenings with Tony."

"But you didn't tell Sergeant Mayhew."

"He didn't know anything about them."

"So you didn't say anything? A police officer was asking about strangers coming in and chatting you up, inviting you out, and you didn't say anything?"

Her nervousness was being supplanted by annoyance. "Listen, Tony is nice to me. He treats me decently. Your sergeant was here on a *murder* inquiry. Do you seriously expect me to give you his name as a suspect?"

He started to say, "If you had ..." Then he stopped and fitted the phrase into another question. "If you hadn't been working yesterday, would you have gone out with Pawson?"

"Probably." As she realized what he was suggesting, she felt her own fingernails pressing deep into her thighs.

"These rumours. Who exactly was putting them about?"

"Some fellows in the pub."

He insisted on more than that. She was forced to admit under more questioning that she had been seriously involved with Matt at one time. Matt obviously interested him. He knew about the old Cortina he drove and his work as a slaughterer. This brought the questioning to an end, but the inspector hadn't finished with her. He wanted her to return with him to the pub and point out Matt.

After DI Briggs had finished questioning him and left, Matt behaved like the star witness meeting the press, holding forth to the entire pub about Tony, referring to him as "our barmaid's fancy man" and insisting that he would be arrested before the day was out for the murders of the two women.

That evening Alison finished work at six and walked in steady rain through the streets of Bridgwater, longing for a few quiet hours at home, free of the tensions in the pub. She was thinking she would not stay in the job much longer.

The sight of Tony's Mercedes outside the house where she lived made her say out loud, "Oh, God!" and reach for a railing for support. Her first impulse was to turn and walk away. But the car door opened and Tony actually ran towards her, opening one of those huge golf umbrellas. "You're drenched. Come under this, for pity's sake."

Controlling herself, she told him she was almost home and didn't care about getting wet, making it as plain as she could that their friendship was at an end.

With no chance of being invited in, he asked if she would step into the car for a moment because there was something he wanted to tell her.

Alison couldn't face explanations. She changed tack completely and used the excuse that she was wet through. She asked him to let go of her arm.

He said, "You believe I killed those women, don't you? I've had two long interviews with the police. Do you think I'd be at liberty now if they knew I was a murderer?"

She said truthfully, "I can't believe you killed anyone."

"You're afraid of me. I can see it in your eyes."

"Tony, all I am is tired. I've had a hard time lately. I just want to get home."

His voice rose at least an octave. "That's why I want to talk to you. I know you've been bothered by the police. I don't blame you if it turns you right off me. I want the chance to say sorry."

"Consider it done. I'm tired and wet through." She started walking away and he stepped in beside her, turning to face her, appealing to her with those soulful brown eyes.

"Tomorrow, then?"

She said, "No. It's over, whatever it amounted to. Let's leave it like that." She was at her front gate.

In an odd, troubled voice that she found chilling, he said, "Can't you understand? I'm not willing to leave it like that."

Frightened now, she ran up the path to the front door, let herself in and slammed it.

Later, she plucked up courage to look out of the window and was relieved to see that the car had gone.

The murder of Angie Singleton, the Langport barmaid, had happened on Saturday night, when Alison would have gone out with Tony if she had not changed her plans. He had been free that evening. The more she thought over what she had learned, the more uneasy she felt. These murdered women had consented to sex, so they must have fancied the man who eventually put his hands around their throats. Suppose it was Tony. Just like her, they could have been attracted by his money, allowed themselves to be driven out into the country, probably treated to a meal somewhere, and gone with him afterwards. The difficulty she had with this was in understanding what turned him from the gentle, diffident man she knew into a strangler. Did sex transform him? Was it something deep in his psyche that made him hate the women he went with? Maybe his reluctance for sex came from a recognition that he couldn't control his violence. By not insisting on a physical relationship, had she saved her own life?

That same evening, she phoned the Glastonbury Police. DI Briggs and Sergeant Mayhew were with her inside the hour. She handed them the paper tissue with the lipstick imprint and explained where it had come from.

"It's been on my conscience. If Tony really is a suspect, it's just possible that this is the mouth-print of the first girl, Emma Charles. I read in the papers that her bag was found beside her. I suppose you can check whether she had a lipstick similar to this."

DI Briggs agreed with an air of resignation that forensic science was equal to the task. "We could have done with this the first time you were questioned. This will take at least another week to check. The lab run all kinds of tests."

"It's still a long shot," Alison pointed out.

"Let us be the judges of that," he said, leaving her with the clear impression that he knew a lot more about Tony's involvement than he was willing to admit. "Meanwhile, if you value your life, have nothing to do with this man. If he pesters you, call us straight away."

Ten days went by and there was no arrest. In the Jellied Eel, Matt was increasingly critical of the police. "They know who did it. We all know who did it. So why don't the buggers pull him in? If they don't act soon, some other woman is going to get stiffed."

Colwell, quick to fuel Matt's complaints against the police, said, "'Tis evidence they lack. These days they want a watertight case, or the Prosecution Service isn't interested. I was talking to a copper not so long ago and he told me there are murderers and child molesters known to the police, no question, and they can't touch them. They just don't have the evidence."

"I gave them evidence enough," said Matt.

"All you gave they is hearsay and rumours," chipped in one old man who was weary of all the bluster. "You don't know nothing of what happened down Meare Green or Westhay."

Matt's credibility was in question and he was loud in his defence of it, hammering the table with his fist. "I don't know nothing, eh? Why do you think we've had the police call here three times, then, questioning a certain party about the company she keeps?"

"They questioned thee, come to that," the old man pointed out, and got a laugh for it.

"Took a statement from I," said Matt, reddening suddenly. "That's different. There's no suspicion attached to me."

"So you tell us."

"I had information, didn't I? Spoke to the driver of that there Mercedes that sat outside on certain occasions when

41

we couldn't get a decent service at the bar. And why couldn't we get served? Because the staff was otherwise occupied, flirting with a fat cat, as she believed. Fat cat be buggered. She were flirting with a bloody tiger."

Alison heard this in silence and pretended not to listen, knowing it would only encourage Matt if she got involved. If only to put a stop to the innuendo, she longed for an early arrest.

"So what did he tell 'ee, that driver?" Colwell asked Matt.

"Told me his boss used to drink in Glastonbury until a few weeks ago."

"Glastonbury?" Colwell was impressed.

"Then he switched to here. He likes this pub."

"The beer?"

"The decor, he reckons." Matt's eyes swivelled towards Alison and a huge laugh went up from the table.

"Doesn't mean he strangles barmaids," said the old man, "else why is young Alison still with us?"

"I warned her in time, didn't I?" said Matt. "Probably saved her life by telling her what she were getting into."

"He hasn't been back since the police were here," said Colwell, as if that confirmed Tony's guilt.

"Made his getaway, I reckon," said Matt. "One of them South American countries that don't do the extra ..."

"Extradition," Colwell came to his rescue. "With his money he can afford to live down in Brazil for the rest of his life."

"In that case, we can all relax," the old man said. "There won't be no more stranglings on Sedgemoor."

Alison knew how mistaken they were. Tony had not left Sedgemoor. In the past week he had tried to phone her at least a dozen times. Anticipating this, she was not answering calls, but she was certain it was Tony because she checked each time with the computer voice that gives the last caller's number. She didn't tell the police. For one thing, she wasn't truly scared of Tony, and for another she now felt ashamed of handing the lipstick stain to DI Briggs. If it turned out to have no connection with the case, she was going to despise herself. She just wished Tony would give up phoning. Her only genuine fear was that he would turn up at the pub. If he ever did, Matt and the others were liable to lynch him - or whatever passed for a lynching on Sedgemoor.

Whenever Matt came in, the conversation turned to the stranglings. Lately the slurs and reproaches had become more dangerous. No longer were they speculating when an arrest would be made. The talk was now of a police force incapable of acting because the legal system was weighted in favour of the criminal. "They're bloody impotent," Matt told his cohorts. "They dare not make an arrest in case it doesn't stick. They know full well who did it, and they can't touch him. He's laughing at them."

"Wouldn't do much good if they nicked him," said Colwell. "Once upon a time a man like that would have been topped. The worst he'll get is life, and that's no time at all these days. He'll be out in five or six years to start all over again, strangling women. A devil like that wants topping."

"He won't get no life sentence," said Matt. "They'll say he isn't right in the head. He'll see a bloody head-doctor and be out inside a year. Rehabilitation, they call it."

"Rehabilitation, my arse," said Colwell. "He wants putting down like a mad dog."

"Who's going to do it, though?" one of them asked. "Not I."

Silence descended like the last edge of the sun.

Colwell started up again, letting the words come slowly, as if he had already calculated their effect. "I could tell you a way. They dealt with a sex pest when I were a lad living up Burnham way, on the estuary. He was a right menace to all the women. Can't recall his name now, but I know the police couldn't do nothing about him. He were soft in the head or something. Anywise, the men took care of him. One night he disappeared off the face of the earth."

"What happened to him?" Matt asked.

"He were never seen again."

"Come off it, John. You just said you could tell us about it."

"And so I did." Colwell seemed to savour the attention he was getting. "He were given a ride on a mud horse."

"What's that?"

"Come closer. I'll tell thee."

The rest was delivered in a voice pitched deliberately low. All Alison heard were some laughs at the end that made her flesh creep.

"When you think on it," Colwell finished up in his normal voice, "it's foolproof."

"If it worked once," said Matt, "it could work again. Save the police a heap of work, wouldn't it?"

Alison seriously thought of speaking to Tony if he phoned again, warning him not to set foot in Bridgwater or anywhere near it. She had no idea what a ride on a mud horse meant, except that it was a death sentence.

The next day, Saturday, Tony didn't phone at all. Alison hoped he had seen sense at last and given up.

This was her day off. She spent it quietly, watching a movie on TV for most of the afternoon, the sort she liked, with pirates and gorgeous women in crinolines and nothing more violent than the baddies being poked with swords and falling into the sea. Later, she went out for some shopping. Among other things, she picked up a copy of the *Bridgwater Mercury*. Seeing the headline, she felt pole-axed. MERCEDES CLUE IN BARMAID STRANGLINGS.

The police had now established that a black Mercedes had been seen parked by the entrance to a field at Meare Green one evening in the week Emma Charles was thought to have been murdered. A similar vehicle had been seen in the car park at the Peat Moor Visitor Centre on the Saturday night Angie Singleton was killed there. The Police National Computer had been used to check on the owners of all Mercedes registered in Somerset.

Until this moment she had not been willing to believe Tony was the strangler. How could she have been so stupid, going out three times with a man like that, and actually inviting him to spend the night with her?

She needed a brandy, or something, just to stop this shaking. The Jellied Eel was only a short walk up the street. She stuffed the newspaper in with the other shopping and made her way there, moaning to herself like a demented person.

The bar was empty except for three old men playing dominos. Karen was on duty, looking bored. She said, "You look terrible, darling. What's up?"

Alison produced the newspaper. "Haven't you seen this?"

"Of course I have. First thing this morning."

"I only just saw it. God, I need a brandy."

Karen reached for a glass and pressed it to the brandy dispenser. "Surely you knew he was odd?"

"He wasn't odd with me."

"You're bloody lucky, then."

"I'll drink to that." Alison shuddered, took a sip, and felt better as her throat warmed.

"Why do you reckon you were spared, then?" Karen asked.

The answer came candidly, with no artifice. "I don't know. He never threatened me, never tried anything heavy. There wasn't a hint of it. He was a slow starter, if you know what I mean." She added in the same honest vein, "The police told me something I suppose I can tell you now. They said he wasn't violent to those women. It wasn't rape. They let him do it to them."

"Go on," said Karen in disbelief.

"So I wonder if they were killed because they hustled too much. You know?"

"Forced the pace?"

"Yes. And if he wasn't much good at it, lacking confidence, or something, maybe he lost control and strangled them."

45

Karen grimaced as she visualised the scene. She drew in a sharp breath. "Nasty."

"As you say, I had a lucky escape."

"You don't know how lucky."

"What do you mean?"

"Only that he was in here asking for you this afternoon."

Alison wondered if she had heard right. "What? Haven't they picked him up? I thought he was under arrest."

Karen shook her head. "But it's all right. He's no danger to you now, love." She glanced across at the domino-players and lowered her voice. "Matt and some of the lads were here. They grabbed the bastard."

"Oh, no!"

"What's the problem? He's guilty as hell. They took him off in Matt's car. He'll be riding a mud horse by now."

"Doing *what*?"

"You must have seen them in Bridgwater Bay - those things the fishermen use to cross the mud. Like something between a surfboard and a sledge?"

Alison knew at once. Simply hadn't linked the name with the contraption. The mud horses were used at low tide to slide over the most treacherous stretches of the flats, where a man would swiftly sink into the ooze if he tried to stand upright. The fisherman would lean on the superstructure, letting it bear his weight while he propelled it with his feet. And they had put Tony on one of these?

The grotesque thing reared up in her mind.

"I'm going to call the police."

Karen shrilled in alarm, "You can't do that. You'll get them all arrested."

"It's vile." She ran across to the public phone.

"Don't be so bloody dense." Karen pushed up the hinged flap on the bar and dashed after her. The domino party suspended play and watched in awe.

Alison had the phone in her hand and was dialling the emergency number. "Keep away from me, Karen."

Karen made a grab for the phone and felt the force of Alison's foot against her belly. The kick would not have disgraced a karate expert. Karen was thrust backwards, tipped off balance and slid across the wood floor.

Alison made her call. It took some explaining, but she conveyed the urgency of the matter.

After a short interval filled with foul language from Karen, who was too winded to fight, a police car arrived outside, with siren wailing. A constable in uniform came in and asked for Alison.

Inspector Briggs was waiting in the back seat of the car. Alison got in beside him and it moved off fast. He had been at a meeting at Bridgwater Police Station when the emergency call came in, he explained. A response car was already on its way to Stolford, the village at the west end of the bay where the mud horses operated.

"He'll be dead by now," said Alison. "They'll have tipped him into the mud and left him to die. I don't care what he's done. That's no way to treat anybody."

Briggs weighed what she had said. He glanced at his watch. "We should be in time."

"No chance. They've been gone for hours."

"You're forgetting something, miss. If they're planning what you say, they have to wait for low tide, and it isn't due for another half-hour."

"I hope to God you're right."

"Still like the man, do you?"

She didn't answer.

Briggs said, "You heard about the sightings of the car?"

"I saw it in the paper."

"That isn't all. This morning we had the result of the lab tests on the tissue you handed in, the one with the lipstick mark you found in his car. It's a variety called Love All by Miss Selfridge. Emma Charles was carrying a lipstick of that brand in her bag, just as you expected. It's the proof we needed."

"Why didn't you arrest him this morning, then?"

"We were just about to nick him. The meeting I mentioned was to finalise the arrest. I'm from Glastonbury, remember. We had to liaise with our colleagues here."

Liaise with colleagues. She didn't trust herself to speak.

Briggs aired his theories as to a motive. "You know why you weren't killed like the others? Because it didn't come to sex. That's when he's dangerous. It's all love and roses until he climaxes, and then some kink in his brain turns him lethal. Maybe he's just bad at sex, and knows it, and takes out his resentment on the women. Or it could be a power thing. Whatever, the reason, you've been dating Jekyll and Hyde."

There was a sense of urgency now. Siren blaring across the countryside, the car swallowed the fast road towards Hinkley Point, only marginally cutting its speed after turning right along a minor road. The hedges along the lanes were eight or nine feet high at this northern edge of the moor, making it impossible to see more than a few yards ahead. Alison knew from her cycle ride to Stockland Bristol through lanes very similar that farm traffic used these ways. The driver seemed to have blind faith that any approaching tractor would hear the siren and have time to move aside, into a passing point.

But cows were less amenable. Suddenly the way was blocked by the back end of one tractor that would not be making way, for it was herding about sixty Friesians back to the field from the milking sheds. Black and white cows filled the lane, ambling along at a leisurely rate. They could not be moved aside, turned back or hustled.

Betraying no emotion, Briggs ordered the siren and light to be turned off in case they panicked the cows. The patrol car was forced to crawl behind the tractor.

A message came over the radio. The first car had reached Stolford. They had spotted some people out on the mud and were going to investigate.

"If they really mean that, they'll regret it," said Briggs in his deadpan voice. "It's suicidal walking on the flats."

Five or six minutes were lost before the cows were all off the lane and the farmer eased the tractor up to the gate and waved the car by.

Stolford was less than a mile off, and still there was no view of the coast. Finally they reached a cluster of farm buildings and cottages that had to be it. The pulsing blue light of the first police car was visible ahead, on the skyline. They crossed a humpback bridge, moved up the ridge that kept the tide from encroaching, and pulled up beside the other police car, and got out. Matt's rusty Cortina was standing nearby.

Beyond a thin bank of shingle and scattered rocks, the mudflats opened out, a vast no-man's-land exposed by the low tide. Somewhere below the grey outline of the Welsh headland, the soft oozy mass met the water of the Bristol Channel. A couple of miles to the left at the western extremity of the bay was the citadel-like structure of Hinkley Point, the nuclear power station, the hum of its turbines carrying to them. Five miles in the other direction was the resort of Burnham-on-Sea.

"I can't see anyone," said Alison.

"They'll be way out. You want field-glasses."

The low sun reflecting on the streams and channels dividing the mudflats produced a pattern like lacework across the scene, but by no stretch of the imagination could it be described as anything but desolate. Gulls and wading birds patrolled the margins.

No one was in the second police car. An elderly man with a dog stood beside it.

"Where did the policemen go?" Briggs asked him.

The old man gestured vaguely across the great expanse of mud with his stick. "They tried, but they had to come back. Then they were off up the coast path like blue-arsed flies."

"Which way?"

He nodded towards Hinkley.

49

"Has the tide turned yet?"

"Any time now."

"Did you see the other men go out?"

The old man nodded. "They took two of my son's mud horses without so much as a by-your-leave. Serve 'em bloody right if they come to grief, I say."

Briggs opened the boot of the car and took out a pair of binoculars.

He made an agonizingly slow scan of the shoreline along the limit of the mud. Then he put down the glasses and said to his driver, "We'll have to cut them off ourselves. They're heading towards Steart."

"With Tony?" Alison asked.

"Pawson? No. He's still out there."

Appalled, she cried out, "Where?"

He pointed. "You could easily take it for a piece of wreckage, but it looks to me like a man up to his waist in mud."

"What? Let me look."

He handed the glasses across and Alison looked through, getting only a blur at first, and then, as she worked the focus control, a clear sight of a large seabird, a herring gull that took flight just as she spotted it. A slight move to her left and she was presented with the disturbing image of a man held fast by the mud with little more than his torso above the surface, his arms held high, and waving. No one was near.

"Oh, my God!"

This, then, was Matt's idea of justice, leaving a man stranded in mud that would hold him helpless until the huge tide rushed over him and drowned him.

"We've got to get out there and save him."

"We can't reach him," Briggs told her in his staid voice. "We'd go under ourselves. The best we can do is radio for help, and I'll see to it. But we can nick the idiots who did this to him. You wait here. For Christ's sake don't do anything stupid. The tide comes in so fast you'd have no chance at all."

He was in the car and had slammed the door before she could react. It reversed and drove away fast. She turned to the old man and asked, "Do you have a phone?"

He shook his head. "What would I want with a phone?"

She turned and looked at the nearest farmhouse and saw the telephone wires leading to it. She wasn't convinced that Briggs wanted Tony to survive; his laid-back manner suggested otherwise. It would be easy for him to delay and say later that he'd been distracted in the chase. She resolved to call the emergency services herself. She dashed down the slope and across the little bridge towards the farmhouse.

Before reaching there, she was aware of a movement to her left and a glimpse of a tall man, smartly dressed, with a black tie and grey suit, standing out of sight against the wall of a barn. She stopped and turned towards him. His face was known to her, yet in her agitated state she couldn't place him until he spoke.

"Were you looking for help, miss?" The voice, quiet, considerate, with just a suggestion of deference, prompted her memory. Of all people, he was Tony's chauffeur, Hugh. It wasn't so remarkable she had failed to recognise him. After all, she knew the back of his head far better than the front.

She blurted out the words, "Tony is -"

"I know," he said, as calm in his way as Briggs. "I was waiting outside the pub when they bundled him into their car and drove off. It's all right. I phoned ten minutes ago from the car. There's a rescue helicopter on its way."

"Thank God," she said. "Oh, Hugh, how could they do this?"

He shook his head. If he knew anything at all about the suspicion Tony was under, he was unlikely to speak of it. So the headshake was in disbelief at the savagery of Matt and his friends. "I followed their car some way and then lost them in the lanes. When I got here they were halfway across the mud."

"Where's your car?"

"Out of sight behind the farmhouse."

"Over there?"

"I'll show you. We can move it closer now."

He led her around the side of the farmhouse to where the Mercedes stood. He opened the front door and Alison got in. This was the first time she had not been seated in style in the rear seat. Hugh got in beside her and started up.

Under the stress she was in, she put her hand over his arm and squeezed. "Thank God you're here."

His pale blue eyes crinkled at the edges in amusement. How is it, she thought, that some men have this capacity to give you confidence?

Instead of turning right, to go over the humpback bridge and up on the ridge beside the police cars, he swung the car towards the road.

"Where are we going?"

"Not far."

Not understanding, she said, "We don't want to go away from here. We want to see what's happening."

He said, "Relax."

Relaxing was far from her mind. They headed off along the lane, out of the village and away from the waterfront where everything was happening. The air rushed through the open roof, blasting her ears and tugging her hair back.

She cried out in alarm, "Hugh, what's going on? I want to be here. I want to get out."

"Shut up."

The rebuke came like an electric shock. Alison did go silent, but only because she was so stunned. Even in this emergency he shouldn't have spoken to her like that.

The Mercedes belted between the high hedges. Anything coming towards them would have no chance of stopping in time.

She gripped the safety belt with both hands, trying to understand what was happening, wondering if Hugh had some plan of his own for going to Tony's aid from a different stretch of beach. What else could explain this?

Then they left the road. A sudden swing of the wheel and they were bumping through an open gate into a field. About thirty yards on, out of sight of the lane, he braked.

Alison felt for the door handle. To her total amazement, Hugh leaned right over and pressed down the lock. Then he grabbed her right arm and forced it under the safety belt. He snatched the slack part of the belt and jerked it so tight that she was held rigid against the seatback. His hand slipped under the collar of her blouse and pressed against her neck, and she understood.

Hugh was the strangler.

He had killed those other women after driving them out to some lonely spot and having sex with them. Suspicion had fallen on Tony because of the car, but it was his chauffeur who was the killer, using the car on days when it wasn't required. The tissue marked with lipstick proved it. Poor Emma Charles must have sat here, in this seat beside Hugh, and placed the used tissue in the glove compartment in front of her.

Now she herself was about to die because she had found him at the scene. He must have been unable to stay away, compelled to watch Tony being dragged across the mud on the mud horse just to be certain that someone else took the rap. No doubt he had fed Matt with lies about Tony's guilt.

His hand was halfway around her throat, choking her. She managed to blurt out the words, "This won't save you. They know all about you." Of course they did not, and of course he knew it.

He swung towards her, still with his right hand gripping her neck, manoeuvering himself out of the driver's seat, across the divider where the handbrake was. He was trying to get fully over her, to get a better grip on her throat. She felt his knee slide across her thighs. His weight was on her, his hot breath in her face, both hands around her neck. He braced, straightening his arms to bear down on her.

With her left hand - the only one that was free - she clutched at his wrist and tried desperately to break the grip that would asphyxiate her in seconds. Hopeless.

She stared up at him, and saw his teeth bared with the effort. His face was outlined by the blue sky. Some instinct for survival sparked an idea in Alison's brain. She realized that his head was poking through the gap in the roof. Instead of clawing at his hands, she groped upwards, behind him, reaching above the windscreen. Her vision was blurred. The blood supply to her brain had almost ceased.

Her middle finger located a button just below the roof. She pressed it. There was a whirring sound as the electrical control activated the sliding roof. She kept her finger on the button.

Hugh gave a yell, more of fury than pain. His grip on Alison's neck loosened. The roof panel had already closed against his chest, and then, as he ducked, it trapped him even more effectively by closing against his neck. There was no way he could bring his head through the gap.

In the car, his stranglehold loosened. Alison gasped for breath, found the catch of the seatbelt and released it. She unlocked the door, squirmed from under Hugh's legs and fell out onto the grass. She didn't stop to see if he had any way of escaping. Sobbing, she stumbled to the gate and up the lane.

About the same time, an RAF rescue helicopter passed over, heading inland towards Woolavington. The crew estimated that Tony Pawson had been within two or three minutes of death when they snatched him from the rising tide.

Two weeks later, Tony took Alison for a meal at the restaurant in Stockland Bristol. They went by taxi.

They had many more meals out before he asked her to marry him. No one could accuse Tony of rushing things. In fact, Matt Magellan and John Colwell were out of prison by then and drinking again at the Jellied Eel, but with one difference. Alison had long since given up her job as barmaid and was spared having to serve them.

She and Tony were married in St Mary's, Bridgwater, the following spring. Hugh the chauffeur was not among the guests. He was a long-term guest elsewhere, with a recommendation that he should remain so for the rest of his life.

The Perfectionist

The invitation dropped on the doormat of The Laurels along with a bank statement and a Guide Dogs for the Blind appeal. It was in a cream-coloured envelope made from thick, expensive-looking paper. Duncan left it to open after the others. His custom was to leave the most promising letters while he worked steadily through the others, using a paperknife that cut the envelopes tidily.

Eventually he took out a gold edged card with his name inscribed in the centre in fine italic script. It read:

> *The most perfect club in the world*
> *has the good sense to invite*
> *Mr Duncan Driffield*
> *a proven perfectionist*
> *to be an honoured guest at its annual dinner*
> *Friday, January 31st, 7.30 for 8pm*
>
> *Contact will be made later*

He was wary. This could be an elaborate marketing ploy. He'd been invited to parties in the past by motor dealers and furniture retailers that turned out to be sales pitches, nothing more. Just because no product or company was mentioned, he wasn't going to be taken in. He read it through several times.

It has to be said, he liked the designation "a proven perfectionist". Couldn't fault their research. He was a Virgo, born under a birth-sign known for its orderly people, strivers for perfection. To see it written down as if he'd already achieved the ideal, was specially pleasing. And to see his name in such elegant script was another fine touch.

Yet it troubled him that the club was not named, nor was there any address, nor any mention of where the function was to be held. Being a thorough and cautious man, he would normally have looked them up before deciding what to do about the invitation.

The phone call came about eight-thirty the next evening. A voice that didn't need to announce it had been to a very good school spoke his name.

"Yes."

"You received an invitation to the dinner on January 31st, I trust?"

"Which invitation was that?" Duncan said as if he was used to getting them by every post.

"A gold-edged card naming you as a proven perfectionist. May we take it that you will accept?"

"Who are you, exactly?"

"A group of like-minded people. We know you'll fit in."

"Is there some mystery about it? I don't wish to join the Freemasons."

"We're not Freemasons, Mr Driffield."

"How did you get my name?"

"It was put to the committee. You were the outstanding candidate."

"Really?" he glowed inwardly before his level-headedness returned. "Is there any obligation?"

"You mean are we trying to sell something? Absolutely not."

"I don't have to make a speech?"

"We don't go in for speeches. It isn't like that at all. We'll do everything possible to welcome you and make you feel relaxed. Transport is provided."

"Are you willing to tell me your name?"

"Of course. It's David Hopkins. I do hope you're going to say yes."

Why not? he thought. "All right, Mr Hopkins."

"Excellent. I'm sure if I ask you - as a proven perfectionist - to be ready at six-thirty, you will, to the minute. In case you were wondering, it's a dinner jacket and black tie affair. I'll come for you myself. The drive takes nearly an hour at that time of day, I'm afraid. And it's Dr Hopkins actually, but please call me David."

After the call, Duncan in his systematic way tried to track down David Hopkins in the phone directory and the Medical Register. He found three people of that name and called them on the phone, but their voices had nothing like the honeyed tone of the David Hopkins he had spoken to.

He wondered who had put his name forward. Someone must have. It would be interesting to see if he recognised David Hopkins.

He did not. Precisely on time, on the last Friday in January, Dr David Hopkins arrived, a slim, dark man in his forties, of average height. They shook hands.

"Is there anything I can bring? A bottle of whisky?"

"No, you're our guest, Duncan."

He liked the look of David. He knew intuitively one of the special evenings in his life was in prospect.

They walked out to the car, a large black Daimler, chauffeur-driven.

"Luxury."

"We can enjoy the wine with a clear conscience," David explained, "but I would be dishonest if I led you to think that was the only reason." When they were both inside he leaned across and pulled down a blind. There was one on each window and across the partition between the driver and themselves. Duncan couldn't see out at all. "This is in your interest."

"Why is that?"

"We ask our guests to be good enough to respect the privacy of the club. If you don't know where we meet, you can't upset anyone."

"I see. Now that we're alone, and I'm committed to coming, can you tell me some more?"

"A little. We're all of your cast of mind, actually."

"Perfectionists?"

He smiled. "That's one of the attributes."

"I wondered why I was asked. Do I know any of the members?"

"I doubt it."

"Then how -"

"Your crowning achievement."

Duncan tried to think which achievement could have come to their notice. He'd had an unremarkable career in the civil service. Sang a bit with a local choir. Once won first prize for his sweet peas in the town flower show, but he'd given up growing them now. He could think of nothing of enough merit to interest this high-powered club.

"How many members are there?"

"Fewer than we would like. Not many meet the criteria."

"So how many is that?"

"Currently, five."

"Oh - as few as that?"

"We're small and exclusive."

"I can't think why you invited me."

"It will become clear."

More questions from Duncan elicited little else, except that the club had been established for over a hundred years. He assumed - but had the tact not to ask - that he would be invited to join if the members approved of him this evening. How he wished he was one of those people with a fund of funny stories. He feared he was dull company.

In just under the hour, the car came to a halt and the chauffeur opened the door. Duncan glanced about him as he stepped out, wanting to get some sense of where he was. It was dark at this time, of course, but this was clearly a London square, with street lights and a park in the centre and plane trees at intervals in front of the houses. He couldn't put a name to it. The houses were terraced, and Georgian, just as they are in almost every other London square.

"Straight up the steps," said David. "The door is open."

They went in, through a hallway with mirrors and a crystal chandelier that made him blink after the dim lighting in the car. David took Duncan's coat and handed it to a manservant and then opened a door.

"Gentlemen," he said. "May I present our guest, Mr Duncan Driffield."

It was a smallish anteroom, and four men stood waiting with glasses of wine. Two looked quite elderly, the others about forty, or less. One of the younger pair was wearing a kilt.

The one who was probably the senior member extended a bony hand. "Joe Franks. I'm president, through a process of elimination."

There were some smiles at this that David didn't fully understand.

Joe Franks went on to say, "I qualified as a member as long ago as 1934, when I was only nineteen, but I joined officially after the war."

David, at Duncan's side, murmured something that made no sense about a body left in a trunk at Brighton railway station.

"And this well set-up fellow on my right," said Joe Franks, "is Wally Winthrop, the first private individual to put ricin to profitable use. Wally now owns one of the largest supermarket chains in Europe."

"Did you say 'rice'?" asked Duncan.

"No. 'Ricin'. A vegetable poison."

It was difficult to see the connection between a vegetable poison and a supermarket chain. Wally Winthrop grinned and shook Duncan's hand. "Tell you about it one of these days," he said.

Joe Franks indicated the man in the kilt. "Alex McPhee is our youngest member and our most prolific. Is it seven, Alex?"

"So far," said McPhee, and this caused more amusement.

"His skene-dhu has more than once come to the aid of the club," added Joe Franks.

Duncan wasn't too familiar with Gaelic, but he had a faint idea that the skene-dhu was the ornamental dagger worn by Highlanders in their stocking. He supposed the club used it in some form of ritual.

"And now meet Michael Pitt-Struthers, who advises the SAS on the martial arts. His knowledge of pressure points is unrivalled. Shake hands very carefully with Michael."

More smiles, the biggest from Pitt-Struthers, who squeezed Duncan's hand in a way that left no doubt of his expertise.

"And of course you've already met our doctor member, David Hopkins, who knows more about allergy reactions than any man alive."

With a huge effort to be sociable, Duncan remarked, "Such a variety of talents. I can't think what you all have in common."

Joe Franks answered, "Each of us has committed a perfect murder."

Duncan heard the statement and played it over in his head. He thought he'd got it right. It had been spoken with some pride. This time no one smiled. More disturbingly, no one disputed it.

"Shall we go into dinner, gentlemen?" Joe Franks suggested.

At a round table in the next room, Duncan tried to come to terms with the sensational claim he had just heard. If it was true, what on earth was he doing sharing a meal with a bunch of killers? And why had they chosen to take him into their confidence? He could shop them to the police and they wouldn't be perfect murderers any longer. Maybe it was wise not to mention this while he was seated between the martial arts expert and the Scot with the skene-dhu tucked into his sock.

The wine glasses were filled with claret by an elderly waiter. "Hungarian," Joe Franks confided. "He understands no English." He raised his glass. "At this point, gentlemen, I propose a toast to Thomas de Quincey, author of that brilliant essay *On Murder, Considered as One of the Fine Arts*, who esteemed the killing of Sir Edmund Godfrey as 'the finest work of the seventeenth century' for the excellent reason that no one knew who had done it."

"Thomas de Quincey," said everyone, with Duncan just a half-beat slower than the rest.

"You're probably wondering what brings us together," said Wally Winthrop across the table. "You might think we'd be uncomfortable sharing our secrets. In fact, it works the other way. It's a tremendous relief. I don't have to tell you, Duncan, what it's like after you commit your first, living in fear of being found out, waiting for the police siren and the knock on the door. As the months pass, this panicky stage fades and is replaced by a feeling of isolation. You've set yourself apart from others by your action. You can only look forward to keeping your secret bottled up for the rest of your life. It's horrible. We've all been through it. Five years have to pass - five years without being charged with murder - before you're contacted by the club and invited to join us for a meal."

David Hopkins briskly took up the conversation. "It's such a break in the clouds, that discovery that you're not alone in the world. To find that what you've done is valued as an achievement and can be openly discussed. Wonderful. After all, there is worth in having committed a perfect murder."

"How do you know you can trust each other?" Duncan asked, without giving anything away.

"Mutual self-interest. If any one of us betrayed the others, he'd take himself down as well. We're all in the same boat."

Joe Franks explained, "It's a safeguard that's worked for over a hundred years. One of our first members was the man better known as Jack the Ripper, who was in fact a pillar of the establishment. If his identity could be protected all these years, then the rest of us can breathe easy."

"That's amazing. You know who the Ripper was?"

"Aye," said McPhee calmly. "And no one has ever named the laddie."

"Can I ask?"

"Not till you join," said Joe Franks.

Duncan hesitated. He was about to say he had no chance of joining, not having committed a murder, when some inner voice prompted him to shut up. These people were acting as if he was one of them. Maybe, through some ghastly mistake, they'd been told he'd once done away with a fellow human being. And maybe it was in his interest not to disillusion them.

"We have to keep to the rules," Wally Winthrop was explaining. "Certain information is only passed on to full members."

Joe Franks added, "And we are confident you will want to join. All we ask is that you respect the rules. Not a word must be spoken to anyone else about this evening, or the existence of the club. The ultimate sanction is at our disposal for anyone foolish enough to betray us."

"The ultimate sanction - what's that?" Duncan huskily enquired.

No one answered, but the Scot beside him grinned in a way Duncan didn't care for.

"The skene-dhu?" said Duncan.

"Or the pressure point," said Joe Franks, "or the allergy reaction, or whatever we decide is tidiest. But it won't happen in your case."

"No chance," Duncan affirmed. "My lips are sealed."

The starters were served, and he was pleased when the conversation shifted to murders in fiction, and some recent crime novels. Faintly he listened as they discussed *The Silence of the Lambs*, but he was trying to think what to say if someone asked about the murder he was supposed to have committed. They were sure to return to him before the evening ended, and then it was essential to sound convincing. If they got the idea he was a mild man who wouldn't hurt a fly he was in real trouble.

Towards the end of the meal, he spoke up. It seemed a good idea to take the initiative. "This has been a brilliant evening. Is there any chance I could join?"

"You've enjoyed yourself?" said Joe Franks. "That's excellent. A kindred spirit."

"It's got to be more than that if you want to be a member," Winthrop put in. "You've got to provide some evidence that you're one of us."

Duncan swallowed hard. "Don't you have that? I wouldn't be here if you hadn't found something out."

"There's a difference between finding something out and seeing the proof."

"That won't be easy."

"It's the rule."

He tried another tack. "Can I ask something? How did you get onto me?"

There were smiles all round. Winthrop said, "You're surprised that we succeeded where the police failed?"

"Experience," Joe Franks explained. "We're much better placed than the police to know how it was done."

Pitt-Struthers, the strong, silent man who trained the SAS, said, "We know you were at the scene on the evening it happened, and we know no one else had a stronger motive or a better opportunity."

"But we must have the proof," insisted Winthrop.

"The weapon," suggested McPhee.

"I disposed of it," Duncan improvised. He was not an imaginative man, but this was an extreme situation. "You would, wouldn't you?"

"No," said McPhee. "I just give mine a wee wipe."

"Well, it's up to you, old boy," Winthrop told Duncan. "Only you can furnish the evidence."

"How long do I have?"

"The next meeting is in July. We'd like to confirm you as a full member then."

The conversation moved on to other areas, a lengthy discussion about the problems faced by the Crown Prosecution Service.

The evening ended with coffee, cognac and cigars. Soon after, David Hopkins said that the car would be outside.

On the drive back, Duncan, deeply perturbed and trying not to show it, pumped David for information.

"It was an interesting evening, but it's left me with a problem."

"What's that?"

"I, em, wasn't completely sure which murder of mine they were talking about."

"Do you mean you're a serial killer?"

Duncan gulped. He hadn't meant that at all. "I've never thought of myself as one." Recovering his poise a little, he added, "A thing like that is all in the mind, I suppose. Which one do they have me down for?"

"The killing of Sir Jacob Drinkwater at the Brighton Civil Service Conference in 1995."

Drinkwater. He remembered being at the conference and the sensation of the senior civil servant at the Irish Office being found dead in his hotel room on the Sunday morning. "That was supposed to be a heart attack."

"Officially, yes," said David.

"But you heard something else?"

"I happen to know the pathologist who did the autopsy. A privileged source. They didn't want the public knowing how Sir Jacob was killed, and thinking it was a new method employed by the terrorists. How did you introduce the cyanide? Was it in his aftershave?"

"Trade secret," Duncan answered cleverly.

"Of course the security people in their blinkered way couldn't imagine it was anything but a political assassination. They didn't know you had a grudge against him dating from years back, when he was your boss in the Land Registry."

Someone had got their wires crossed. It was a man called *Charlie* Drinkwater who'd made Duncan's life a misery and blighted his career. No connection with Sir Jacob. Giving nothing away, he said smoothly, "And you worked out that I was at the conference?"

65

"Same floor. Missed the banquet on the Saturday evening, giving you a fine opportunity to break into his room and plant the cyanide. So we have motive, opportunity."

"And means?" said Duncan.

David laughed. "Your house is called *The Laurels*, for the bushes all round the garden. It's well known that if you soak laurel leaves and evaporate the liquid, you get a lethal concentration of cyanide. Isn't that how you made the stuff?"

"I'd rather leave you in suspense," said Duncan. He was thinking hard. "If I apply to join the club, I may have to give a demonstration."

"There's no 'if' about it. They liked you. You're expected to join."

"I could decide against it."

"Why?"

"Private reasons."

David turned to face him, his face creased in concern. "They'd take a very grave view of that, Duncan. We invited you along in good faith."

"But no obligation, I thought."

"Look at it from the club's point of view. We're vulnerable now. You're dealing with dangerous men, Duncan. I can't urge you strongly enough to co-operate."

"But if I can't prove that I killed a man -"

"You must think of something. We're willing to be convinced. If you cold-shoulder us, or betray us, I can't answer for the consequences."

A sobering end to the evening.

For the next three weeks he got little sleep, and when he did drift off he would wake with nightmares of fingers pressing on his arteries or skene-dhus being thrust between his ribs. He faced a classic dilemma. Either admit he hadn't murdered Sir Jacob Drinkwater and was a security risk to the club; or concoct some fake evidence, bluff his way in, and spend the rest of his life hoping they wouldn't catch him out. Faking evidence wouldn't be easy. They were intelligent men.

"You must think of something," David Hopkins had urged.

Being methodical, he went to the British Newspaper Library and spent many hours rotating the microfilm, studying accounts of Sir Jacob's murder. It only depressed him more, reading about the involvement of Special Branch, the Anti-Terrorist Squad and MI5. "The files remain open" the papers said. Open to whom? With all that high security involvement how could any ordinary man acquire the evidence the club insisted on seeing?

More months went by.

Duncan weighed the possibility of pointing out to the members that they'd made a mistake. Surely, he thought in rare optimistic moments, they would see that it wasn't his fault.

He was just an ordinary bloke caught up in something out of his league. He could promise to say nothing to anyone, in return for a guarantee of personal safety. Then he remembered the eyes of some of those people around the table, and he knew how unrealistic it was.

One morning in May, out of desperation, he had a brilliant idea. It arose from something David Hopkins had said in the car on the way home from the club. *"Do you mean you're a serial killer?"* At the time it had sounded preposterous. Now, it could be his salvation. Instead of striving to link himself to the murder of Sir Jacob, he would claim another killing - and show them some evidence they couldn't challenge. He'd satisfy the rules of the club and put everyone at their ease.

The brilliant part was this. He didn't need to kill anyone. He would claim to have murdered some poor wretch who had actually committed suicide. All he needed was a piece of evidence from the scene. Then he'd tell the Perfectionists he was a serial killer who dressed up his murders as suicide. They would be forced to agree how clever he was and admit him to the club. After a time, he'd give up going to the meetings and no one would bother him because they'd think their secrets were safe with him.

It was just a matter of waiting. Somebody, surely, would do away with himself before the July meeting of the club. Each day Duncan studied the Telegraph, and no suicide - well, no suicide he could claim as a murder - was reported. At the end of June, he found an expensive-looking envelope on his door- mat and knew with a sickening certainty who it was from.

The most perfect club in the world
takes pleasure in inviting
Mr Duncan Driffield
a prime candidate for membership
to present his credentials after dinner on July 19th, 7.30
for 8 p.m.

Contact will be made later

This time the wording didn't pamper his ego at all. It filled him with dread. In effect it was a sentence of death. His only chance of a reprieve rested on some fellow creature topping himself in the next two weeks.

He took to buying three newspapers instead of one, still with no success.

Mercifully, and in the nick of time, his luck changed. News of a suicide reached him, but not through the press. He was phoned one morning by an old civil service colleague, Harry Hitchman. They'd met occasionally since retiring, but they weren't the closest of buddies, so the call came out of the blue.

"Some rather bad news," said Harry. "Remember Billy Fisher?"

"Of course I remember him," said Duncan. "We were in the same office for twelve years. What's happened?"

"He jumped off a hotel balcony last night. Killed himself."

"Billy? I can't believe it!"

"Nor me when I heard. Seems he was being treated for depression."

"I had no idea. He was always cracking jokes in the office. A bit of a comedian, I always thought."

"They're the people who crack, aren't they? All that funny stuff is just a front."

"His wife Sue must be devastated."

"That's why I'm phoning round. She's with her sister. She understands that everyone will be wanting to offer sympathy and help if they can, but for the present she'd like to be left to come to terms with this herself."

"OK." Duncan hesitated. "This happened only last night, you said?" Already, an idea was forming in his troubled brain.

"Yes. He was staying overnight at some hotel in Mayfair. A reunion of some sort."

"Do you happen to know which one?"

"Which reunion?"

"No. Which hotel."

"The Excelsior. Thirteenth floor. People talk about thirteen being unlucky. It was in Billy's case."

Sad as it was, this *had* to be Duncan's salvation. Billy Fisher was as suitable a "murder victim" as he could have wished for. Someone he'd actually worked with. He could think of a motive, make up some story of an old feud, later.

For once in his life, he needed to throw caution to the winds and act immediately. The police would have sealed Billy's hotel room pending some kind of investigation. Surely a proven perfectionist could think of a way to get inside and pick up some personal item that would pass as evidence that he had murdered his old colleague.

He took the five-twenty-five to London. At this time most other travellers were going up to town for an evening's entertainment. Duncan sat alone, avoiding eye contact and working out his plan. First he needed to find out which room on the thirteenth floor Billy had occupied, and then devise a way of getting in there. Through the two-hour journey he was deep in concentration, applying his brain to the challenge. By the time they reached Waterloo, he knew exactly what to do.

A taxi ride brought him to the hotel, a high-rise building near Shepherd Market. He glanced up, counting each set of windows with its wrought-iron balcony outside, and thought of Billy's leap from the thirteenth. Personally, he wouldn't have gone so high. A fall from the sixth would have killed anyone, and more quickly.

Doing his best to look like one of the guests, he stepped briskly through the revolving doors into the spacious, carpeted foyer and over to the lift, which was waiting unoccupied. No one gave him a second glance. It was a huge relief when the door slid across and he was alone and rising.

So far, the plan was working beautifully. He got out at the twelfth level and used the stairs to reach the thirteenth. It was now around seven-thirty, and he was wary of meeting people on their way out to dinner. He paused to let a couple ahead of him go through the swing doors. They didn't turn round. He moved along, looking for a door marked "Staff Only" or something similar. There had to be a place where the chambermaid kept her trolley, and he found it just the other side of those swing doors.

At this time of day the rooms were made up and the maid had gone off duty. Duncan found some worksheets attached to a clipboard hanging from a nail in the wall. All the thirteenth-floor rooms were listed, with ticks beside some of them showing, presumably, those that had needed a complete change of linen and towels. On the latest sheet, number 1307 had been struck out and marked "not for cleaning". No other room was so marked. He had found Billy Fisher's hotel room. Easy as shelling peas.

He took a look at the door of 1307 before returning to the lift. No policeman was on duty outside. It wasn't as if a man had been murdered in there.

Down in the foyer, he marched coolly up to the desk and looked at the pigeon hole system where the keys were kept. He'd noticed before how automatically reception staff will hand over keys when asked. The key to 1307 was in place.

Deliberately Duncan didn't ask for it. 1305 - the room next door - was also available and he was given it without fuss.

Up on the thirteenth again, he let himself into 1305, taking care not to leave fingerprints. His idea was to get out on the balcony and climb across the short gap to the balcony of 1307. No one would suspect an entry by that route.

The plan had worked brilliantly up to now. The curtains were drawn in 1305. He didn't switch on the light, thinking he could cross to the window and get straight out to the balcony. Unfortunately his foot caught against a suitcase some careless guest had left on the floor. He stumbled, and was horrified to hear a female voice from the bed call out, "Is that you, Elmer?"

Duncan froze. This wasn't part of the plan. The room should have been unoccupied. He'd collected the key from downstairs.

The voice spoke again. "Did you get the necessary, honey? Did you have to go out for it?"

Duncan was in turmoil, his heart thumping. The plan hadn't allowed for this.

"Why don't you put on the light, Elmer?" the voice said. "Now I'm in bed I don't mind. I was only a little shy of being seen undressing."

What could he do? If he spoke, she would scream. Any minute now, she would reach for the bedside switch. The plan had failed. His one precious opportunity of getting off the hook was gone.

"Elmer?" The voice was suspicious now.

In the civil service, there had been a procedure for everything. Duncan's home life was similar, well-ordered and structured. Now he was floundering, and next he panicked. Take control, something inside him urged. Take control, man. He groped his way to the source of the sound, snatched up a pillow and smothered the woman's voice. There were muffled sounds, and there was struggling, and he pressed harder. And harder. And finally it all stopped.

Silence.

He could think again, thank God, but the realisation of what he had done appalled him.

He'd killed someone. He really had killed someone now.

His brain reeled and pulses pounded in his head and he wanted to break down and sob. Some instinct for survival told him to think, think, think.

By now, Elmer must have returned to the hotel to be told the room-key had been collected. They'd be opening the door with a master key any minute.

Must get out, he thought.

The balcony exit was still the safer way to go. He crossed the room to the glass doors, slid them across and looked out.

The gap between this balcony and that of 1307 was about a metre - not impossible to bridge, but daunting when you looked down and thought of Billy Fisher hurtling towards the street below. In his agitated state, Duncan didn't hesitate. He put a foot on the rail and was up and over and across.

Just as he expected, the doors to 1307 were unfastened. He pushed them open and stepped inside. And the light came on.

Room 1307 was full of people. Not policemen, nor hotel staff, but people who looked familiar, all smiling.

One of them said, "Caught you, Duncan. Caught you good and proper, my old mate." It was Billy Fisher, alive and grinning all over his fat face.

Duncan said, "You're ...?"

"Dead meat? No. You've been taken for a ride, old chum. Have a glass of bubbly, and I'll tell you all about it."

A champagne glass was put in his shaking hand. Everyone closed in, watching his reaction - as if it mattered. He knew the faces.

"Wondering where you've seen them before?" said Billy. "They're actors, mostly, earning a little extra between engagements. You know them better as the Perfectionists. They look different out of evening dress, don't they?"

He knew them now: David Hopkins, the doctor; McPhee, the skene-dhu specialist; Joe Franks, the trunk murderer; Wally Winthrop, the poisoner; and Pitt-Struthers, the martial arts man. In jeans and T-shirts and a little shame-faced at their roles in the deception, they looked totally unthreatening.

"You've got to admit it's a brilliant con," said Billy. "Retirement is so boring. I needed to turn my organising skills to something creative, so I thought this up. Mind, it had to be good to take you in."

"Why me?"

"Well, I knew you were up for it from the old days, and Harry Hitchman - where are you, Harry?"

A voice from the background said, "Over here."

"I knew Harry wouldn't mind playing along. So I rigged it up. Did the job properly. Civil service training. Got the cards printed nicely. Rented the private car and the room and hired the actors and stood you all a decent dinner. I was the Hungarian waiter, by the way, but you were too preoccupied with the others to spot my false moustache. And when you took it all in, as I knew you would - being such a serious-minded guy - it was worth every penny. I wanted to top it with a wonderful finish, so I dreamed up the suicide, and" - he quivered with laughter - "you took the bait again."

"You knew I'd come up here?"

"It was all laid on for your benefit, old sport. You were totally taken in by the perfect murder gag, and you were bound to look for a get-out, so I fabricated one for you. Harry told you I'd jumped off the balcony, but I wasn't the fall-guy."

"Bastard," said Duncan.

"Yes, I am," said Billy without apology. "It's my second career."

"And the woman in the room next door - is she an actress, too?"

"Which woman?"

"Oh, come on," said Duncan. "You've had your fun."

Billy was shaking his head. "We didn't expect you to come through the room next door. Is that how you got on the balcony? Typical Duncan Driffield, going the long way round. Which woman are you talking about?"

From the corridor outside came the sound of hammering on a door.

Duncan covered his ears.

"What's up with him?" said Billy.

Interior, With Corpse

Her chestnut brown hair curved in an S shape across the carpet, around a gleaming pool of blood. She was wearing an old-fashioned petticoat, white with thin shoulder straps. The lace hem had been drawn up her thigh, exposing stocking-tops and suspenders. The stockings had seams. Her shoes, too, dated the incident; black suede, with Louis heels. One of them had fallen off and lay on its side, close to the edge of a stone fireplace. The hearthstones were streaked with crimson and a blood-stained poker had been dropped there.

But what really shocked was the location. Beyond any doubt, this was Wing Commander Ashton's living room. Anyone who had been to the house would recognise the picture above the fireplace of a Spitfire shooting down a Messerschmitt over the fields of Kent in the sunshine of an August afternoon in 1940. They would spot the squadron insignia and medals mounted on black velvet in the glass display cabinet attached to the wall; the miniature aircraft carved in ebony and ranged along the mantelpiece. His favourite armchair stood in its usual place to the right of the hearth. Beside it, the old-fashioned standard lamp and the small rosewood table with his collection of family photographs. True, some things had altered; these days the carpet was not an Axminster, but some man-made fibre thing in dark blue, fitted wall-to-wall. And one or two bits of furniture had gone, notably a writing desk that would have been called a bureau, with a manual typewriter on it - an Imperial - and the paper and carbons under the platen. It was now replaced with a TV set and stand.

DI John Brandon stared at the scene in its gilt frame, vibrated his lips, stepped closer and peered at the detail. He had to act. Calls had been coming in all morning about the picture in the window of Mason's Fine Art Gallery. Some, outraged, wanted it removed. Others, more cautious, enquired if the police were aware of it.

They were now. Brandon understood why people were upset. He'd drunk sherry in the Wing Commander's house many times. This oil painting was a near-perfect rendering of the old fellow's living room. Interior, with corpse.

Brandon wasn't sure how to deal with it. Defamation, possibly. But defamation is usually libel or slander. This was only a picture. Nothing defamatory had been said or written down.

He went into the gallery and showed his ID to Justin Mason, the owner, a mild, decent man with no more on his conscience than a liking for spotted bow-ties.

"That painting in the window, the one with the woman lying in a pool of blood."

"The Davey Park? Strong subject, but one of his finest pieces."

"Park? He's the artist?"

"Yes. Did you know him? Local man. Died at the end of last year. He had his studio in that barn behind the Esso station. When I say 'studio', it was his home as well."

"Did he give the picture a title?"

"I've no idea, inspector. He wasn't very organised. It was left with a few others among his things. The executors decided to put them up for sale, and this was the only piece I cared for. The only finished piece, in fact."

"How long ago was it painted?"

"Couldn't tell you. He kept no records. He had some postcards made of it. They're poor quality black and white jobs, nineteen-fiftyish, I'd say."

"You realise what it shows?"

"A murder, obviously. You think it's too gory for the High Street? I was in two minds myself, and then I remembered that series of paintings by Walter Sickert on the subject of the Camden Town murder."

"I wouldn't know about that," Brandon admitted.

"I only mention them to show that it's not without precedent, murder as the subject of a painting, I mean."

"This is a real location."

"Is it? So was Sickert's, I believe."

"It's Wing Commander Ashton's living room."

Mason twitched and turned pale.

"Take my word for it." said Brandon. "I've been there several times."

"Oh, good Lord!"

"People have been phoning us."

"I'll remove it right away. I had no idea. I'd hate to cause offence to Wing Commander Ashton. Why, if it weren't for men like him, none of us would be living in freedom."

"I'll have to take possession of it. You can have a receipt. Tell me some more about the artist."

"Park? A competent professional. Landscapes usually. Never a big seller, but rubbed along, as they do. Not an easy man to deal with. We expect some eccentricity in artists, don't we?"

"In what way?"

"He drank himself to death, so far as I can make out. Was well known in the Crown. Amusing up to a point, and then after a few more beers he would get loud-mouthed and abusive. He was more than once banned from the pub."

"Doesn't sound like a chum of the Wing Commander's," Brandon commented. The Battle of Britain veteran, not far short of his ninetieth birthday now, was eminently respectable, a school governor, ex-chairman of the parish council and founder of the Town Heritage Society. He'd written *Scramble, Chaps*, reputed to be the best personal account of the Battle of Britain. "They knew each other in years past, I believe, but they hadn't spoken for years. There must have been an incident, one of Davey's outbursts, I suppose. I couldn't tell you the details."

"I wonder who can - apart from the Wing Commander?"

Brandon left soon after with the painting well wrapped up. Back at the police station, he showed it to a couple of colleagues.

"Nasty," said DS Makepeace.

"Who's the woman supposed to be?" said DC Hurst.

"A figment of the artist's imagination, I hope," said Brandon. "If not, the Wing Commander has some awkward questions to face."

"Have you spoken to him?"

"Not yet. It's difficult. He's frail. I'd hate to trigger a heart attack."

"You're going to have to ask him, guv."

"He's a war hero. A gentleman through and through. I've always respected him. I need more background before I take this on."

"Try Henry at the Crown. He knew Davey Park better than anyone."

Henry Chivers had been landlord for most of his life, and he was seventy now. He pulled a half of lager for the inspector and gave his take on Davey. "I heard about the painting this morning. A bit of a change from poppy fields and views of the church. Weird. Davey never mentioned it in here. He'd witter on about most things, including his work. He had an exhibition in the old Corn Exchange a year or so before he died. Bloody good artist. None of that modern trash. It was outdoor scenes, mostly. I'm sure this one with the woman wasn't in the show. The whole town would have talked."

"They're talking now. He must have been inside the Wing Commander's house, to paint it so accurately. It's remarkable, the detail."

"In years past they knew each other well. I'm talking about the fifties, now, half a century ago. They had interests in common - cricket, I think, and sports cars. Then they fell out over something pretty serious. Davey wouldn't speak of it, and whenever the Wing Commander's name was mentioned in the bar, he'd look up at the beam overhead as if he was trying to read the names on the tankards. Davey had opinions on most subjects, but he wouldn't be drawn on the Wing Co."

"Could it have been a woman?"

"The cause of the argument? Don't know. Davey had any number of affairs - relationships, you'd call them now. The artistic temperament, isn't it? A bit saucy for those days. But the Wing Co wasn't like that. He was married."

"When?"

"In the war, to one of those WAAFs who worked in the control rooms pushing little wooden markers across a map."

"A plotter."

"Right."

"She must have died some years ago, then. I don't remember her."

"You wouldn't. They separated. It wasn't a happy marriage. He's a grand old guy, but between you and me, he wouldn't move on mentally. He was still locked into service life. Officially he was demobbed in 1945, and took a local job selling insurance, but he wouldn't let go. R.A.F. Association, British Legion, showing little boys his medals at the Air Training Corps. And of course he was writing that book about the Battle of Britain. I think Helen was suffocated."

"Suffocated?"

"Not literally."

"What became of her, then."

"Nobody knows. She quit some time in the fifties, and no one has heard of her since."

"That's surprising, isn't it?"

"Maybe she emigrated. Sweet young woman. Hope she had a good life."

"Dark haired, was she?" Brandon asked. "Dark, long hair?"

"Now don't go up that route, inspector. The old boy may have been a selfish husband, but he's no murderer."

Brandon let that pass. "You haven't answered my question."

"All right, she was a brunette. Usually had it fastened at the back in a ponytail, but I've seen it loose."

"You said Davey Parks was a ladies' man. Did he ever make a pass at Helen Ashton?"

Chivers pulled a face. "If he did, she wasn't the sort to respond. Very loyal, she was. Out of the top drawer."

"That's nothing to go by," said Brandon. "So-called well-brought-up girls were the goers in those days."

"Take my word for it. Helen wouldn't have given Davey the come-on, or anyone else."

"She couldn't have been all that loyal, or she'd never have left the Wing Commander."

"I bet it wasn't for another man," said Chivers. "You'll have to ask the old boy yourself, won't you?"

Brandon could see it looming. How do you tell a ninety-year-old pillar of the community that half the town suspects he may have murdered his wife? Back at the police station, he studied that painting again, trying to decide if it represented a real incident, or was some morbid fantasy of the artist. The detail was so painstaking that you were tempted to think it *must* have been done from memory. The index and middle fingernails of the left hand, in the foreground, were torn, suggesting that the woman had put up a fight. The rest of the nails were finely manicured, making the contrast. Even the fingertips were smudged black from trying to protect herself from the sooty poker.

Yet clearly Davey Park couldn't have set up his easel at a murder scene. The background stuff, the Spitfire picture, aircraft models and so on, could have been done from memory if he was used to visiting the house. The dead woman - whoever she was - must have been out of his imagination, unless Park had *been there*. Was the picture a confession - the artist's way of owning up to a crime, deliberately left to be discovered after he died?

If so, how had the killing gone undetected? What had he done with the body?

The interview with the Wing Commander had to be faced. Brandon called at the house late in the afternoon.

"John, my dear fellow! What a happy surprise!" the old man innocently greeted him. "Do come in."

The moustache was white, the hair thin and the stance unsteady without a stick, but for an old man he was in good shape, still broad-shouldered and over six feet. Without any inkling of what was to follow, he shuffled into his living room, with the inspector following.

The room was disturbingly familiar. Little had changed in fifty years.

"Please find somewhere to sit. I'll get the sherry." He tottered out again.

Brandon didn't do as he was asked. This would be a precious interval of at least three minutes at the old man's shuffling rate of progress. With a penknife he started scraping at the dark strips of cement between the hearthstones. If any traces of dried blood had survived for half a century, this was the likely place. He spent some minutes scooping the samples of dust into a transparent bag and pocketed it when he heard the drag of the slippers across the carpet.

He was upright and admiring the dogfight picture over the fireplace when the Wing Commander came in with the tray.

"My, this is a work of art."

"Don't know about that, but I value it," said the old man. "Takes me back, of course."

"Did you ever meet the artist?"

"No, it's only a print. There are plenty of aviation artists selling to dotty old critters like me, nostalgic for the old days. We had a copy hanging in the officers' mess at Biggin Hill."

"I suppose it comes down to what will sell, like anything else. There was an artist in the town called Park, who specialised in landscapes. Died recently."

"So I heard," said the Wing Commander with a distinct change in tone.

"You knew him, didn't you?"

"Years ago." There was definitely an edge to the voice now.

"He painted a pretty accurate interior of this room. It was found among his canvases after he died."

"Did he, by jove? That's a liberty, don't you think? Abuse of friendship, I call that."

"He didn't remain your friend, I heard."

"We fell out."

"Do you mind telling me why?"

"Actually, I do, John. It's a closed book."

In other circumstances, Brandon would have put the screws on. "But you must have been close friends for him to know this room so well."

"I suppose he'd remember it. Used to drop in for a chat about cricket. We both played for the town team." The Wing Commander poured the sherry and handed one to Brandon. "Are you here in an official capacity?"

It had to be said. "I'm afraid so. The picture I mentioned wasn't just an interior scene." He hesitated. "I wish I didn't have to tell you this. It had the figure of a woman in it, lying across the carpet, apparently dead of a head wound."

"Good God!"

"There was a poker beside her. You don't seem to keep a set of fire irons any longer."

"It's gas now." The Wing Commander had turned quite crimson. "Look here, since you've come to question me, I think I have a right to see this unpleasant picture. Where is it?"

"At the police station, undergoing tests. I can let you see it, certainly, later in the week. What bothers me is whether it has any foundation in real events."

"Meaning what? That a woman was attacked here - in my living room?"

Brandon had to admire the old man's composure. "It seems absurd to me, too, but he was an accurate painter -"

"An alcoholic."

"... and wasn't known to paint anything he hadn't seen for himself."

"Don't know about that. Painters of that time used to use their dreams as inspiration. What do they call it - surrealism?"

"I have to ask this, Wing Commander. You separated from your wife in the nineteen-fifties."

"Helen? She left me. We found out we were incompatible, as many others have done."

"Did you ever divorce?"

"No need. I didn't want another marriage."

"Didn't she?"

"Evidently not."

"You're not in touch?"

"When it's over, it's over."

He's lost none of his cricketing skills, thought Brandon. He could stonewall with the best.

The dust samples went to the Home Office forensic department for analysis. In three days they sent the result: significant traces of human blood had been found. Normally, he would have been excited by the discovery. This was a real downer.

So a gentle enquiry was transformed into a murder investigation. Wing Commander Ashton was brought in for questioning and a scene of crime team went through his house. More traces of dried blood were found, leaving no question that someone had sustained a serious injury in that living room.

The Wing Commander faced the interrogation with the dignity of a veteran officer. He had lost contact with his wife in 1956 and made no effort to trace her. There had been no reason to stay in contact. They had no children. She had been comfortably off and so was he. No, her life had not been insured.

Brandon sensed that the old man held the truth in high regard. It was a point of honour not to lie. He wasn't likely to volunteer anything detrimental to himself, but he would answer with honesty.

When shown the painting that was the cause of all the fuss, he gave it a glance, no more, and said the woman on the floor didn't look much like his wife, what you could see of her. He was allowed to go home, only to find a team of policemen digging in his garden. He watched them with contempt.

A public appeal was made for the present address of Mrs Helen Ashton, aged 79. It was suggested that she might be using another name. This triggered massive coverage in the press. Davey Parks's painting was reproduced in all the dailies with captions like: IS THIS A MURDER SCENE? and PROOF OF MURDER OR CRUEL HOAX?

The response was overwhelming and fruitless. Scores of old ladies, some very confused, were interviewed and found to have no connection with the case. It only fuelled the suspicion that Helen Ashton had been dead for years.

The investigation was running out of steam. Nothing had been found in the garden. There were no incriminating diaries, letters or documents in the house.

"What about the book?" someone asked. "Did he have anything mean to say about his wife?"

Brandon had already skimmed through the book. Helen wasn't mentioned.

The answer to the mystery had to be in the picture. If the artist Davey Park knew a murder had been committed, and felt strongly enough to have made this visual record, he'd wanted the truth to come out. Then why hadn't he informed the police? Either he had killed Helen Ashton himself, or he felt under some obligation to keep the secret until he died. The picture was his one major work never to have been exhibited.

Either way, it suggested some personal involvement. He'd been known to have numerous affairs. Had Helen Ashton refused his advances and paid for it with her life?

Brandon stared at the picture once more, systematically studying each detail: the bloodstained fireplace, the pictures, the medals, the photos on the table, the armchair, the typewriter on the bureau, the dead woman, the blood on the carpet, her clothes, her damaged fingernails, her blackened fingertips. By sheer application he spotted something he'd missed before.

She wasn't wearing a wedding ring. The hand in the foreground was her left and the ring finger was bare.

"I deserve to be sacked," he said aloud.

Park had been so careful over detail that he wouldn't have forgotten to paint in the ring. And in the fifties, most married women wore their rings at all times.

"You're joking, guv," said DS Makepeace when Brandon asked him to make a list of the women Davey Park had been out with in the nineteen-fifties.

"I'm not. There are people in the town who remember. It was hot gossip once."

"Did he keep a diary, or something?"

"If he had, we'd have looked through it weeks ago. All he left behind were pictures and unpaid bills. Start with Henry Chivers, in the Crown."

After another week of patiently assembling information, Brandon had the Wing Commander brought in for further questioning.

Sergeant Makepeace thought he should have waited longer, and didn't mind speaking out. "I think he'll stall, guv. You won't get anything out of him."

"No," said Brandon firmly. "He's one of those rare witnesses you can rely on. A truth-teller. With his background it's a point of honour to give truthful answers. He won't mention anything that isn't asked, but he won't lie, either."

"You admire him, don't you?"

"That's what makes it so painful."

So the old man sat across the desk from Brandon in an interview room and the tape rolled and the formalities were gone through.

"Wing Commander Ashton, we now believe the woman who was attacked in your house was not your wife."

A soft sigh escaped. "Isn't that what I told you from the beginning?"

"The woman in the picture doesn't have a wedding ring. I should have looked for it earlier. I didn't."

The only response was a slight shrug.

Brandon admitted, "When I realised this, I was thrown. The victim could be anybody - any dark-haired young woman without a ring. There had to be some extra clue in the painting, and there is. She was the woman who typed your book. Her name was Angela Hamilton. Is that correct?"

He said stiffly, giving only as much as his moral code decreed, "I had a typist of that name, yes."

"She was murdered in your house in the manner shown in the painting. Davey Parks saw the scene just after it happened and painted it from memory."

The Wing Commander spread his hands. "The existence of this painting was unknown to me until I saw it here a few days ago."

"But you confirm that Miss Hamilton was the victim?"

"Yes."

"I'm interpreting the picture now. It gives certain pointers to the crime."

"Like the typewriter."

"Just so. And the reason she was partially dressed is that you and she had been making love, probably in that room where she typed for you. Precisely where is not important. Your wife came home - she was supposed to be out for some considerable time - and caught you cheating on her."

The Wing Commander didn't deny it. He looked down at his arthritic hands. The passions of fifty years ago seemed very remote.

Brandon continued: "We think what happened is this. To use an old-fashioned phrase, Angela Hamilton was a fast woman, an ex-lover of the artist Davey Park. Park heard she'd been taken on by you as a part-time typist and found out that she didn't spend all her time in front of the machine. Perhaps she boasted to him that she'd seduced the famous Battle of Britain hero, or perhaps he played Peeping Tom at your window one afternoon. Anyway, he decided to tell your wife. He'd been trying to flirt with her, with no success. He thought if she found out you were two-timing, she might be encouraged to do the same. She didn't believe him, so he offered to prove it. They both turned up at your house when you and Angela were having sex. Is that a fair account?"

"They caught us in some embarrassment, yes," said the Wing Commander.

"You were shocked, guilt-stricken and extremely angry. The worst part was seeing Park and realising he'd told your wife. Did you go after him?"

"I did, and caught him in the garden and let fly with my fists." At last, the Wing Commander was willing to give more than the minimum of information. "I was so incensed I might have injured him permanently."

"What stopped you?"

There was an interval of silence, while the old man decided if at last he was free to speak of it. "There was a scream from the house. I hear it now. Like no other scream I have ever heard. The fear in it. Horrible. We abandoned the fight and rushed inside."

"Both of you?"

"Yes. He saw it too. Angela, dead on the floor, with blood seeping from her head and the poker beside her, just as it is in the picture. Helen had already run out through the back. Such ferocity. I never knew she had it in her."

"What did you do?"

"With the body? Drove it to a place I know, a limestone quarry, and covered it with rubble. It has never been found. I blamed myself, you see. Helen had acted impulsively. She didn't deserve to be hanged, or locked up for life. You'll have to charge me with conspiracy."

"I'll decide on the charge," said Brandon. "So you felt you owed it to your wife to cover up the crime. What did she do?"

"Packed up her things and left. She wanted no more to do with me, and I understood why. I behaved like a louse and got what I deserved."

"You truly didn't hear from her again?"

"I have a high regard for the truth."

"Then you won't know the rest of the story. Your wife took another name and moved, first to Scotland, and then Suffolk. Davey Parks, always scratching around for a living, saw a chance of extorting money."

"Blackmail?"

"He set out to find her, and succeeded. We've looked at a building society account he had. Regular six-monthly deposits of a thousand pounds were made at a branch in Stowmarket, Suffolk, for over twenty years."

"The fiend."

"He painted the picture as a threat. Had some postcards made of it. Each year, as a kind of invoice, he would send her one - until she died in 1977."

"I had no idea," said the Wing Commander. "He was living in my village extorting sums of money from my own wife. It's vile."

"I agree. Perhaps if you'd made contact with her, she would have told you."

He shook his head. "Too proud. She was too proud ever to speak to me again." His eyes had reddened. He took out a handkerchief. "You'd better charge me before I make an exhibition of myself."

Brandon shook his head. "I won't be charging you, sir."

"I want no favours, just because I'm old."

"It would serve no purpose. You'd be given a suspended sentence at the very worst. There's no point. But I have a request. Would you show us where Angela Hamilton was buried?"

The remains were recovered and given a Christian burial a month later. Brandon, Sergeant Makepeace and Wing Commander Ashton were the only mourners.

On the drive back, Makepeace said, "One thing I've been meaning to ask you, sir."

"Ask away."

"That picture contained all the clues, you said. Davey Park made sure."

"So he did."

"Well, how did you know Angela Hamilton was the victim?"

"She was on your list of Clark's girlfriends."

"It was a long list."

"She was the only one who temped as a typist. The typewriter was in the picture. A big clue."

"Yes, I know, but -"

"You're not old enough to have used an ancient manual typewriter," Brandon added. "If you remember, her fingertips were smudged black. At first I assumed it was soot, from the poker, but the marks were very precise. In those days when you wanted more than one copy of what you typed, you used carbon paper. However careful you were, the damned stuff got on the tips of your fingers."

Dr Death

I am alone in the house with a madman, and I don't know what to do. My poor husband Charles has been murdered, his throat cut after he went to open the door. Please God, may I be spared!

I am at the mercy of the monster who has butchered no fewer than twelve people in their own homes since March of 1873. The newspapers call him Dr Death. Of course he cannot be a doctor. That is a wicked slur against the medical profession. He is a murderer who knocks on doors and kills at random with a cut-throat razor, attacking whoever comes to the door. In the streets the children chant a horrid rhyme:

> Dr Death will cure your ills.
> He's very quick.
> He calls, he kills.
> He never gives you stomach pills.
> He just turns up
> And calls, and kills.

Our night of terror began at twenty-five past nine, less than half an hour ago. Charles and I were in the drawing room playing cribbage, as we do most Sunday evenings. Some will disapprove of cards on the sabbath; I can only say in mitigation that this is the only evening we have together. From Monday to Saturday Charlie supplements our meagre income by working long hours as a billiard-marker at the Amateur Athletic Club premises at Lillie Bridge. It is a humble occupation, keeping the score for gentlemen of leisure in the hope that they will be generous with gratuities, but in these difficult times a man is glad of anything that keeps him from the workhouse. We live - thank God - in a nice detached house on Putney Hill. Charles's family has owned the house for generations. We were playing cribbage, then, and eating some nuts I had kept from Christmas, enjoying the modest comfort of a wood fire and a chance to be alone, with just our little Shetland Terrier, Snowy, for company. We have no servants.

There was a knock on the door, an urgent rat-a-tat that startled us both and caused Snowy to bark. I was in no state to receive a visitor. I had taken a bath earlier in the evening and had not gone to the bother of dressing again. In my nightdress and dressing gown I was relaxing with my dear husband. One feels so secure, so content in one's privacy, at home behind locked doors and thick curtains.

"Who can that be?" Charles said.

I shook my head and spread my hands. It did not cross my mind that Dr Death was on our doorstep.

One Sunday evening a few weeks ago we talked about him. I asked Charles what he would do if the madman called at our house and Charles said, "I would protect you, of course."

"But what if I were alone, as I am most evenings?"

"Don't answer the door. It's bolted and the windows are shuttered. You're safe here."

I believed him.

Tonight, we were proved wrong.

He got up and reached for his jacket. "I expect it's William."

His brother William is our mainstay, our Good Samaritan. He gives us money, pays our doctor's bills and even hands on his old suits to Charlie. He found Charlie the job at Lillie Bridge. Without his help, we would have been on the streets years ago. I call him Sweet William.

Charles said, "You'd better leave the room, just in case it's someone else."

I obeyed willingly. It was possible Charles would feel obliged to admit the caller and I had no wish to receive anyone dressed as I was. I withdrew at once to the dining room. In there, without a fire, it was chilly, but I could remain out of sight until Charles had dealt with the visitor. I hoped it was just some hawker who could be sent on his way at once. People come quite late hoping to interest us in anything from bootlaces to kittens, or even expecting us to pay them something to remove their caterwauling hurdy-gurdy to another street. I suppose they think we must be comfortably placed, living in a house with a gravel drive. Little do they know the long hours Charles has to work to keep us from penury. He walks two miles to work every day, to save the fares.

Charles withdrew the bolt on the front door and opened it. From the dining room I strained to hear who the caller was. The words were modulated at first, and then they increased in volume and although I could not hear them distinctly I was sure they were not friendly in tone. In vain my poor husband, who is not the most patient of souls, tried to get rid of the visitor. The exchange of opinions turned to ranting. Still I had no suspicion as to who the caller might be. Then, to my horror, the argument was joined by sounds of a physical struggle. Some piece of furniture in the hall - probably the umbrella stand - was toppled over. Then a picture or a mirror fell and shattered. I cowered in a corner, shaking uncontrollably. How I wish now that I had gone to Charles's assistance; feeble as I am, I might have created some distraction enabling him to gather his resources. You see, horrible as it was to hear sounds of violence, I had no conception that anything so dreadful as murder was being done.

Neither did it cross my mind that we were being invaded by Dr Death. Why should he choose our house, of all the homes in London? I know the answer now, of course. He didn't choose it at all. He calls and kills indiscriminately, men and women, taking perverted pleasure in the power he feels when he produces his razor and sees the uncomprehending terror in their eyes. He'll knock at anyone's door. It must give him a sense of power, not knowing who will be next to feel the blade across their throats. That is why the police are having such difficulty catching him. He is unpredictable.

I should have been alert to the danger. Like everyone else,

I have read about the killings in the newspaper and tut-tutted and shaken my head, but I never seriously thought we would be his next victims.

There was a blood-curdling scream that stopped abruptly, followed by silence. I shall hear it for ever if I live through this experience, the scream and the silence. It must have been the moment my beloved Charlie's throat was cut. Then the thump of his body hitting the floor, followed by the beast-like panting of his killer.

Petrified, I pressed my fists against my teeth, trying to understand what had just happened. There could be no doubt that terrible violence had been done. I wanted to shriek in terror, but the slightest sound would have revealed me as a witness, and put me in danger.

I waited, trying desperately not to swoon and praying that this evil presence would leave the house. Presently I heard a door being opened. Then, faintly, the sound of running water. He had gone to the kitchen to wash away the worst of the blood, as I now realise.

It was my opportunity. Without regard to the risk, I left the dining room and went to assist my poor husband. Broken glass crunched under my carpet slippers. My heart sank fathoms when I saw the scene, the lifeless form lying across the hall with a dark pool spreading beneath his head, and blood all over the wall, running down in streaks. The smell of it was sickening. It must have gushed from an artery. No one could survive such a massive loss.

Now I knew for certain that Dr Death had called, and killed. Numb, petrified, ready to faint, I could not bring myself to touch my poor husband. I just stood staring at the back of his head.

Then I heard the tap turned off in the kitchen and steps across the tiled floor. What was I to do? Charlie was beyond help. The madman would kill me next. I had seen in the papers that he has twice before slit the throats of a man and his wife together.

I ran up the stairs. It was a stupid action, I admit, for where could I go if he pursued me? I went to our bedroom and looked for a place to hide and in my distracted state I could think of nothing more original than the wardrobe, a huge mahogany thing we inherited with the house. Charlie's late father was quite well-to-do; he was deeply disappointed when Charlie failed his exam for the Civil Service and had to seek unsalaried work. We are not all good at passing exams. I was so grateful that he left us the house in his will. It is the one secure thing in our existence. The family money, the stocks and shares and so on, were left to William, who is a chartered accountant, and understands the world of finance, and helps us to survive. We have practically no money, but we have a roof over our heads. It was a wise decision.

Here I squat, at the bottom of the wardrobe, trying to hide under the spare blanket. I have been here ten minutes at least, weeping silently, trying to tell myself not to give way to my troubled thoughts. I must stay in control.

If Dr Death comes looking for me, I am going to die. I pray that he will leave the house. Surely his desire for blood is sated. Yet I know he is still here. Occasional sounds come from downstairs. I suppose he is looking for money, or valuables. He won't find any.

Suddenly there is a sound nearby, here, in the bedroom. My flesh prickles. I want to scream.

It is not a heavy sound, but it is close, extremely close. The wardrobe door rattles. There is a scratching sound outside, followed by whimpering.

Snowy.

My little dog has found me. If I don't do something about him, he'll give me away, for sure. He will start barking any second.

I open the wardrobe door and get a terrible shock. Snowy has a gash across his middle, from the top of his back to right under his stomach. It seems unspeakably cruel. Then I look closer and see that what I am looking at is not a wound, but a streak of my poor husband's blood. Snowy climbs up and nudges against me, seeking comfort, and some of it marks my nightdress. He continues to whimper. The sound will surely bring the killer upstairs.

I must think of something. I can't stay here, now that Snowy has found me, and I can't silence him. If the madman comes anywhere near, Snowy will bark. He barks at the slightest thing. Oh God, am I starting to panic?

I dare not go downstairs again.

Above me, there is the attic, but I can't get up there without the stepladder, and that is kept in the cupboard under the stairs. If there was a balcony to this bedroom, I would step outside, but there is not.

I have just remembered the fire escape. It is at the back of the house. You get to it from the little bedroom, the one we use as a box room. If I can open the window, I can climb down the ladder to the ground and run for help. That is what I must do.

With as much stealth as I am capable of, I emerge from my hiding place and cross the bedroom to the landing. Snowy follows me. Mercifully he is silent.

Then - Oh God! - I hear footsteps on the stairs. Dr Death has heard me and is coming.

Abandoning caution, I rush across the landing to the box room and fling open the door. Our box room is, of course, crammed with portmanteaux and trunks filled with bric-a-brac, summer curtains, old clothing, rolls of carpet, discarded ornaments, cracked mirrors, a dressmaker's dummy. There is scarcely room for a person to move in there, and I must get to the window.

I slam the door after me, hoping to hamper my pursuer. Finding strength I did not know I possessed, I slide an enormous cabin trunk across the doorway and heap things on it, at the same time clearing a route to the window. Snowy is beside me, barking furiously now. I don't know what I shall do with him. He will have to be left here and take his chance. In my frenzy I knock over a tower of hat boxes, and they crash against some brass stair rods with a clatter that sounds all over the house. I must get to the window.

I have to climb over an old armchair heaped with magazines to reach it. My foot slides on the paper and I fall against an iron bedstead. Pain shoots through my arm and shoulder. I try again.

Now Dr Death is at the door, rattling it. Brave little Snowy barks and growls. I don't look round. I am at the window trying to get my fingers under the brass handles. The sash cord is broken, I think. I have to force it upwards by brute strength if I have any left. It is very stiff, but it moves a few inches and I wedge a book into the gap and try again.

I can hear the madman straining outside the door. He has it open a fraction and is crashing his shoulder against it.

I succeed in heaving the window upwards and putting my leg over the sill. It is pitch black out there. I tug my nightdress to the top of my legs, all decorum abandoned, and get a foot onto one of the top rungs of the fire escape ladder. Squeezing myself under the window I climb fully out. The window slams down, just missing my hand. The last thing I hear is my little dog still inside the room. He has stopped barking and is whimpering.

On the ladder, I feel the chill of the night air. I am so hot from my exertions that I welcome it. Down the iron rungs I hurry, feeling chips of rust flaking off under my already sore hands. My feet hurt terribly. Slippers were never meant for this sort of activity. I don't know how far down I am when the window above me is thrust open. I suppose he is looking down, deciding whether to come after me. All I can do is keep descending until I feel the ground under my feet.

At last I am down, and running around the side of the house to the front, where it is better lit. I shall stop the first person I see. I run across the drive, sobbing now. I can't stop myself from crying.

On Putney Hill the gas lamps show me an empty street. Nobody is about. What can I do except run to my neighbours? I cross the road to the Tyler's house. We don't know them well, but they have two grown-up sons. Surely one can be sent to summon the police.

Their manservant opens the door.

"Help me," I say. "My husband is murdered and the man is still inside the house." I point towards where we live.

He asks me to wait, but I follow him inside.

Mr and Mrs Tyler are magnificent. They grasp the urgency of the matter at once and the men go out to deal with the emergency. One son will go for the police, just a short way down Putney Hill. The others will keep watch. Mrs Tyler wraps me in a blanket and brings me brandy. I have given way to weeping hysteria again, but by degrees I lapse into a shocked silence.

I can't say how much time passes before the front door opens. I jump at the sound, but it is only Mr Tyler, with a policeman. Mr Tyler has Snowy tucked under his arm.

"It's all over, my dear," he says, releasing my little dog, who runs to me and licks my ankle. "This is Inspector Reed."

"You caught the man?"

"Yes," says the policeman. "He's in custody now. We forced an entry into the house and took him. You must be in a state of shock, ma'am, but I need to speak to you."

I take Snowy into my arms. "It's all right. I feel much better."

"Did you see the man who came to the house?"

"See him? No. Charles, my husband, went to the door. It was savage, what happened. He was murdered almost at once."

"We saw for ourselves, ma'am."

"I heard everything. I was in the next room."

"Heard what was said?"

"No, that was indistinct. Raised voices, and the sound of violence."

There is a pause, as if they hesitate to tell me some new horror.

"Your husband had a brother William. Is that correct?"

I frown and hug Snowy to my chest. "What does William have to do with it?"

"He's older than your husband?"

"Yes. He's twenty-eight, I think."

"Comes to visit you, does he?"

"Yes, he takes a brotherly interest in our lives. He's a lovely man, generous and caring." I don't mention that William sometimes helps us with money. That's private, and the Tylers don't have to hear of it.

"It was William who came to your house this evening."

I am astounded. "What? William? I don't understand."

"He came out of a sense of responsibility, ma'am. We've spoken to his wife and she told us they were deeply troubled by your husband's conduct."

"This can't be true!" I say.

"Will you hear me out, ma'am? People at Lillie Bridge, where your husband is known - he works there sometimes, I believe - saw him last week using the bathing facilities, washing blood from his hands and arms on the day the man was murdered in Chelsea."

"No!"

"They reasoned that a billiard-marker doesn't get bloody hands. They suspected him of the crimes we've heard so much about. It was only suspicion, so they didn't come to us as they should have done. They went to your brother-in-law."

"To William?"

"William came to your house tonight to seek an explanation and was savagely attacked. Your husband must have had his cut-throat razor at the ready, in his jacket pocket. He murdered William."

"No," I cry out. "You're mistaken. It's Charlie who is dead."

"Did you look at the face of the dead man?"

I am speechless. I *didn't* look at his face. I couldn't bear to see the cruel gash across his throat. How could I mistake my own husband for his brother? My brain is racing now. They have similar coloured hair. William is slightly taller, but their physique is similar. And Charlie wears William's handed-down suits. Black pin-stripes always, as you would expect a professional man to wear.

The policeman says, "Your husband is alive. He's the man we have in custody, ma'am."

Mr Tyler says, "It's true."

I scream, a long, piercing scream, a scream of horror, and despair, and mental agony.

Mrs Tyler tries to comfort me. I push her away. I stare at them all, shaking my head, sobbing convulsively.

Over my sounds of grief, the policeman adds, "We believe him to be responsible for the deaths of thirteen people. You're going to ask me why he did it and I can only say that he's obviously insane."

"He's not," I plead. "He's a perfect husband to me."

"He has a double life, then," the policeman insists.

Now Mr Tyler tries to make me understand. "My dear, such cases are not unknown to those who study the criminal mind. They are perfectly reasonable ninety-nine per cent of the time. Then something happens in the brain. An uncontrollable anger makes them attack innocent people for quite trivial reasons. It seems that tonight your husband's brother came to face him with the truth, a brave, but misguided action. There was a struggle and William was killed with a vicious slash across the throat, just like the other victims."

The policeman says, "He would have killed you, too."

"Never. Not Charlie."

Will I ever believe it? I stare at the policeman, hating him for what he is saying, and knowing, deep inside, that he is right.

Mr Tyler says, "It's going to be hard for you to accept. However intimate we are with another human being, we never know them fully."

Wise, intolerable words. I have the rest of my devastated life to reflect on them.

The Four Wise Men

One December morning in the year 1895, Sherlock Holmes tossed aside *The Times* and said to me with some abruptness, "Stop dithering, Watson. It's your duty to go down to Somerset for Christmas, regardless of the plans you made."

I stared at him in astonishment. I had spoken not a syllable of the matter that was exercising me.

He amazed me even more, by adding, "An old soldier's loyalty to his senior officer is a commitment for life. He needs your support and you are not the man to withhold it."

"Holmes," said I, when I found my voice again, "your feats of deduction are well known to me, but to discover that you are also a mind-reader is truly a revelation, not to say unnerving."

He made a dismissive gesture with his long, limp hand. "My dear fellow, I can think of few things I should less enjoy than peering into the minds of my fellow-creatures. My advice to you is based on observation alone." As if to provoke me further, he stopped speaking, thrust his unlit pipe in his mouth and looked out of the window at the traffic passing along Baker Street.

I waited. It became obvious that he proposed to say nothing more unless I pursued the matter.

I was lath to give him the satisfaction, but at length my curiosity prevailed. "I hesitate to trespass on your time -"

"Then don't."

Some minutes passed before I steeled myself to begin again. I do believe he, too, was finding the silence intolerable, though he would never have admitted as much.

"I thought I knew your methods, Holmes. In this matter, I confess myself mystified."

He continued to stare out of the window.

"I would appreciate some explanation."

He sighed heavily. "There are times, Watson, when I despair of you. You are blind to your own behaviour. When I told you to stop dithering, it was after you had removed that letter from its envelope for the third time and perused it with much frowning. By now you know the contents. You can only be re-reading it to see if you can think of some half-decent way of avoiding Christmas in Somersetshire."

"How on earth do you know about Somerset?"

"The Taunton postmark."

"Ha!" I chuckled at my own naivety, and I should not have done so, for Holmes took it as dismissive of his brilliance. Recovering my tact, I continued, "But the other things. Your statement - which I have to declare is accurate - that my presence is required by an old army colleague."

"I said your senior officer."

"And you are right, by jove. Have you been reading my correspondence?"

He emitted a sound of impatience. "How could I? It hasn't been out of your possession since the moment you tore open the envelope. The explanation will, of course, disappoint you, as these things do."

"I'm sure it will not."

With a show of reluctance, he enlightened me. "The festive season is approaching. We're all aware of that. A time of invitations."

"You made an inspired guess?"

Now a look of extreme disfavour clouded the great detective's features. "I do not guess."

"I said 'inspired'."

"It does not lessen the insult. Guessing is the province of charlatans. I make deductions. I was about to point out that when you first perused the letter you turned to look over my shoulder at the front page of *The Times*, which has nothing to interest you except the date."

"So I did!"

"Today's date told you how close we are to Christmas, how many days are left. You're an active fellow, with much to attend to in the coming days. You had to calculate the time at your disposal."

"Absolutely true."

"An invitation to the country for Christmas. Need I say more?"

"Please do." His statements had the force of logic, as always. "What mystifies me most is how you divined that the invitation comes from one of my regiment - and his senior rank."

"Oh, that," he said, knocking his pipe against the window-ledge and producing a cloud of ash. "It's training, Watson."

"Training in the deductive method?"

"Not my training. Yours. In the army. The drilling every soldier undergoes. What did you do when you met a superior officer?"

"Saluted. But I didn't salute just now."

"No, no, but when you saw who the letter was from, your free hand snapped to your side with the fingers lightly clenched, the thumb pointing down the seam below your trouser pocket in the military fashion. Highly indicative."

"Good Lord," I said. "Am I so transparent?"

"Quite the reverse."

"Opaque?"

He looked away and I believe there was a gleam of amusement in his eye. "You have made your decision, I see. You will go to Taunton. Loyalty demands it, even though duty no longer applies."

I took the letter from its envelope once more. Holmes had delivered his advice, and I saw the sense of it, but I felt that a more considered opinion might be forthcoming. The invitation was, indeed, from my old Commanding Officer in the Fifth Northumberland Fusiliers, Colonel Sloane, M.C., a hero of the Afghan campaign. I offered to read it aloud.

"*My Dear Watson*, (it began),

Some years have passed since we were last in contact, but your admirable strengths impress me still. I always regarded you as utterly dependable."

"True," Holmes generously interposed.

"I never expected to ask for your support after we retired from Her Majesty's Service, but a strange contingency has arisen here in the village of Bullpen, near Taunton, where I reside."

"Would you repeat that?" Holmes requested.

"Bullpen, near Taunton. May I continue?"

He nodded. I had all his attention now.

"I can forgive you if you have never heard of the Bullpen Nativity Service, but it has some celebrity in these parts. Each year on the Sunday preceding Christmas it is the custom for the villagers to take part in a masque and procession to the church, where our Nativity Service takes place. We take turns to play the parts of the characters in the age-old story, and this year I have the honour to be Balthazar, one of the Three Kings."

"Wise Men," Holmes interjected again.

"It says 'Kings'."

"Kings are not mentioned in any of the Gospel accounts."

"Really?"

"The figure of three is not specified either, for that matter," said he, displaying a hitherto unrevealed acquaintance with the New Testament.

I resumed reading: *"It is a role of some responsibility, for by tradition Balthazar carries the Star. I should explain that the Star is a representation in silver and precious stones of the Star in the East, of Biblical renown. It is about the size of a dinner plate and is carried high, mounted on a seven-foot pole, so that the impression is given that we Kings - and, indeed, the shepherds - are being guided towards Bethlehem. The star is of mediaeval workmanship, beautifully constructed of Welsh silver and set with seven rubies. It is kept in the strong-room of the United Bank in Taunton. Without exaggeration it is one of the most valuable mediaeval treasures in England, rivalling even the Crown Jewels in workmanship and beauty. Last summer, it was put on exhibition at the British*

Museum, and insured for twenty thousand pounds. My task - my honour - is to collect the star from the bank, travel with it in a closed carriage to my home, the manor house, where the principal actors assemble to put on their robes and the procession through the street to the church begins. I carry the Star aloft on the stave, keeping it in my possession until the moment during the service when it is placed over the crib. The responsibility then passes for a brief time to Joseph, who returns it to me after the service."

"Ha!" said Holmes with animation. "He wishes you to be his Joseph."

I nodded.

"And you will go." As if the matter no longer held any interest, he reached for his scrapbook and opened it. "Have you seen my paste-bottle?"

"Behind you on the mantelpiece."

"And scissors?"

"Where you left them, in the top pocket of your dressing gown."

"So I did. There's an item of passing interest on page three about the theft in Paris of a necklace that belonged to Marie Antionette. It has features that lead me to suspect my old adversary Georges Du Broc is active again."

"Du Broc?" I repeated. "You've never spoken of Du Broc before."

"The Jackdaw. A chirpy little fellow half your size. The most brazen thief in Europe."

"He is unknown to me."

"Be thankful, then. He'd have the shirt off your back without your noticing. Have I not mentioned the case of the Tsarina's ankle-chain?"

"Not to me," said I. "I should have remembered a case like that, I'm certain."

"How discreet I have become," mused Holmes.

He exasperated me by saying no more of Du Broc, the Tsarina, or the ankle-chain. But he was good enough to announce, "I shall attend the Bullpen Nativity Service."

We took the train together from Paddington on the Saturday before Christmas. A dusting of snow in London became quite an Arctic scene as we steamed towards the West Country. I still hoped to return to London by Christmas Eve, but my confidence ebbed when I saw the snowflakes getting larger by the minute. At Bristol, we changed to the Exeter and Plymouth line.

"I doubt if they'll cancel it," said Holmes, reading my thoughts with ease (he was capable of it, I swear). "A tradition that has lasted five hundred years isn't going to be ended by a few inches of snow."

"Perhaps they'll dispense with the street procession and go straight to the church."

"My dear fellow, Joseph and Mary travelled scores of miles over mountains and across deserts from Nazareth to Bethlehem through the most inclement conditions and you complain at the prospect of a ten-minute walk in the snow."

I turned aside and faced the window.

We were greeted at Taunton by Colonel Sloane himself, little changed from the gallant officer I had last seen in Kabul, six feet tall, with a fine, erect bearing and a cropped iron-grey moustache. He walked with a marked limp, the result of a stray bullet that had shattered his left kneecap. I had patched him up myself, and he always maintained that I saved the leg from amputation.

I introduced Holmes.

"I have heard of you, of course, Mr Holmes," said the Colonel. "What brings a man of your reputation to our humble village?"

"A bird I seek," Holmes answered cryptically.

This was news to me. I had never heard my illustrious friend discussing ornithology.

"Most of them migrated months ago," said Sloane. "You'll see a few sparrows and chaffinches, no doubt. A robin or two."

Holmes appeared uninterested. He makes no concession to the social graces.

Colonel Sloane had come for us in a four-wheeler. His former batman, Ruff, a strapping fellow I faintly recalled from Kabul, stepped forward to assist with our luggage. I gathered that the Colonel lived as a bachelor in Bullpen Manor House and was looked up to as the squire.

With Ruff at the reins, we were smoothly conveyed through the lanes towards the village. It was like riding on a sleigh, for the hooves and wheels made little sound on the snow.

The Colonel wasted no time in explaining my duties. "You will have gathered that I put the highest priority on securing the safety of the Bullpen Star. I have engaged two sergeants of the Taunton police to act as bodyguards. My batman is big enough to handle most emergencies, but I see this as a full-scale military operation, which is why I detailed you to be Joseph. I shall hand the star to you at the appropriate time in the church."

"When is that?"

"You will be standing beside the Crib with Mary and the Angels. You are not in the procession."

I could not resist a triumphant glance at Holmes, who gazed back stonily.

"You may stand easy during the service," the Colonel continued, "but mentally you will be at attention, if you understand me. The procession will march up the aisle with me at the front."

"*March?*" said Holmes.

"With me at the front holding the Star," Sloane reiterated, "and the two policemen, disguised as shepherds, in close attendance. The congregation will be singing a carol, *Once In Royal David's City*. As the *Amen* is sung, I shall take two paces forward to the Crib. The Rector will say the words, 'It came and stood over where the young child was' - whereupon I shall hand you the staff on which the Star is mounted. You will grasp it firmly with both hands."

"Military fashion," murmured Holmes.

My companion's irony was threatening to discompose the Colonel. I gave him a sharp glance of disapproval.

"This is of the utmost importance, Watson," Colonel Sloane stressed. "Do not let go of that staff until the service is over and I take it from you. No one else must be in possession of the Star at any time. Is that understood?"

"Absolutely, sir."

"Do you still have your service revolver?"

The question somewhat surprised me.

"Not with me."

"No matter. I have guns. I shall see that you are armed."

"In church?"

"The enemy are no respecters of the Lord's house."

"The enemy? Who do you mean precisely?"

"The criminal class, Watson. They will rob us of the Star if we give them the opportunity."

Holmes raised an eyebrow.

"Are you expecting an ambush, Colonel?"

"Deplorably, there is the possibility," Sloane answered gravely. "Did I mention that the Star was loaned to the British Museum for several months in the summer? Thousands of visitors saw it. The newspapers wrote of it. The *Illustrated London News* and the *Graphic* printed line-engravings of it. More of the public know of its existence than ever before. Our simple Nativity Service was fully described. Isn't it a tailor-made opportunity for the wickedly-disposed to attempt a grand larceny?"

"You may well be right," Holmes was fair enough to concur. "You are wise to be alert."

The guest-room of the Feathers Inn had been booked for us. Bullpen was a modest-sized village of about two hundred souls, of whom a fair proportion crowded into the public bar that night. We joined them. In the course of the evening we met Andrew Hall, the farmer who was to play Melchior in the masque, a massively built individual with the reddish, leathery complexion of one who makes his living in all weathers.

"We take it by turns," Farmer Hall told us, speaking of the casting of the players. "I were a simple shepherd two year back. Now I'm carrying the gold."

"Real gold?" I enquired.

"Lord, no. Don't get ideas, just because our Star is valuable. 'Tis only a box of trinkets I carry."

"Who plays the other Wise Man, Gaspar?" Holmes asked.

"The frankincense man? Our landlord, Jeb Wiggs."

"You're all well known in the village - you, Wiggs and the Colonel?"

"That's a fact, sir. Parts are played by villagers, according to tradition."

I was beginning to feel uneasy about my role as Joseph, but Farmer Hall reassured me by saying. "Them's the walking parts I'm speaking of, kings and shepherds. It's they the crowds come to see and it's they that gets handed mince-pies and mulled wine along the route. We don't mind who plays Joseph and Mary - stuck in the church for upwards of two hours. They're non-imbibing parts. We got a Joseph from London this year, old army friend of the Colonel."

I was about to make myself known when Holmes spoke up first: "And what of Mary? Who plays Mary?"

"Any young girl of sixteen, provided she has a pious expression and a spotless reputation. This year 'tis young Alison Pugh, the church warden's youngest."

"And the infant Jesus?"

"A china doll."

"Does anyone else take part?" Holmes asked, at pains to get the entire cast-list.

"The angels. Girls who wanted the part of Mary and had to be overlooked for various reasons. There are only two this year. The Dawson sisters. Winsome little things. Just a mite too winsome, I reckon."

We spoke no more of the Dawson sisters. By the end of the evening we had a useful understanding of the entire arrangements. At five the next evening, the players in the procession would assemble at the manor house.

"I shall follow the procession," Holmes declared before we retired.

"Are you sure you wouldn't care to dress up as a shepherd?" I asked. "You enjoy going in disguise."

"Dressing-up is not disguise," said he witheringly.

So it was that by five the following afternoon I found myself standing berobed in a "manger" in Bullpen Church, ankle-deep in straw that scratched my feet distractingly through the sandals. Had I been in the procession, I should have been allowed to wear my own shoes, but as a non-moving player I earned no concession. At my side in virginal blue, seated on a bale, was young Alison, in the role of Mary. She kept her eyes downcast and said little. The Dawson sisters, playing the angels, were more sociable. Cicely, the older of the two, gold-en-haired and extremely pretty, invited me more than once to adjust the angle of her wings, which involved unbuttoning her bodice a little way at the back and retying the satin straps over her shoulders. But when her parents joined the congregation and sat in the front pew, she needed no more adjustments.

The animals around us were constructed by a local carpenter, flat wooden figures of full size that the angels were at some risk of knocking over with their wings. In fact, a donkey fell against me when the organist startled us by launching suddenly into *The First Noel*.

The service was beginning, but my thoughts were outside, on the snow-covered street, where the procession must already have left the manor house with Colonel Sloane at its head, proudly carrying the Bullpen Star, its rubies glittering in the light of scores of flaming torches. I hoped the Colonel was not being too literal about the "march" and setting a pace out of keeping with the occasion. As a spectacle, it should have been stately and devout, like an Epiphany procession I once saw in one of the Latin countries.

We reached the last verse of the carol and the Rector made his way up the aisle to receive the procession at the West door. The gas was turned so low that we could barely see the words in the hymn-books, and the dimness contributed to the charmed atmosphere, the air of anticipation.

A draught of cold December air gusted through the church when the door was opened. The organist started a *diminuendo* rendering of *Once In Royal David's City*, with just the trebles in the choir singing, and I do not mind admitting I was moved almost to tears. Hastily I reminded myself that I was on duty for the Colonel and ought to be at full alert.

The procession entered the church. With deep satisfaction I saw the Star above the heads, gleaming proudly in the unbroken tradition of five centuries or more. The lights were turned up gradually and the silver fairly shone as it was borne up the aisle.

My role in the service was about to begin. Along the aisle I saw Balthazar gripping the staff with the Star aloft, dressed in a robe of glittering fabric with an ermine collar that would not have looked out of place at a coronation. He sported a crown, of course, fashioned in the eastern style; and a black beard that gave him a splendid Oriental appearance, so his limp did not take anything away from the effect.

Beside him, the two policemen dressed as shepherds were moving with the heavy tread of officers on duty, but this was noticeable only to me, with the advantage of knowing who they were. I spotted my drinking companions of the night before, as sumptuously arrayed as the Colonel, playing Gaspar and Melchior with great conviction.

The carol drew to a close and the *"Amen"* was sung. The Rector spoke his few words about the star standing over the stable. Balthazar stepped forward like a colour-sergeant about to hand over the regimental standard. His lush black beard quite covered three-quarters of his face, but our eyes met briefly and I believe I conveyed confidence. I put out my hands to receive the precious Star and it was handed across. Resolutely I gripped the staff with both hands.

The Three Kings - or Wise Men, as Holmes would have it - by turns presented Mary with their offerings of gold, frankincense and myrhh. Having stepped back, they knelt, allowing the shepherds to come forward. When everyone was kneeling

I had a clear view of the congregation and I was pleased to observe that Holmes had found a seat at the end of one of the pews. It would do him no harm to have a good view of me at the centre of proceedings, loyally carrying out my duty, just as the Colonel had instructed. For once in his life, I reflected, Mr Sherlock Holmes was obliged to play second fiddle.

There followed more verses from St Matthew and then the Rector, an elderly man with a fine crop of white hair and a rather monotonous voice, said, "Let us pray." I had better explain that I am not in the habit of praying standing up and with my eyes open. On this occasion (may I be forgiven), I made an exception. Primed for any occurrence, I looked steadily ahead, whilst every other head was bowed. I was resolved not to relax my vigilance for a second, even though it was difficult to conceive of anything untoward happening whilst we were at our devotions.

I was mistaken.

There was an interruption, and the offender, of all people, was Holmes!

I spotted a movement along the aisle and to my mortification saw him crawling rapidly and with uncanny stealth, Indian-fashion, over the flagstones and the monumental brasses in my direction, or at least towards the kneeling shepherds and Wise Men in front of the crib. When he was near enough to touch their robes, he dipped even closer to the floor like a ferret.

That it was Holmes, I had not the slightest doubt, or I would have raised the alarm there and then. I knew the man. I knew what he was wearing, the Inverness cape and the brown suit and the goloshes. No one but my Baker Street companion could move with such remarkable agility.

Aghast, I held onto the Star, craning to see what he was doing. He appeared to strike a match.

"And now let us pray for the health and happiness at Christmas of Her Majesty the Queen," intoned the Rector.

Holmes blew out the match, turned, and was back in his pew before the "*Amen*". There was the merest wisp of smoke indicating where he had been. Some of his fellow-worshippers must have been aware of some movement close to them, and there were a few glances his way, but by then he was joining lustily in *"God rest ye, merry gentlemen, let nothing you dismay."*

The Grace was spoken and the service ended. The organ soared in a Christmas anthem and people began to file out. Naturally, I remained staunchly at my post. In all the movement I lost sight of the Three Wise Men, and I must say I felt a trifle neglected. The Colonel had promised to relieve me of the treasured Star at the first opportunity.

One of the angels (the winsome Cicely, in fact) asked me if I was going to the vestry to change out of my costume. I shook my head.

She said without much maidenly coyness that she was tired of being an angel and hoped I would help her remove her wings.

Not without regret, I said I must guard the Star until the Colonel came. To Cicely, this was unreasonable. She responded with a toss of her pretty curls that I should please myself.

I remained at my post. Almost everyone had filed out, leaving two church-wardens collecting hymn-books, and me, still in my costume. My feet itched from the straw and my legs ached from standing up for so long. I am bound to record, self-pitying as it must appear, that I felt neglected. Presently Cicely Dawson and her sister came from the vestry dressed in their own clothes and strutted past and out of the church without even wishing me goodnight.

I could understand the Colonel forgetting about me, but how could he have neglected to remember the Star he had been at such pains to protect?

Then a voice echoed through the church. "Come, Watson, time is short!"

It was Holmes. He, at least, had remembered me. He was standing in the doorway.

"I can't leave," I called back. "I'm guarding the Star."

"That thing on the pole?" he said, striding up the aisle towards me. "Paste and nickel-plate. That isn't the Bullpen Star! The Star is well on its way to Taunton by now. If we hurry we may yet save it."

"No," I insisted. "This is the Star and those are my orders."

To my horror he reacted by grabbing the staff above my handhold and shaking it violently. The Star, loosened from the shaft, fell, hit the flagstones and shattered into three pieces.

"Does solid silver break like that?" he demanded, eyes blazing.

I stared at the fragments in amazement. He was manifestly right. The plaster of Paris was laid bare. I had spent the evening guarding a fake replica of the mediaeval treasure.

"Where's the Colonel?" I asked hoarsely. "We must inform him at once."

"No time, Watson, no time. Do you have that gun he gave you?"

"Under my robe."

"Capital. I've borrowed Farmer Hall's dog-cart. We must be in Taunton before the next train leaves for Bristol."

"I'm not dressed."

"Nonsense."

Without a notion as to the reason, I presently found myself seated beside Holmes exposed to the elements on a light cart behind a black gelding that fairly raced through the night. Fortunately the snow had stopped in the last hour. A full moon and a clear sky made the going possible. I was chilled to the marrow in my biblical apparel, yet eager for information.

"Who exactly are we pursuing, Holmes?"

"The thief," he said, through bared teeth.

An appalling thought struck me. "Not Colonel Sloane?"

"No. Sloane isn't our man."

"But what happened to him? He promised to see me after the service."

"He's at home, at the manor house. Could be dead, but I think not." He cracked the whip, urging the horse on.

"Good Lord!"

"Trussed up, more likely. He never left home."

"How can that be so? I saw him in the church. He handed me the Star."

"No, Watson. That wasn't your Colonel. That was the thief."

"Are you sure?" I asked in disbelief. "He was limping like the Colonel."

"Naturally he was. The robbery was planned to the last detail. Almost the last, anyway," Holmes added on a note of self-congratulation that I picked up even with the wind rushing in my ears.

I hazarded a guess. "Was he limping on the wrong side?"

"Ha! Nothing so obvious," said he.

"Wearing a built-up shoe? I saw you creeping up the aisle behind him and lighting a match."

"No, Watson. His shoes were a perfect pair. That was the detail I went to some trouble to ascertain. Whilst Balthazar knelt in prayer, I examined his heels. The heel of a lame man always shows wear on the edge of the shoe that takes most weight. This pair of heels was evenly worn. So the wearer was not lame. Whoa!"

We were going too fast, and the wheels skidded towards a hedge. Holmes pulled on the reins in time to avert a disaster.

"Deucedly clever," I said. "But you must have had your suspicions already."

"I knew if the Star was to be stolen, it would be well-planned. The weak point in the Colonel's arrangements was when he had brought the Star from the bank to his house. He needed to change into his costume. He wouldn't want the bodyguards in his bedroom watching him dress."

"Lord, no."

"But he wanted the Star in his possession at all times, so he took it in with him."

"And that was when the thief struck?"

"Yes. He was hidden in the room, waiting. I hope he didn't injure the Colonel seriously. My guess is that he tied and gagged him."

"If that was what happened, why didn't this scoundrel - whoever he may be - escape with the Star across the fields at once?"

"Too risky. The bodyguards were outside the bedroom waiting. The hue and cry would have been raised within minutes. His plan was more ingenious. Under Balthazar's robes and behind the black beard, he was well disguised. He'd gone to the trouble of making that cheap, but convincing replica of the Star. He made the substitution, tucked the real Star under his robes and went out to lead the procession."

"What nerve!"

"He's audacious, I grant you."

"And resourceful. How did he know what the Star looked like, to manufacture the fake replacement? Of course!" I found myself answering my own question. "He saw it for himself in London last summer, and used the illustrations in the press as blueprints. Diabolical."

"And at the end of the service," said Holmes, "he walked quietly away, dismissed the bodyguards, slipped off Balthazar's robes behind the church wall - where I found them a few minutes too late - and helped himself to one of the carriages lined up in the lane."

"And escaped!"

"Just so."

Our dog-cart slithered over the snow for some minutes more. The lights of Taunton were showing across the fields.

"Holmes."

"Yes?"

"How shall we recognize the thief?"

His answer was cryptic. "He'll be waiting at the railway station - if we're in time." He whipped up the horse again.

The streets of Taunton, being more used by traffic than the country lanes, glistened black under the street-lamps and our wheels clattered over the cobbles as we raced the last minutes through the town and into the station yard, where several carriages were waiting.

"Take out the gun and be ready to use it," Holmes ordered. He sprang down from the dog-cart and strode into the booking hall, his cape billowing. At such times, in pursuit of wrong-doing, he was like a terrier, fearless and unstoppable.

I followed as well as I was able, hampered by my New Testament robes. I wondered how well I could use a revolver these days. Of one thing I was certain: my heart had not forgotten how to thump as it always did in battle.

"Has the last train left for Bristol?" Holmes demanded of the ticket collector.

"Due in two minutes, sir," came the answer.

We hurried onto the "Up" platform, which appeared deserted, save for an elderly couple.

"He's hiding up," said Holmes.

"The waiting rooms?" said I.

"We don't have the time to check. He'll have to make a dash for the train when it comes in. Take up a position halfway along and to the right. I'll be up here."

"Shall I use the gun?"

"Wing him, if you have to."

The sound of the approaching express carried down the line before the engine came into view. My throat was dry and my legs felt like jelly. I'm sure Holmes, at the other end of the platform, was as steady and primed as a hunting lion. I looked about me, at the waiting rooms and cloakrooms of different classes from which the thief might emerge.

The rasp of the locomotive increased. It would be in sight now, snorting pink steam and sparks into the night sky, but my eyes were on the doors nearest to me, expecting a figure to dart out any minute and dash for the train.

Somebody did emerge from the ladies' waiting room, but it was a young woman carrying a child. I saw nobody else.

116

The train steamed in and came to a halt. Several people opened doors and got out, bringing confusion on the platform. I couldn't possibly use my gun.

"Watson!"

I turned, hearing the shout from Holmes.

"Behind you, man! The end of the platform!"

I swung about, in time to see a tall, male figure in the act of opening a compartment door near the front, away from all the station buildings. He must have left it to the last moment to climb over the paling that extended along the platform. I gave chase. When I got to the compartment and swung open the door, no one was inside. He had gone straight through, opened the door on the other side and jumped onto the line, dashing along the rails. I followed, shouting to him to halt.

The man turned, saw me, a horrified look in his eye, and redoubled his running.

As I tried gamely to catch up, a movement at his side caused him to veer off course. He was powerless to evade the tackle. Holmes felled him with a grab that was as good as anything I ever saw on a football field.

I hastened towards them, gun at the ready, but Holmes, a master of baritsu, the Japanese system of wrestling, already had his man in a stranglehold. And there in the snow, between the railway lines, lay the precious Bullpen Star, thankfully undamaged.

"You see who this scoundrel is?" said Holmes.

In the poor light I had some difficulty recognizing the fellow, particularly as most of his face was pressed into the snow. However, I hazarded a guess. "Is it the Jackdaw, Georges Du Broc, the most brazen thief in Europe?"

"No, Watson, it is not," said Holmes on a petulant note. "I told you Du Broc is a short man. He couldn't possibly impersonate Colonel Sloane, who is quite six feet in height. This is Ruff, the Colonel's own batman."

"Oh, my hat!" I exclaimed in horror.

"Only a servant," Holmes charitably pointed out.

The shock I felt was nothing to the Colonel's when he was apprised of the news. He had known Ruff for twenty years and the man had given no hint of dishonesty.

"Yes, but when did he become your civilian employee?" enquired Holmes, over a late glass of claret in the manor house.

The Colonel had by this time recovered from being trussed and gagged, and lying in his bedroom, just as Holmes had deduced.

"About eight months ago. He turned up one afternoon. I was delighted to see him again, the first time in years."

"By which time you were already chosen for the part of Balthazar in the masque, I presume?"

"That is true," the Colonel admitted. "The service has to be arranged a long time in advance."

"And it was in the press?"

"Yes."

"So he learned of the opportunity and insinuated himself into your employment." Holmes flapped his long hand as if that answered all questions.

"You're an amazing detective, Mr Holmes."

"If you insist."

"But one thing still puzzles me," the Colonel went on.

"What is that?"

"You said when you arrived that you had come in search of a bird."

"Yes, indeed."

"Did you find it?"

"Certainly. You may not be aware, Colonel, that there is a member of the sandpiper family known as a ruff."

"Oh."

Not one of us had thought of that.

We returned to London by an early train next morning. The landscape was still seasonably white, without any overnight snowfall. The prospect of Christmas at home cheered my spirits no end after the shocks of the night before.

Holmes, too, was in festive mood, and appeared to have acquired a present in his short stay in Somersetshire, for there was a large, interesting parcel on the luggage-rack above his head.

With Holmes in a buoyant mood, I taxed him on a matter that had not been explained to my satisfaction.

"Now that we're alone, old friend, will you admit that it was pure chance that the thief's name happened to be that of a variety of sandpiper?"

He laughed. "Total coincidence, Watson."

"Then your remark to the Colonel - the one about seeking a bird - was the merest eyewash."

He gave me a long, disdainful look. "Is anything I ever say eyewash? Of course I was seeking a bird in the country. And I found one." He pointed upwards to the parcel on the luggage rack. "Thanks to Farmer Hall, who you will remember as Melchior, the Wise Man, we shall have a twenty pound goose for Christmas luncheon."

I shook my head in admiration. "Truly, Holmes, there was a fourth Wise Man this year, and he is sitting opposite me."

Away With the Fairies

"Location, location, location" is supposed to be the mantra of home-buyers. If so, Miss Jackson hadn't heard of it. The cottage was not practical for a lady in her seventies who knew nobody. It stood a good half-mile outside the village, in a clearing in the woods with access along a track that would test the suspension of any car. Picturesque, admittedly. Over the years a succession of people had been tempted into ownership, but few had lasted more than a couple of years, and there had been some long spells when it was empty and up for sale. The estate agents danced on their desks after the old lady walked into their office and said she wanted the place because she'd lived there as a little girl.

30 May, 1938
I HATE it here. Hate the spiders and all the creepies. Hate the cottage and the smell of the oil lamps and the candles and the dark corners of the rooms. Hate the ugly pig called Tim and hate Mummy for marrying him.

She moved in one August afternoon and soon there were new lace curtains at the windows and a small yellow Citroen Special outside. People walking their dogs past the cottage caught glimpses of a short, wiry woman with permed silver hair. Her long-haired white cat was always on view, eyeing the dogs indifferently from an upstairs window.

A few elderly villagers remembered Bryony Jackson from before the war. They spoke of her with reserve, and it was evident that none of them planned to visit and talk about old times. Although she'd attended the village school she had never been accepted as local. She wasn't from a village family. Her people, like so many previous owners of the cottage, had been suburban Londoners beguiled by the idea of a thatched home in the woods. They moved in, realised their mistake and left after a year or so. They weren't even Wiltshire folk.

This was before the electricity was laid on and the bathroom was installed, so they must have found the conditions difficult. The parents had used bikes to get their shopping and the child had walked through the woods to school. Nobody thought anything of it at the time.

"She were strange," Mrs Maizey, mother of the shopkeeper, recalled. "You couldn't get friends with her if you tried. She weren't exactly stuck-up, just didn't want to join in things, so we let her be. There wasn't bullying as I recall. Nothing worse than pulling of her pigtails that all of us girls had to put up with."

10 June, 1938

Miss Stirling says I have to join in their stupid games, but I can't understand their silly singing, and they only laugh when I try, so why should I? This school is horrid. Children of all ages are in the same class and some of them have itchy things in their hair and don't bring hankies and some don't even wear shoes. I can't wait for the summer holiday. But then what will I do? Spend more time with Mummy and HIM? No thank you!!!

After a month or so when she must have been busy sorting out the house, Miss Jackson started taking walks through the woods. The narrow footpaths ensured that if she met someone, she or they would have to step aside. She made it clear from the brisk way she thanked people and moved on that she wasn't interested in lingering to talk. Nobody was getting much out of her. If Thomas the postman couldn't persuade her to open up, no one would. She did her shopping at a supermarket in Devizes rather than the village shop. Admittedly the local vegetables couldn't compare with what Safeway offered, but everyone suspected she still wouldn't have used the village even if everything was fresh each day.

It was interesting how Miss Jackson's determination to stay aloof only encouraged the locals to find out more. She was spotted buying a garden spade in Devizes and the entire village discussed it. What would an old biddy be wanting with a spade when she had no garden? The ground around the cottage was simply the coarse turf that had been there for centuries. Surely she wasn't going to give herself extra work by cultivating it?

One morning as early as 7 a.m., Thomas the postman saw the new spade resting against the wall of the cottage. There was fresh mud on the blade, indicating that Miss Jackson had left it out. Fair enough. She'd bought the thing, so she must have had a use for it. No, what intrigued Thomas (and everyone he told) was that there was no sign of digging in the vicinity of the cottage.

26 July, 1938

The holidays are here at last and hooray, I have found a secret place where I am writing this. I'll come here whenever I can and lie in a sunbeam, listening to the water trickle over the stones. It's a nice sound, like the fairies talking. I take off my sandals and socks and dip my feet in the cool stream. There are bright red toadstools and I found some lovely stripy feathers, blue, white and black, that I'm using to decorate my magic place. I'm happy here.

"She could be digging up plants," suggested the younger Mrs Maizey. "Folk do, and it's illegal now. Primroses and things are protected."

"Why would she dig up plants?"

"To sell 'em. Townspeople pay good money for a primrose."

"Violets," said the older Mrs Maizey.

"Wild orchids," said the younger.

"Where would she keep 'em?" Thomas the postman asked.

"In the spare bedroom. She's got plenty of room in that cottage."

Most of the village had been inside Glade Cottage at some time in their lives, through knowing the owners, or through a window at the back in years when the place stood empty.

"That's daft," said Thomas. "Plants wouldn't survive indoors. Besides, how would she get 'em to a plantsman in that poky French car of hers?"

"All right, cleverclogs. What's your theory?"

"I don't think it's plants," said Thomas. "I think something is buried in the wood."

"Something valuable?"

"Something she's dead keen to find, if it's worth buying a spade for. She knows a thing or two the rest of us don't. That's for sure."

"What would Bryony Jackson know? She hasn't lived here for the past sixty years."

"You'll have to ask her, won't you?"

"Are you thinking she saw something when she was a child?"

The senior Mrs Maizey chuckled and wheezed. "Don't you know what she saw?"

Thomas the postman shook his head. "Before my time."

The young Mrs Maizey said, "Tell him, Mother."

Old Mrs Maizey was pink-faced. "Do you ever eat a boiled egg, postman?"

"Course I do."

"And after you scoop it out from the shell, do you poke your spoon through the bottom?"

"I do."

"And why? Do you know why?"

"Couldn't say. We've always done it in our family."

The old lady nodded. "Ours, too. Tis country lore. If you leave an eggshell unbroken there's a danger the little folk will take it away and put wheels on it and turn it into a coach."

"The fairies?" said Thomas with a wide smile.

She drew a sharp, disapproving breath. "You said it. In our family we never use the word."

"They're said to make all kinds of mischief," the younger Mrs Maizey explained, "like snatching babies from their cradles and putting changelings in their place. I don't believe a word of it myself."

"Load of rot," Thomas confirmed.

Old Mrs Maizey smiled wickedly. "Well, them's what Bryony Jackson saw. She said she saw them regular. She swore blind and it was in all the papers."

1 August, 1938

I was in my secret place all afternoon watching the pretty dragonfly things with blue wings that hover over the stream and I missed tea and got back when they were listening to the news on the wireless. Mummy was very cross and I wouldn't tell them where I had been. She said my clothes were in a dreadful state. I was sent to bed early and the pig sucked on his smelly horrible pipe and smiled.

The mystery of Miss Jackson and her digging continued to intrigue the locals. Those who hadn't been around in 1938 were treated to vivid accounts of the fairy sightings from Mrs Maizey, old Ben Harmer, Olwen Sparrow, Walter Williams and other veterans - in fact, from everyone except Bryony Jackson herself. Even if she had been on speaking terms with the villagers, it was too embarrassing a matter to raise with her. The memories varied as to detail, but the essentials were pretty well agreed. Some time in the summer holidays of 1938, Bryony's solemn little face was on the front page of the local paper over a report that she had often seen and spoken to fairies in the wood where she lived. No one would have believed the child except that her stepfather, Timothy Walkinshaw, claimed to have seen one of them himself and had signed an affidavit that was reproduced in the Observer, and the other national papers when they took up the story from the local press.

Bryony became a celebrity. She took a photographer from the *Daily Mirror* to get a picture of the fairies. He thought he saw something, but somehow the camera didn't capture it.

3 August, 1938
Yesterday as a punishment for spending so long in the woods and getting my clothes in a mess I was kept in all day, and today I was not allowed out of sight of the cottage. The pig was watching me from the window while I made a long daisy chain. I know he was hoping he could tell on me and get me into worse trouble. Mummy said she would smack my bottom if I disobeyed her, and I'm sure he wanted it to happen so he could be there to watch. So I did just as I was told, all day long. It was a boring, horrid day, but at least the pig was bored too and didn't get what he was hoping for, ha ha. Anyway, when Mummy smacks me she always makes sure he isn't about. He isn't even allowed to see me in the bath.

The new theory about Miss Jackson originated with someone other than the Maizeys - probably Olwen Sparrow, who had a morbid turn of mind. She was old enough to have been at school with Bryony. The theory was that shortly before the family left Glade Cottage in 1940, or thereabouts, Bryony got pregnant. Of course it would have been a great scandal. Abortions were illegal and (according to Olwen) Bryony kept the pregnancy a secret for a long time. Finally a baby was born. It didn't survive. Bryony's mother - who was known to be narrow-minded, even by the standards of the time - was said to have buried it secretly in the woods.

Olwen - in outlining this theory - was extremely vague. She didn't know for sure if the pregnancy had been true. She just thought she'd heard her parents discussing it. She would only hint that Bryony had murdered the child.

No one else remembered Bryony being pregnant, but then the war was on, and there was so much else to occupy everyone's attention. Mrs Maizey senior said she thought the child had been too young to bear a child. But others thought it possible. The idea that she had returned after all these years to dig up her dead baby had a certain poignancy. Maybe her conscience had given her no peace and she wanted to give the child a proper burial. Maybe she would persuade the vicar to find a place for it in the churchyard.

"When does she do this digging?" Olwen's son Derek asked.

"At first light, before anyone is up," said Mrs Maizey.

"I'm up," said Derek. "I'm an early riser. Happen I might take a walk through the woods tomorrow."

3 August, 1938

Another day making daisy chains. Mummy says if I promise to keep my clothes clean and be back by tea-time I can play in the woods tomorrow. I know what will happen. I saw her look at the pig when she was talking to me and he winked at her. She wants him to spy on me. When we were having dinner, he asked me what games I play in the wood. I told him I don't play games. I said I visit the fairies. He told me it's wicked to make things up and I said I wasn't making anything up. There really were fairies in the wood and they were my friends. He says he doesn't believe me, but I think he does, a little bit. Well, I say let him try and spy on me because I have a SECRET PLAN.

Derek Sparrow got up before five and was waiting within view of Glade Cottage and listening to the dawn chorus and wondering if he was on a fool's errand when Miss Jackson came out wearing green wellingtons and carrying her spade. She headed off purposefully down one of the footpaths between the bracken. When it was safe to follow, Derek took the same route.

4 August, 1938

Mummy left early to go shopping and I went out soon after. The pig was wearing boots and gaiters and had his field-glasses on the table, so I knew he was going to try and follow me. I could easily have run on and lost him, only I didn't. I walked to another part of the woods a long way from my magic place. When I got to a fallen tree I sat down and pretended to hide something in a hole in the trunk. I knew he was not far off, watching me with the glasses, because I saw the sun flash on them. In a minute I pretended to move on, but really I hid behind some bushes and got ready. Just as I thought, nosy Pig came to look in the hollow. AND WHAT A SURPRISE HE GOT!

Derek could hear the sound of digging ahead, so he approached stealthily, using the trees as cover. Presently he caught sight of the old lady at a lower level where a stream coursed downwards among stones. Evidently she had been working here before, because a large heap of scrub lay to one side. She had cleared an area of about three square metres at the side of the stream and was now scraping the surface with the spade, shifting stones and roots. It looked hard work for someone of her age.

Once she stopped and leaned on the spade and sighed so loudly that he heard her from where he was. Then she turned and looked straight in his direction, just as if he had sighed. He ducked and kept very still and she went back to the work.

After half an hour it was obvious that she was digging deeper, taking divots from one small area. It was slow progress; she had to rest every few minutes. Derek could have shifted the earth in half the time. He kept thinking she could bring on a heart attack doing heavy work at her age. He was getting sorry for her.

At the depth of little more than the spade-length the edge of the blade struck something metal. The sound was unmistakable. She put down the spade and knelt beside the hole and shifted some earth with her hands.

Derek crept towards a bramble just large enough to shelter behind.

Miss Jackson picked up the spade and tried to lever something out. She wasn't much good at it. All she got was a metallic scraping sound. After a number of tries she flung down the spade and said, "Oh, God help me!"

By now Derek's admiration for the old lady's efforts had reached a point when he felt compelled to respond. He couldn't bear to watch her pathetic efforts any longer. So he played God. Standing up, he stepped down the bank towards her and said, "Morning, Miss Jackson."

She stared at him open-mouthed.

"Can I help?" he asked.

She shook her head and took a step back from the hole.

"What have you got here?" Derek asked. "Buried treasure?"

"What are you doing here?"

He said something about early morning walks. He crouched by the hole and looked into it. "It looks like a tin box of some sort."

Miss Jackson had snatched up the spade and lifted it to shoulder height, threatening him. "Get away from there! It's mine."

He backed off, trying to calm her. "Easy. I'm only trying to help. I'm Derek - Mrs Sparrow's son."

"Olwen Sparrow?" She lowered the spade a little.

"You remember?"

"Some things, yes."

"Mother was at school with you. I happened to see you here and thought you were in trouble."

"It's just something I buried a long time ago."

"Want me to get it out?"

She sighed, lowered the spade, and gave a nod.

To Derek's eye, the box appeared too small to hold a dead baby. It was coffin-shaped, certainly, narrow and oblong, but it was only about nine inches long. He flicked away some dirt and saw the words "Sharp's Toffees" on the lid.

"What's inside?"

"Memories," she said.

He used a sharp-edged stone to force out enough earth to get his fingers underneath. Then he lifted it from the hole. It felt light in weight, but there was definitely something inside.

Miss Jackson grabbed it from him and held it to her chest.

"Aren't you going to open it?"

"Not here. Would you pass me the spade?"

"I'd better carry it for you, if you're going to hang on to the tin." She was gripping that box in a way that left no doubt she would not let go of it.

They walked together through the woods towards her cottage. Derek asked, "What was it like, growing up here in the war?"

"Before the war," she said. "We came before the war."

"And lived in Glade Cottage?"

"Yes."

"Just you and your Mum and Dad?"

"He wasn't my father. My father died in London when I was quite small."

"How long were you here?"

"Two or three years. They parted - my mother and stepfather - and we went back to Wimbledon, mother and me."

Derek got nothing more from Miss Jackson. At the cottage door she could have invited him in for a coffee after the good turn he'd done, but she didn't.

He said, "I'd like to know what we dug up."

She said, "It's private."

5 August, 1938

I never thought I would feel sorry for the pig, and I don't. But I almost do. Mummy didn't believe him when he said he'd seen a fairy in the wood. She likes people to tell the truth, however bad it is. He was scared to say he'd seen me undressed, because that's rude and Mummy's really modest and it would have made her very upset and angry, so he told her what I made him say - that it must have been a fairy he saw. Mummy laughed at first and asked what this fairy looked like and I butted in and said it was quite big and wasn't wearing any clothes and he had to agree. Mummy frowned then and got cross when he kept saying it really happened. In the end, she said he would never get her to believe it, and he said would she believe him if it was in the paper? So a lady from the paper came this afternoon and talked to us about the fairy. I said I'd seen fairies lots of times in the wood and the pig said he'd seen this one yesterday at a place where I took him. Now they want to try and get a photograph for the paper.

8 August, 1938

It was in the paper, all about the fairy. No picture, of course, but there's a picture of me with Tim the pig. He looks so uncomfortable, just like he's sitting on a hedgehog. Now more papers want to come and talk to us this afternoon. It's very funny. And the funniest thing of all is that Mummy STILL doesn't believe a word of it. But she isn't cross with me. She thinks the pig must have made me say it, about the fairy. They are having HUGE arguments.

Alone in the cottage, Bryony Jackson lifted the lid from the tin and took out an object wrapped in oilskin cloth. It was her diary of 1938. For some time, she had been reading in the papers about recovered memories - people who had gone to counsellors and psychiatrists and discovered dark truths they had suppressed all their adult lives. She wanted to know if her stepfather, Tim, had abused her as a child. Else why had the marriage ended so abruptly with his quitting the house in 1938? You heard so much about wicked things happening to children. It had begun to worry her after she heard about women recovering childhood memories, and the worry had increased until it almost reached the level of mental torment. But she would never go to a psychiatrist.

Anyway, there were counter-claims about something called false memory syndrome.

The childish handwriting was still legible. She spent the next hour totally absorbed, thankful for the chance to unlock her past in privacy, reassured when she was certain no sexual abuse had taken place, but appalled to learn how manipulative a jealous child can be.

10 August, 1938

The pig left us this morning. Mummy says he's gone to live somewhere else. She asked me lots of questions about what happened in the woods and if I had anything I wanted to tell her. Of course there was nothing. Nothing happened except me giving him the fright of his life by coming from behind a tree in my birthday suit, but I can't tell her that now, can I? Tim the pig didn't dare tell Mummy he'd seen me like that. She would have thought it was his fault for sure. She hates rude people, specially rude men. She's always warning me about nasty men. So he had to tell her what I told him to say. Seeing a fairy might have sounded silly to a grown-up, but it wasn't rude or nasty, because fairies don't wear clothes usually. Mummy says she and I won't have to live here much longer. She doesn't like the place any more. That's a pity, in a way. I think I could get to like it now.

Showmen

"Getting rid of the bodies was never a problem for me, sir. Sure, we got rid of so many I lost count."

"Sixteen, they said."

The cracked lips parted and curved. Sixteen was a joke. Everyone knew the official count had been too low.

"You got away with it, too."

"I wouldn't say that."

"Come now, you're a free man, aren't you? Thirty years later, here you are, drinking whisky in the Proud Peacock."

"God bless you, yes."

"A reformed character."

"Well, I'm not without sin, but I've not croaked a fellow creature since those days. I was wicked then, terrible, terrible."

"Does it trouble you still?"

"Not at all."

"Really?"

He roared with laughter. "Jesus, if I thought about it, I'd never get a peaceful night's sleep."

Talking of trouble, it had taken no end of trouble to find the fellow. Rumour had it that he was now an Oxford Street beggar - but trying to find a particular beggar in Oxford Street in 1860 was like looking for a pebble on Brighton beach. From Hyde Park to Holborn a parade of derelicts pitched for pennies, pleading with passers-by, displaying scars and crippled limbs, sightless eyes and underfed infants. They harrassed the shoppers, the rich and would-be rich, innocents up from the country trying to reach the great drapery shops, Marshall & Snelgrove and Peter Robinson.

It took a long morning and most of an afternoon of enquiries before William Hare was discovered outside Heath's the Hatmakers, a lanky, silver-haired, smiling fellow offering bootlaces for sale and not above accepting charity from those who didn't need laces. "A spare wretch, gruesome and ghoulish", the court reporters had once called him, but at this stage in his declining years his looks frightened no one. Animated, grinning and quick of tongue in his Irish brogue, he competed eagerly for the money in the shoppers' pockets.

To listen to Hare trading on his notoriety, discussing his series of murders, was supposed to be "high ton", the latest thing in entertainment, the best outside the music halls. He was a good raconteur, as the Irish so often are, with a marvellous facility for shifting the blame onto others, notably his partner, Burke, and the anatomist, Dr Knox.

Of course, he had to be persuaded to talk. He denied his own identity when first it was put to him. The promise of a drink did the trick.

Now, in the pub, he was getting gabbier by the minute.

"Did y'know I was measured by the well-known bumps-on-the-head expert, Mr Combe, at the time of the trial, or just after? Did y'know that?"

"The phrenologist."

"You're right, your honour. Phrenologist. There's something called the bump of ideality and mine is a bump to be marvelled at, prodigious, greater than Wordsworth's or Voltaire's. With a bump like mine I could have done beautiful things if my opportunities had been better."

"You made your opportunities."

"Indeed I did." The mouth widened into the grin that was Hare's blessing and his curse.

"You robbed others of their opportunities."

"That's a delicate way of putting it, sir."

"No one murdered so many and lived to tell the tale."

He almost purred at that. "A tale I don't tell very often."

"Unless you're paid."

That nervy smile again. In court, all those years ago, the incessant twitch of his lips had displeased the judge and

133

drawn hisses of contempt from the public gallery. The people of Edinburgh had hated him. The grin inflamed them.

It seemed Hare didn't feel comfortable with his new patron, despite the whisky in his hand. "Tell me, sir, is it possible we met before?"

"Why do you ask?"

"The familiar way you talk to me."

The nerve of the man - as if his crimes had made him one of the elect. "You're notorious, Hare. I know all about you, if that's what you mean."

"I bet you don't, sir, not all. You know the worst, but no one ever told you the best. People shouldn't believe what they read in the newspapers. The queer thing is, I never planned it, you know. The papers made me out to be a monster, but I was not. It was circumstances, sir, circumstances." He was into his flow now. "The first one, the very first, wasn't one of those we turned off. He was an old soldier, a lodger in the house, the lodging house my woman had in West Port. He faded away of natural causes."

This caused some macabre amusement. "Come now."

"I swear before God, that's the truth," Hare insisted, planting a fist on the table, "Mag and I didn't hasten his leaving at all. We wanted him to live a few days more. His rent was due. Four pounds. And fate cruelly took him to his Maker before his quarterly pension was paid. How can you run a lodging house without the rent coming in?"

"So the circumstance was financial?"

"You have it in a nutshell, sir. He left nothing I could sell. I couldn't go up to the Castle and ask the military for his pension. I was forced to go elsewhere for the arrears."

"By selling the corpse."

Hare nodded. "With the help of another lodger, my fellow countryman, Mr Burke, whose name has since become a byword for infamy. Sure and William Burke was no angel, I have to admit. But I couldn't have managed alone. We removed old Donald from his coffin and weighted it with a sack of wood and gave it a pauper's burial. After dark that evening we carried the body up to the College on the South Bridge, with a view to donating it to science."

"Selling it, you mean."

"To recover the rent. All of Edinburgh knew the schools of anatomy couldn't get enough corpses. At the time I speak of, 1827, there were seven anatomists at work in the city, doing dissections to educate the students, and that wasn't enough. The dissecting rooms were like theatres, sir, vast places, crammed to the rafters with students, five hundred at a time. Is it any wonder there was a trade in bodysnatching? Not that Burke and Hare rifled graves. Say what you like about us, we never stooped to that. Ours were all unburied. We had this innocent corpse, as I told you, and we went in search of Professor Monro."

"Why Monro?"

"You have an item to sell, you're better off going to the top, aren't you? And here's a strange twist of fate. We were standing in the quad with our booty between us in a tea-chest when a student happened to come by. I asked him the way to the School of Anatomy. This is where fate interfered, sir. The student wasn't a pupil of the professor. He was one of Dr Knox's canny little boyos. He sent us down to Cowgate, to 10 Surgeons' Square, the rival establishment." He drew himself up. "That, sir, is the truth of how we got drawn into the web of the infamous Dr Knox. If we'd got to the professor first, the story might have ended differently."

"Why is that?"

"Because of what was said, sir."

"By Dr Knox?"

"His accolytes, the people at Surgeon's Square. We didn't get to see the old devil that night. We dealt with three of his students. You have to admire his organisation. He had students on duty into the night meeting visitors like ourselves and purchasing bodies, and no questions asked. They paid seven pounds ten. We should have insisted on ten, but we had no experience. The students seemed well pleased with what they got, and so were we, to speak the truth. And then they spoke the words that touched our Irish hearts: 'Sure, we'd be glad to see you again when you have another to dispose of.' Ha - and didn't our ears prick up at that!"

"'*Glad to see you.*' Glad to see the contents of your tea-chest, more like."

A cackle greeted this. "And do you know who those students were that night? They became three of the most eminent surgeons in the kingdom. Sir William Fergusson, Thomas Wharton Jones and Alexander Miller. And here am I, who assisted so handsomely in their education, reduced to begging on the streets."

"Shall I fetch another whisky?"

"I won't say no."

Left alone at the table, William Hare pondered his chances of extracting something more than drink. He had a suspicion the expenses were being met by a newspaper. There was still plenty of macabre interest in the story of Burke and Hare. It was like old times: the law of supply and demand at work again. A paper with an interest in famous crimes ought to be paying him a decent fee for this interview. He might even negotiate a week in a proper hotel.

"Would you mind telling me who you represent?" he asked his companion when he returned to the table.

"Myself."

"You wouldn't be from the press?"

"Certainly not. I'm a showman."

Hare stood up, outraged. "I'm not going into a freak show."

"Please calm down. I haven't the slightest intention of offering you employment. This is simply a quiet tête-à-tête over a whisky."

He remained standing. "What's the show?"

Dismissively, the showman said, "It's totally unconnected with this conversation. If you must know, I am employed for my voice, in a circus, acting as interlocutor, lecturer and demonstrator for a travelling party of Ojibbeway Indians from North America."

If anything could silence Hare, it was a man who spoke for a troupe of Ojibbeway Indians.

He resumed his seat. "What do you want with me, then?"

"I'm curious about what happened."

"It's all been told before."

"I know that. I want to hear it from the lips of the man who did it. Tell me about your method. How was the killing done?"

"For the love of God, lower your voice," said Hare. "I don't want the whole of London knowing my history." He'd suffered enough in the past from being named in public.

More quietly, the showman said, "You've always insisted that Burke was the prime mover in the business."

Leaning across the table, Hare responded in a low voice, "He did the suffocating, and that's the truth. He always held the pillow."

"But you assisted."

"Only in a passive manner, sir, by lying on the subject, to discourage the arms and legs from interfering. I did it well, too. There was never a mark of violence. Never. That was what saved me from the hangman."

"That, and your gift of the gab."

Hare sniffed. "You're a fine one to comment, by the sound of things. Say what you like, we were professionals, through and through. We didn't take any Tom, Dick or Harry. They were hand-picked. They were not missed usually, being derelicts, simpletons and women of the unfortunate class. And it didn't matter what sort of scum they were when they were lying on Dr Knox's slab. He called them his subjects." He laughed. "Straight, that's the truth. His subjects. You'd think he was the king himself."

"What did you call them? Your victims?"

"Our shots. Did I say a moment ago that none of them were missed? I'd better correct that. We did have an enquiry from the daughter of one of our shots, a grown woman, a whore. She came looking for her mother." He paused. His timing was part of the act. "We got sixteen pounds for the pair."

"Did you ever sell a corpse to anyone else?"

"No, sir. Only to Dr Knox. I'll say this for him - and I won't say much for that odious sawbones - he knew how to guard his reputation. There was one we took to his rooms known in the city as Daft Jamie, a bit of a character this one had been. Jamie always went barefoot, winter and summer, and they were queer feet, if you understand me, mis-shapen. Well, when we pulled him out of the tea-chest in the dissecting-room, three or four people, including the janitor, said, 'That's Daft Jamie!' But Dr Knox would have none of it. He said it couldn't be. Burkey and I guarded our tongues and took the money."

"You believe Dr Knox was pretending?"

"I'm sure of it."

"Why?"

"Because later there was a bit of a hue and cry about Jamie. His mother and sister went around the town asking questions. And as soon as old Knox heard of that, he ordered the corpse to be dissected and the parts dispersed. Mr Fergusson took the feet away and one of the others had the head, so that if the police came calling, no one would know the rest of the body from Adam's."

There was a pause in the conversation. The appalling details didn't make the sensation that Hare expected. Surely the story was worth another drink? But no. "And this lucrative career of yours came to an end after only nine months."

"You must have been a-checking of your facts," he said caustically. "Yes, it was no fault of mine. I was having trouble with Burke. There was a falling-out at one point, you know. In the summer, Burkey went visiting his woman's people in Falkirk, and when they returned, he smelt a rat. Thought I'd done a little work on my own account, taken a shot to Dr Knox and pocketed the reward without telling him. The leery devil trots off to Surgeons' Square to get the truth of it. When he's told they paid me eight pounds for a female, he leaves my lodging-house in a huff. Found new lodgings."

"That must have put a blight on your arrangements."

"Not for long, sir. Burkey got short of money and came skulking back with a new proposal. A cousin of his woman's, a young girl he'd met in Falkirk, came to stay. He asked me to take the first steps in the matter, the girl being a relative."

"You did the smothering on this occasion?"

"As a kindness to his family. A ten pound shot. But Burke never lodged with us any more."

"You were back in business, though."

A twitchy smile. "We did a few more, and then the fates put a stop to our capers. Burke asked me and my woman Mag to his lodging to celebrate Halloween. What a disaster! If only I'd had the sense to refuse. He'd found another shot, of course, some old beggar woman called Docherty. Sure, she was Irish, like Burkey and myself, and only too willing to join the party. But all he had was the one room to do it in. What's more he had lodgers, a family called Gray, who slept on straw on the floor. To simplify matters, I said the Grays could remove to our place that night, and they did. So it was just Burke and his Nell, me and my Mag, and old Mrs Docherty. Well, we all had a few drinks too many, and the old woman screamed 'Murder!' and one of the neighbours went to look for a policeman."

"You were arrested?"

"No, sir." The smirk again. "You know how it is with the guardians of the law. They're like the bloody omnibuses. You can never find one when you want one. What did for us was Burke's incompetence. When the Gray family came back next morning, the corpse was still in the room, under the straw they slept on. Can you believe that? Like a bat out of hell Gray goes to the police."

Hare's companion took a thoughtful swig of his drink. He wasn't writing any of this down. "You don't have to talk about the trial," he said. "How you turned King's Evidence to escape the noose."

"To assist the law, sir. They had no case without me. As I told you a moment ago, there wasn't so much as a scratch on the bodies."

"You had a few more brains in your head than Burke."

"He swung, as you know, sir."

"And his corpse, fittingly enough, was presented to Professor Monro to be dissected."

"Yes," said Hare cheerfully. "And did you hear about the lying-in-state?"

"The what?"

Hare laughed. "Burkey was never so popular as when he was on the slab. The judge in his wisdom decreed that he should be anatomized in public and the public demanded to see the result. Thirty thousand filed through the room. Most of Edinburgh, if you ask me. The line stretched for over a mile."

"Your companion, flayed, salted and preserved, packed into a barrel - for science, as you would put it. His skin cut into pieces and sold as souvenirs. I believe his skeleton can still be seen at the University."

This was not part of the script, the audience taking over. Hare didn't care for it. Moreover, he had detected a note of censure. He stated emphatically, "It was no bed of roses for me, sir. They tried their damnedest to make me go the way of Burke. A private prosecution, followed by a civil action. They failed, but it was mental persecution. And when I finally got my liberty I was in fear of my life from the mob outside. They wanted to lynch me."

"And no wonder."

"I had to be smuggled out of the gaol, disguised. I was put on the southward mail coach. As bad luck would have it, one of my fellow passengers had featured in the trial as a junior counsel, and he recognised me, and blabbed to the others. The news was out. At Dumfries, I was practically mobbed. It was ugly, sir, uncommon ugly. I holed up in the King's Arms for a time, but it wasn't safe. The authorities removed me to the gaol for my own safety, and the jackals outside bayed for my blood all night. It took a hundred specials to disperse them."

"But you got away."

"Under armed guard. The militia escorted me across the border."

"You're a fortunate man, Hare."

"You think so? A ruin, more like. Look at me. I'll tell you who was a fortunate man, and that's the piece of excrement they called Knox. He was in it up to his ears, as guilty as Burke, and guiltier than me."

"Why so?"

"Knox was the instigator, wasn't he? He knew everything, everything. He dealt with us in person a dozen times. Oh, he denied it of course. For pity's sake, where did he think the bodies were coming from, freshly dead and regular as clockwork? The people weren't fooled, just because he was a doctor."

"Surgeon, in fact. You should be careful with your choice of words. The people you just referred to were the same crowd you described as the mob a moment ago."

Hare laughed. "Mob they may have been, but they knew all about Knox. I know for a fact that they met on Calton Hill and made an effigy of the bastard, and carried it in procession all the way to his house in Newington Place, where they burned it in his garden and smashed all his windows."

"So they did."

"You heard of it, too?"

"Indeed," said the showman. "Moreover, they attacked his dissecting-rooms. Like you, he fled. He was thought to have gone into hiding in Portobello, so they made another effigy and hanged it on a gibbet at the top of Tower Street there. You were not alone in being an object of hatred."

"He got his job back," Hare pointed out. "The same year he was back in Surgeons' Square cutting up bodies."

"Ah, but he was obliged to suffer the indignity of a University committee of inquiry. They found nothing actionable in his past conduct. There's the difference, Hare. You stand condemned - or you should have, if there were any justice. Dr Knox was exonerated of blame in the matter."

"Absurd," muttered Hare.

"What do you mean?"

"They would never sack him. He was a god to his students. They adored the bastard. His classes numbered over five hundred."

"However, his career was blighted. You may not know this, but he twice applied for Chairs of the University, and was twice humiliated. He was compelled to relinquish his career at Edinburgh. He moved to Glasgow."

"And I'm moved to tears," said Hare. "I hope he died spitting blood in the poorest tenement in the Gorbals."

"You're still a bitter man."

"I've reason to be bitter. Dr Knox underpaid us for the last one."

"The last one? I don't understand."

"The old Irish woman I was telling you about. Mrs Docherty, on Halloween. You see, we delivered her to Knox the day the game was up. We had to get rid of it. He only paid us half. Said we could have the rest on Monday. We never got our second five pounds."

"And that still irks?"

"No man has treated me with anything but derision ... until today."

"Just a couple of drinks so far."

The "so far" emboldened Hare to say in the wheedling tone that worked best for him, "Would you see your way to the price of a bed in return for all the inside information I've given you in confidence, sir?"

"I can do better than that. If I give you money, you'll only blow it on drink. I can offer you accommodation. I have rooms in Hackney. A humble address, but better than the places you inhabit, I'll warrant."

"Hackney. That's not far."

"Shall we treat ourselves to a cab-ride?"

Hare beamed. "Why not, sir? And if you want to introduce me to your friends and neighbours, I won't object."

"That won't be necessary."

"I am the only man to be exhibited in the Chamber of Horrors in his lifetime. Baker Street - my other address," he joked, "- care of Madame Tussaud."

"Shall we leave?"

"If you're ready, then so am I." Hare finished the last of the whisky and stood up. He reached out with his right hand, groping at the space between them. "It would help me if I took your arm, sir."

"Of course." The showman enquired with what sounded like a note of concern, "How did you come to lose your sight?"

"That was after I came south, sir. I got a job. Labouring - that's my occupation. It was all right for a time. I got on well enough with the others. Then - pure vanity - I confided in one of my mates that I was the smarter half of the old partnership. Smart! You know what? They set upon me. Threw me into a lime-pit. Vicious. Destroyed my eyes. I've been a vagrant ever since. Do you know what I most regret?"

"I've no idea."

He permitted himself another smile. "I shall never see myself in the Chamber of Horrors."

"Careful, there's a step down."

"Down to what, sir?" quipped Hare. "A meeting with Old Nick?"

143

They made their way out of the pub and took the first cab that came along. Heading east, it was soon lost to view in the Oxford Street traffic.

The encounter just described is a fantasy based on accounts of the case, but the story can end with facts. William Hare, who combined with Burke to commit the West Port Murders of 1828, was said to have been a familiar figure, blind and begging in Oxford Street until about 1860.

The famous anatomist Dr Robert Knox also ended his days in relative obscurity, as a general practitioner in Hackney, and latterly as "lecturer, demonstrator, or show-man to a travelling party of Ojibbeway Indians". He died of a stroke in 1862 at the age of 71.

Hare just disappeared.

The Word of a Lady

Denise Wolsey woke suddenly and felt the touch of a hand on her bare shoulder, fingers curving over, squeezing. She'd been well asleep, and alone in the house ... she thought. The nights were a trial in Shillinghurst, a great Elizabethan country house in its own park. She wasn't raised in a place where the boards creak and the plumbing gurgles and hidden creatures rustle in the tall chimneys and there are rooms no one has looked into in months. She'd spent the first eighteen years of her life in a two-bedroomed terraced house in Fulham, sharing a room with her sister.

Petrified, she lay there while her brain caught up. She hadn't heard anyone come in - but would she? Shillinghurst was so huge you could have held an auction downstairs and cleared all the furniture and she wouldn't have heard.

She drew breath to scream.

A man's voice. "It's only me."

"What?"

"Adrian."

Her husband. He switched on the bedside lamp.

She turned her head on the pillow, looked up through squeezed eyelids and breathed a great sigh of relief. "Oh. I thought ..."

"It's all right, wench."

He hadn't used his pet name for her for a long time. It was an endearment, part of their private language. Tonight the tone of his voice wasn't playful. He was nervous.

"What time is it?"

"Don't know - after midnight."

"You didn't say you were coming home."

"Right."

His faraway voice, thinking of other things. *That* was more typical of Adrian. He could cut off like a phone put down, and then it hurt. She didn't need reminding that he was from another world - Eton, Oxford, the peerage - and to be fair he didn't make much of it, but when his voice altered and his eyes glazed over, she took it personally. Then she felt like a piece of low life. She would never have met him except for her skill at drawing and painting that had led to a career in stage design. Their coming together had been so clichéed she didn't care to talk about it, being asked to produce the sets for an Albee play Adrian happened to be backing; and bumping into him, literally, at the first night party and having red wine poured down her. He'd insisted on replacing the dress, which was a cheap frock out of the January sales, with the latest creation from Galliano, and escorting her to Bond Street to choose it. Then he wanted to see her wearing it at a party, he said, and she sensed with pleasure that he wasn't merely being the gentleman. He fancied her.

"What is it, Adrian?"

"What?"

"Something's happened. Why are you here? I thought you were staying over in London." They had this flat in Eaton Square. She had stayed there often.

"Did you?" Still on autopilot.

After meeting Adrian she'd been scooped into the champagne whirlpool of a society she knew nothing about: dinner parties, Ascot, Cowes. She survived, thanks to Adrian. He never left her side. And she adored swanning from event to event, meeting the same articulate young people in their fine clothes. They accepted her warmly because she was Adrian's choice; or most did. One or two of the women stared her out and cut her in the powder room, but she understood why and she could handle that. She was increasingly attracted to Adrian, his black, unruly hair, the strong features that put her in mind of a Gypsy rather than a lord, and the infinite trouble he took to make sure she was comfortable among his friends.

They got engaged the same year. Her photo was in all the magazines. The ring was from Cartier, a large emerald, set in diamonds. Emerald was her birth stone (she was a May child) and signified success in love, people told her.

The following April, they married in Bath Abbey and had their reception in the Assembly Rooms where Jane Austen had danced and Johann Strauss and Liszt had played. The honeymoon was a three-month tour of the great European cities, ending in Venice in July. By then she'd fully expected to be pregnant. She'd learned enough about high society to know that producing an heir was a wife's first duty after marriage. Adrian said it didn't concern him in the least that she was not expecting, and then suggested she saw a specialist if nothing happened before Christmas.

She stopped work. The theatre simply didn't fit in with life in the country. The house and staff occupied much of her time. They had a butler, cook, three maids and four gardeners. Adrian was on various boards and committees and couldn't supervise the running of the house. Thoughtfully, he'd let her sister Janice live free of rent in the gatekeeper's lodge. She was supposed to be company for Denise, but it hadn't worked out. Instead of being grateful, Janice had got jealous, and now the sisters rarely spoke.

The gynaecologist had said there was no reason why Denise shouldn't bear children. He was kind and encouraging and seemed to think it was far too soon in the marriage to be concerned.

Another year went by.

Adrian was increasingly called away to London for meetings. Sometimes he had to stay over. That was when Denise wished she were back in the Fulham terrace, on the lone nights in the great house. None of the servants slept in. Even the butler lived in the village.

Here was Adrian trying to tell her something. For once he was not the polished Old Etonian.

"Horrible. Bloody nightmare. Believe me, it wasn't anyone's fault."

"What wasn't?"

"The accident."

She clasped the front of her nightdress, gathering it in a bunch. "Oh, God. Are you -"

"No. Some stupid hitchhiker on the A337, that road through the Forest. Rain bucketing down. Visibility poor. He stepped in the road."

"You hit him?"

He gave a nod.

"Badly?"

"Dead."

"Oh, Adrian." She was appalled.

He muttered, barely audible, "The point is, I didn't report it. Stopped - oh, yes, I stopped. There was nothing I could do for him. There was a girl with him, hysterical. He was dead all right. I got back in the car and drove on."

Now her eyes opened wide. "You left them there? Why?"

"Can't you smell it on my breath? Had a few after the meeting. You know how it is. If they breathalyse me, it's a prison sentence."

Denise stared up at her husband. "You left this girl by the roadside?"

Adrian wasn't thinking about the girl's distress. "She wouldn't know me again. She was frantic. Quite a few cars came past. No one stopped, but I'm terrified some busybody noted my number and called the police."

"They'll come looking for you."

"You think I haven't worked that out for myself? If they do - and it's only a possibility -" He paused, and a different, gentler note came into his voice. "- would you be an angel and say I was home with you all evening?"

"Tell a lie?"

He gave a loud, frustrated sigh. "I *know*. You were brought up to tell the truth - the simple working class morality - but you're my wife, for God's sake. If I can't rely on you, who can I turn to?"

She felt the tug of loyalties. She had a deeply ingrained respect for the truth. She'd never succumbed to the sophistries that were common currency among his class. "Surely, if they do come asking questions, they'll want to see the car, and they can tell -"

"It isn't damaged. They're built like tanks."

"If you killed him ..."

"He bounced off the bullbars like a ninepin. I've checked the bodywork. Not a scratch. If they come asking, there's nothing to show. It's up to you to tell them I was home by seven and here all evening."

She was shaking now. "Adrian, in the state you're in, you may not have noticed marks on the car. I think I'd better look."

"Go ahead. If I'm right, and there's nothing, will you back me?"

Probably she would, she thought, and despise herself - as well as Adrian - for the rest of her life. She pulled on her dressing gown.

He'd left the car on the drive. They went out with a flash-lamp. He was right. There were no obvious marks. Denise said they ought to put the car out of sight in the garage.

"Good thinking. Would you do it? In my state I might scrape the side." He gave her the keys and went over to the garage to open it.

She stepped inside the car, took one breath and changed her mind. No way was she going to save him.

Back in the house, he said he needed another drink. Denise went upstairs and called the police from the phone by her bed. She said her husband had come home drunk saying he'd killed a man on the A337.

When he came in, whisky in hand, she said, "Who is she?"

"I beg your pardon?"

"The woman who was with you in the car tonight. It reeked of her cheap perfume."

He denied it. Not for long. He was too drunk to lie with any conviction. Yes, he'd offered a lift home to a friend, he said. Just doing a good turn. She was going his way and he'd offered. She'd been really upset when the accident happened. After it, he'd driven her home and then come straight here.

"Who is she, this tart?"

"It's not like that at all, my love."

"You were going to spend the night with her. You didn't tell me you were coming home. You're only here because of what happened, to get an alibi from me."

"Get a grip, wench. It's not worth getting upset."

"Tell me her name, Adrian."

"I can't remember."

"What do you take me for, you two-timing jerk?"

"Calm down, will you?"

"I've been alone for weeks in this barn of a place, while you were off with other women. 'Meetings in London'. Where - in hotel bedrooms?"

"Denise, this isn't the time. The police could be on their way here."

"They are."

"What?" His bloodshot eyes widened.

"I called them just now. Told them about you."

"Oh, come on." He didn't believe her.

"They'll be coming up the drive any minute. You'll see the blue light flashing."

He lurched across the bedroom and pushed open the big windows to the balcony. Standing out there with his hands on the balustrade, he said, "You're pathetic. It's your own sister, Janice. I took her for dinner at the Savoy. We've been lovers for months."

Janice!

Maddened, she rushed at him like the car at that poor hitch-hiker. He turned, and her hands hit his chest and pushed. He tipped backwards and the balustrade caught the backs of his legs. Over the top he went, and down, two stories, to the paved area below. She heard his skull crack as he hit the stones.

She had her story ready when the police arrived. She was waiting for them beside her dead husband, playing to perfection the part of the well-bred lady refusing to break down. She'd drunk two straight brandies to steady her nerves.

"You're too late. I tried to stop him, but he was suicidal."

They felt for a pulse and decided to call a doctor, but only to confirm the death.

"How did this happen, Lady Wolsey?"

"He came home in a terrible state and told me he'd had a car accident and killed someone and panicked and left the scene. I tried to calm him, but he opened the bedroom windows and threw himself off the balcony."

"Blamed himself, did he?"

"Yes. He said the man is dead." Something in the policeman's look made her hesitate. "That *is* correct?"

"We have a report that a man was killed on the A337 tonight, yes. And someone got the number of the vehicle, and it's registered in your husband's name."

So her story was watertight. "Dreadful. So sudden, and tragic."

"Yes, my lady. And now I'd like to look at the car."

She told him Adrian had put it in the garage.

Twenty minutes later, the policeman was back in the house. "Was everything all right between you and your husband, Lady Wolsey?"

"Perfectly." She didn't want scandal about their private life on top of the fuss the papers would make out of the hit-and-run incident.

"It was a happy marriage?"

"Absolutely."

"How much have you drunk tonight, my lady?"

She gave a withering glare. "Some wine earlier. Brandy, for the shock. I know what I'm saying."

"We need to breathalyse you."

"Whatever for? I haven't been driving. I haven't been near the car all evening."

"Before you say any more, Lady Wolsey, I think I should tell you this. The hit-and-run car was driven by a woman.

151

Two witnesses agree on that. And the young girl who was with the victim said a man got out to see if her friend was dead, but a woman was at the wheel."

A woman? Adrian must have let Janice drive him. Idiot.

"If it wasn't you, no problem. We'll check the fresh prints on the door and the steering wheel and compare them with yours. It does smell of scent inside."

She'd backed the car into the garage. Her prints were all over it. What could she do? Tell them about Janice, and reveal her own motive for killing Adrian? What was it to be - murder, or manslaughter?

"I killed him," she said with the dignity of a grand lady. "I was at the wheel. I killed the hitchhiker. Adrian was devastated. He knew I'd go to prison for it and he couldn't bear to be parted from me. That's the reason he killed himself."

She served two years for involuntary manslaughter. They accepted the word of a lady.

Star Struck

On that September evening the sun was a crimson skull cap, and a glittering cope was draped across the surface of the sea. I was leaning on the rail at the end of the pier where the fishermen liked to cast. By this time they had all packed up and gone. A few unashamed romantics like me stood in contemplation, awed by the spectacle.

I wasn't aware of the woman beside me until she spoke. Her voice was low-pitched, instantly attractive.

"You can already see a star."

"Jupiter," I said.

"For sure?"

"Certainly."

"Couldn't it be Venus? Venus can be very bright."

"Not this month. Venus is in superior conjunction with the sun, so we won't see it at all this month."

"You obviously know," she said.

"Only enough to take an interest." Up to now I hadn't looked at her. All my attention had been on the sky. Turning, I saw a fine, narrow face suffused with the pink light. She could have modelled for Modigliani.

"This is an ideal place to stand," she said. "It's my first time here."

"I thought I hadn't seen you before. Did someone recommend it?"

Her eyes widened. "How did you know?"

"A guess."

"I don't think so. You must be intuitive. I always read my horoscope in the local paper, the *Argus*. This week, it said Friday was an evening to go somewhere different that gives a sense of space. I couldn't think of anywhere that fitted better than this."

"Nor I." The polite response. Privately I haven't much time for people who take astrology seriously.

As if she sensed I was a sceptic, she said, "It's a science, you know."

"Interesting claim."

"The zodiac doesn't lie. If mistaken readings are made, it's human error. Anyone can call himself an astrologer, and some are charlatans, but the best are extremely accurate. I've had it proved again and again."

"Right. If it has a good result, who cares? You came here and saw this wonderful sunset."

Only later, hours later, still thinking about her, did I realise what I should have said: Did the horoscope tell you what to do next? The perfect cue to invite her out for a meal. I always think of the lines too late.

She'd made a profound impression on me - and I hadn't even asked what her name was.

Idiot.

I played the scene over many times in the next few days. She'd spoken first. I should have made the next move. Now it was too late unless I happened to meet her again. I went back to the pier and watched the next three sunsets. Well, to be truthful I spent most of the time looking over my shoulder. She didn't come.

I couldn't concentrate on my job. I'm a sub-editor on the *Argus*. My subbing was so bad that week that Mr Peel, the editor, called me in and pointed out three typos in a single paragraph. "What's the matter with you, Rob? Get your mind on the job, or you won't have a job."

Still I kept thinking about her. I can't explain the effect she had on me. I'd heard of love at first sight, but this was more like infatuation. I'm thirty-two and I ought to be over adolescent crushes.

It took a week of mental turmoil before I came to my senses and saw that I was perfectly placed to arrange ʰᵉʳ ᵐᵉeting. The one thing I knew about her was that ᵃⁿd acted on - her horoscope in the *Argus*. My

The horoscopes were written by a freelance, some old darling in Tunbridge Wells. The copy always arrived on Monday, banged out on her old typewriter with the worn-out ribbon. Vacuous stuff, in my opinion, but she was a professional. The word-count was always spot on. Each week I transferred the text to my screen almost without thought.

This week I would do what I was paid to do - some sub-editing.

First, I looked at last week's astrology piece and found the phrase my mysterious woman had mentioned. *Go somewhere different on Friday. A sense of space will have a liberating effect.* She was an Aquarian. Finally I knew something else about her. She had a birthday in late January or the first half of February.

I picked up the piece of thin paper that had just come in from Tunbridge Wells with this week's nonsense. Aquarians had a dreary week in store. *A good time for turning out cupboards and catching up with jobs.* I could improve on that, I thought.

"Saturday," I wrote, *"is the ideal time for single Aquarians to make a rendezvous with romance. Instead of eating at home in the evening, treat yourself to a meal out and you may be treated to much more."*

One word in my text had a significance only a local would understand. There is a French restaurant called Rendezvous on one of the corners of the Parade, above the promenade. I was confident my lady of the sunset would pick up the signal.

The day after the paper appeared, I wasn't too surprised to get a huffy letter from The Diviner - as our astrological expert in Tunbridge Wells liked to be known to readers. It was addressed to the Editor. Fortunately Mr Peel's secretary Linda opened it and put it in my tray before the boss saw it. Was the newspaper not aware, The Diviner asked in her letter, that each horoscope was the result of hours of study of the dispositions and influences of the planets? In seventeen years no one had tampered with her copy. She demanded a full investigation, so that the person responsible was identified and "dealt with accordingly". If she was not given a complete reassurance within a week she would speak to the proprietor, Sir Montagu Willingdale, a personal friend, who she knew would be "incandescent with fury".

Rather over the top, I thought. However, I valued my job enough to compose an abject letter from Mr Peel stating that he was shocked beyond belief and had found the perpetrator - a schoolboy on a work experience scheme who had mistakenly deleted part of the text on the computer and in some panic improvised a couple of sentences. It had gone to press before anyone noticed. *"Needless to say,"* I added, *"the boy will not be experiencing any more work at the Argus office."* And I added more grovelling words before forging Mr Peel's signature.

After that, I just hoped my initiative would produce the desired result.

You have to be confident, don't you? I booked a table for two on Saturday evening at the Rendezvous.

They opened at seven and I was the first in. The manager consulted his reservations book and I stood close enough to see he had plenty of names besides mine.

"I expect you're busy on Saturdays," I said.

"Not usually so busy as this, sir. It's remarkable. We're popular, of course, but this week we were fully booked by Thursday lunchtime. It's like Valentine's Day all over again."

I hoped so.

Before I was shown to my seat, others started arriving, men and women, mostly unaccompanied, and nervous. I knew why. I was amused to see how their eyes darted left and right to see who was at the other tables. I would have taken a bet that they all had the same birth-sign.

The power of the press.

In the next twenty minutes, the restaurant filled steadily. One or two bold souls at adjacent tables started talking to each other. In my quiet way, I was quite a matchmaker.

Unfortunately none of the women resembled the one I most hoped to see. I sat sipping a glass of Chablis, having told the waiter I would wait for my companion before ordering.

After another twenty minutes I ordered a second glass. The waiter gave me a look that said it was about time I faced it - I'd been stood up.

Some of the people around me were on their main course. A pretty red-head alone at a table across the room smiled and then looked coyly away. Maybe I should cut my losses and go across, I thought.

Then my heart pumped faster. Standing just inside the door handing her coat to the waiter was the one person all this was set up for. In a long-sleeved blue velvet dress, she looked stunningly beautiful.

I got up and approached her.

"You again?" I said. "We met at the end of the pier a few days ago. Do you remember?"

"Why, yes! What a coincidence." Her blue eyes shone with recognition - or was it joy that her sun sign had worked its magic?

I suggested she joined me and she said nothing would please her more.

At the table we went through the preliminaries of getting to know each other. Her name was Helena and she worked as a research chemist at Plaxton's, the agricultural suppliers. She'd moved down from Norfolk three years ago, when she got the job.

I told her I've lived in the area all my life. "As a matter of fact, I'm a journalist. Freelance. Which Sunday paper do you take?"

"The *Independent*."

"You've probably read some of my stuff, then." A slight distortion, but I didn't want to mention the *Argus* in case she got suspicious.

"Do I know your name?" she asked.

"I don't expect so. It's Rob - Rob Newton."

"It sounds familiar."

"There was a film star. Called himself Robert. Dead now."

"I know! Bill Sikes in *Oliver Twist*."

"Right. And Long John Silver. He cornered the market in rogues."

"But you're no rogue, I hope?"

"No film star, either."

"What brought you here tonight? Do you come regularly?"

"No," I answered, trying my best to give an other-worldly look. "It was quite strange. Something mysterious, almost like an inner voice, told me to make a reservation. And I'm so pleased I acted on it. After we spoke at the pier, I really wanted to meet you again."

The waiter came over, and I ordered champagne before we looked at the menu. Helena said something about dividing the bill, but I thanked her and dismissed the idea. After all, I had my own words to live up to: *you may be treated to much more*. The champagne was just the beginning.

"How about you?" I asked after we'd ordered. "What made you come here tonight?"

"It was in the stars." She could look other-worldly, too.

"Do you really believe they have an influence?"

She smiled with confidence. "I'm certain of it." But she didn't mention the horoscope directly.

After the meal, we walked by the beach and looked at the stars. Helena pointed to the group that formed Aquarius, her own constellation. "Let me guess," she said. "Are you an Aquarian also?"

I shook my head. "Capricorn - the goat."

She giggled a little at that.

"I know," I said. "But I'm well behaved, really."

"Pity," she said, and curled her hand around my neck and kissed me. Just like that, without a move from me.

I had to be true to the stars, didn't I? I took her back to my flat and treated her to much more. She was a passionate lover.

We went out each night for the next week, clubbing, skating, the cinema and the theatre. We always ended at my place. It should have been perfect and it would have been if I'd been made of money. It was champagne all the way for Helena. She had expensive tastes, and since that first evening she didn't once offer to go halves. It was very clear she expected to be treated to much more - indefinitely.

On the Friday it all turned sour.

We'd been to London because Helena wanted a meal at the Ivy, and the Royal Ballet after. I should never have agreed. I had to take money out of my savings account. Even so, I was horrified at how much it all cost. She didn't even offer to pay her train fare.

"So where shall we go tomorrow?" she asked in the train at the end of the evening.

"How about a night in for a change?"

"*Saturday night?* We can't stay in."

"I've got no choice," I said. "After tonight I'm cleaned out." Which should have been her cue to treat *me* for a change.

"You mean you can't afford to take me out?"

"It's been an expensive week, Helena."

"You don't think I'm worth it? Is that what you're saying?"

"That doesn't come into it. I can't go on spending what I haven't got."

"You're a freelance journalist. You told me. The national papers pay huge money just for one article."

At this stage I should have told her I was only a lowly sub-editor on the *Argus*. Stupidly I didn't. I tried bluffing it out. "Yes, but to earn a fat fee I have to have a top story to sell. It means months of research, travel, interviewing people. It's the old problem of cash flow."

"Come off it," she said. "You're a typical Capricorn, money-minded, with the heart and soul of an accountant. I bet you keep a cashbook and enter it all in."

"That isn't fair, Helena."

She was silent for a time, staring out of the train window at the darkness. Then she said, "You've been stringing me along. I really thought you and I were destined to spend the rest of our lives together. I gave myself to you, body and soul. I don't throw myself at any man who comes along, you know. And now you make me feel cheap, keeping tabs on every penny you spend on me. It puts a blight on all the nice things that happened."

"What a load of horseshit."

"Pig!"

When we reached the Station she went straight to the taxi-rank and got into a waiting cab. I didn't see her again. I walked home. At least I didn't fork out for her fare.

I forgot about Helena when I started going out with Denise. Do you remember the red-head who smiled at me in the Rendezvous? She was Denise. I saw her in a bus queue one afternoon and there was that double-take when each of us looked at the other and tried to remember where we'd met. I clicked my fingers and said, "The restaurant."

We got on well from the start. I was completely open with her about my bit of astrology-writing in the *Argus*, and she thought it was a great laugh. She admitted she always read her horoscope and had gone along that Saturday evening in the hope of meeting someone nice. Such openness would have been impossible with Helena, who was so much more intense. I told Denise about Helena, and she didn't mind at all. She said any woman who expected the guy to pay for everything wasn't living in the real world. To me, that was a pretty good summing-up of Helena.

"Was she out of a job, or something?" Denise asked.

"No. She has a good income, as far as I know. She's a scientist with Plaxton's, the agricultural people."

"You wouldn't think a scientist would believe in star signs."

"Believe me, she takes it very seriously."

I don't think we discussed Helena again for some time. We had better things to do.

At work, I'd been keeping a look-out for letters postmarked Tunbridge Wells, just in case The Diviner decided to write back to Mr Peel, but nothing came in except her weekly column – which of course I set without adding so much as a comma. My brown-nosing apology had done the trick. I continued with my boring duties, looking forward to the weekend, when I had another date with Denise. So when a packet arrived for The Diviner, care of the *Argus*, I did what I routinely do with all the other stuff that is sent to us by people wanting personal horoscopes, or advice about their futures – readdressed it to Tunbridge Wells and tossed it into the mailbag.

On our date, Denise told me she'd had an ugly scene with Helena. "It was Monday lunch-time, in the sandwich stop in King Street. I go there every day. I was waiting in line and felt a tap on on my arm. She said, 'You're going out with Rob Newton, aren't you?' – and made it sound really hostile. I shrugged and said, 'Yes,' and then she told me who she was and started telling me you were – well, things I won't repeat. I tried to ignore her, but she kept on, even after I'd bought my baguette and drink and left the shop. She was in a real state. In the end I told her there was nothing she could tell me I didn't know already. I said I had no complaints about the way you'd treated me."

"Thanks."

"Ah, but I only made it worse. Talking about you *treating* me was like a trigger. She wanted to know what my birth-sign is. I didn't say I was Aquarius, but she said I must be,

161

and started to tell me about the piece she'd read in the *Argus*. I said, 'Listen, Helena, before you say any more, there's something you should know. Rob works for the *Argus*. He wrote that piece himself because he fancied you and knew you believed in astrology.' That really stopped her in her tracks."

"I can believe it."

"Well, it's time she knew, isn't it? She's a damaged personality, Rob.

"What did she say?"

"Nothing after that. She went as pale as death and just walked away. Did I do wrong?"

"No, it's my fault. I ought to have told her the truth at the time. It's a good thing she knows. Her opinion of me can't get any lower."

I woke on Saturday to the sound of my mobile. Denise, beside me, groaned a little at the interruption. "Sorry," I said as I reached across her for it. Can't think who the hell this is."

It was my boss, Mr Peel. "Job for you, Rob," he said. "Have you heard the news?"

I said, "I've only just woken up."

"There's been a letter-bomb attack. A woman in Tunbridge Wells. She's dead."

"Tunbridge Wells isn't local," I said, still half asleep."

"Yes, but it's a story for the Argus. The dead woman is The Diviner, our astrology writer. Get there fast, Rob. Find out who had anything against the old dear."

I could have told him without going to Tunbridge Wells.

The police arrested me last Monday morning and charged me with murder. I've told them everything I know and they refuse to believe me. They say I had a clear motive for killing the old lady. Among her papers they found a copy of the letter to Mr Peel complaining about her column being tampered with and demanding that the person responsible was "dealt with accordingly." They spoke to Linda, Mr Peel's secretary, and she confirmed she'd passed the letter to me. Also in the house at Tunbridge Wells they found my reply with my poor forgery of Mr Peel's signature. They say I was desperate to keep my job and sent the letter and must have sent the letter-bomb as well. Worst of all, a fingerprint was found on a fragment of the packaging. It was mine.

I told them why I handled the package when it arrived at the Argus office addressed to The Diviner. I said I now believe the bomb was meant for me, sent by Helena under the mistaken impression that I was the writer of the astrology column. I said I'd gone out with her for a short time and she was a head-case. I also told them she's a scientist with access to agricultural fertilisers, which any journalist would tell you can be used to make explosives. She's perfectly capable of constructing a letter bomb.

To my horror, they refuse to believe me. They've interviewed Helena and of course she denies any knowledge of the letter bomb. She says she stopped going out with me because I'm a pathological liar with fantasies of being a top London freelance. Do you know, they believe her! They keep telling me I'm the head-case, and I'm going to be remanded for a psychological assessment. My alteration to the astrology column proves I'm a control freak. Apparently it's a power thing. I get my kicks from ordering people to do pointless things – and from sending letter bombs to old ladies.

Will nobody believe I'm innocent? I swear everything I've just written is true.

The Amorous Corpse

I'd been in CID six months when the case of the amorous corpse came up. What a break for a young detective constable: the "impossible" evidence of a near-perfect murder. You've probably heard of that Sherlock Holmes story about the dog that didn't bark in the night-time. Well, this was the corpse that made love in the morning, and I was the super sleuth on the case. I don't have a Dr Watson to tell it for me, so excuse me for blowing my own trumpet. There's no other way I can do it.

It began with a 999 call switched through to Salisbury nick at 9.25 one Monday morning. I was in the office waking myself up with a large espresso. My boss, a deadbeat DI called Johnny Horgan, never appeared before 10, so it was up to me to take some action. An incident had just occurred at a sub-post office in a village called Five Lanes, a short drive out of the city. The call from the sub-postmistress was taped, and is quite a classic in its way:

"Police, please ... Hello, this is Miss Marshall, the sub-postmistress at Five Lanes. Can you kindly send someone over?"

"What's the emergency, Miss Marshall?"

"Well, I've got a gentleman with a gun here. He asked me to hand over all the money, and I refused. I don't care for that sort of behaviour."

"He's with you now?"

"Yes."

"Threatening you with a gun?"

"At this minute? Don't be silly. I wouldn't be phoning you, would I?"

"He's gone, then?"

"No. He's still here as far as I know."

"In the post office?"

"On the floor, I believe. I can't see him from where I'm speaking."

"Are you injured, Miss Marshall?"

"No. I'm perfectly all right, but you'd better send an ambulance for the man."

I decided CID should be involved from the beginning. Having told the switchboard to inform DI Horgan, I jumped into my Escort and burned rubber all the way to Five Lanes. I'm proud to say I got there two minutes before uniform showed up.

The crime scene was bizarre. The post office door was open. A man lay on the floor in front of the counter with a gun beside him. He was ominously still. *And two old women were buying stamps.* They must have walked around the body to reach the counter. The doughty Miss Marshall was serving them. Crazy, but I suppose they remembered doing things like that in the war. Business as usual.

We put tapes across the entrance to stop a queue forming for stamps and I took a deep breath and had a closer look at the git-em-up-guy. He was wearing a mask - not one of those Lone Ranger jobs, but a plastic President Nixon. I eased it away from his face and didn't care much for what I saw. I can't handle death scenes. I felt for a pulse. Nothing.

My boss, Johnny Horgan, arrived soon after and took over. He was supposed to be the rising star of Salisbury CID, an inspector at thirty-one, one of those fast-track clever dicks, only two years older than me. "Did you call the hospital?"

"I just got here, guv."

"The man is obviously dead. What's the ambulance outside for?"

The sub-postmistress spoke up. "I sent for that."

DI Horgan phoned for the meat wagon and a pathologist. Meanwhile, we got the full version of the hold-up from Miss Marshall:

"No one was here at the time. The man walked in wearing some kind of mask that made him look very peculiar."

"Nixon."

"I beg your pardon."

"Nixon, the ex-President of America."

"He didn't sound like an American. Whoever he is, we don't walk about wearing masks in Five Lanes, so I was suspicious. He pointed a gun and said, 'This is a gun.' I said, 'I can see that.' He said, 'Give us it, then.'"

"How did you respond?"

"I told him not to be ridiculous, to which he replied, 'Hey, come on. I'll blow your frigging head off.'"

"He actually said 'frigging'?"

"I may be unmarried, but I'm not mealy-mouthed, inspector. If he'd said something stronger, I'd tell you."

"So what did you say to that?"

"I said, 'Go on. Pull the trigger. You won't get the money if you do. I'm all locked in. And don't even think of trying to smash the glass.' He said, 'Lady, who do you think you are? It's not your dosh.' I said, 'It's not yours, either. You're not having it.' To which he replied, 'Jesus, are you simple? This is a stick-up.'"

"What happened then?"

"I led him to believe that I'd pressed an emergency button and the police were already on their way. He said, 'Frigging hell.' He took a step back from the counter and I thought for a moment he was about to give up and go away. Then he said, 'I'm not quitting. I'm not a quitter.'"

"Just like Nixon," I remarked.

My boss glared at me.

Miss Marshall continued, "He lurched forward again, and I wondered if he was the worse for drink, because he reached for the glass wall of my serving area, as if for support. Then he lowered the gun, I think, and said, 'Oh, shit.'" She gave Johnny Horgan a look that said how about that for a maiden lady.

"You hadn't touched him?"

"What are you suggesting? That I assaulted him? I was shut in here."

"And nobody else was in the shop?"

"Nobody except him and me. To my amazement, he swayed a little and started to sink down, as if his knees had given way. It was like watching a lift go down. He disappeared from view. The last thing I saw was the hand pressed against the glass. I expect there are fingerprints if you look."

"And then?"

"I looked at the clock. It was twenty past nine. Sitting on my stool here I had the same view I always do, of those notices about ParcelForce and the postage rates. The man had disappeared from sight. To tell you the truth, I half believed I'd imagined it all. It's a fear you live with when you run a post office, having to deal with an armed robber. I was tempted to unlock my door and have a look, but what if he was bluffing? So I stayed here and called 999."

"Good move."

The local pathologist, Dr Leggatt, arrived and didn't take long with the stethoscope. "Calling the ambulance was optimistic," he told us.

"Wasn't me," said Johnny Horgan. "I knew he'd croaked as soon as I saw him."

"You can't tell by looking."

I said, "I checked for a pulse."

"We all agree, then," said the pathologist with just a hint of sarcasm. "This is a dead man."

"But what of?" said Johnny Horgan.

Dr Leggatt answered curtly, "I'm a pathologist, inspector, not a psychic."

"Heart?"

"Weren't you listening?"

"He's not a young man."

"Do you know him, then?"

Fat chance. Johnny didn't know anyone in the county. He was fresh from Sussex, or Suffolk, or somewhere. He turned to me. I'm the local guy. But I was trying not to look at the body. Green in more senses than one, I was.

I saw my boss wink at the pathologist as he said, "His first one." His eyes returned to the corpse. "Fancy dropping dead in the middle of a hold-up."

"It could happen to anyone." Like most people in his line of work, Dr Leggatt had a fatalistic streak.

"Anyone stupid enough to hold up a post office."

"Anyone under stress," said Leggatt - and then asked Johnny with a deadpan look, "Do you sleep well?"

The DI didn't respond.

The doctor must have felt he had the high ground now, because he put some sharp questions to us about the conduct of the case. "Have the scene of crime lads finished?"

"All done," said Johnny.

"Pockets?"

"He wasn't carrying his calling card, if that's what you mean."

"What's the gun?"

"Gun? That's no gun," said Johnny, glad of the chance to get one back. "It's a toy. A plastic replica." He turned to the postmistress, who up to now had preferred to remain on her side of the counter. "Did you know the man, Miss Marshall?"

"I haven't seen him."

"But you told us -"

"Without the mask, I mean."

"You'd better come round here and look."

Miss Marshall unlocked, emerged from the serving area and took a long squint at the body. She was less troubled by the sight of death than me. "He's a stranger to me. And I didn't know it was a toy gun, either."

"You were very brave," Johnny told her, and muttered in an aside to Dr Leggatt and me, "Silly old cow."

He went on to say more loudly that he'd like her to come to the police station and make a statement.

"What did you call her?" Leggatt asked, after she had been escorted to the police car.

"I meant it," said Johnny. "She might have had her stupid head blown away for the sake of Post Office Counters Limited."

Leggatt gave Johnny a look that was not too admiring. "What happened to good citizenship, then? Some of you coppers are born cynics. You've no idea what it takes for a woman to stand up to a gunman."

"Have you?" Johnny chanced it.

"As it happens, yes. My sister stood up to one - and didn't get much thanks from you people. You don't know how often Miss Marshall will wake up screaming, reliving what happened this morning."

"Hold on, doc," said Johnny. "I said she was brave."

The pathologist didn't prolong it. "If you don't mind, I'd like to get this body to the mortuary."

"Yes, and we've got to find his next of kin," said Johnny.

When he said 'we', he meant me. He'd already decided there wasn't anything in it for him.

I may be squeamish with dead bodies, but I'm fearless with the living, especially blondes. It was the day after the hold-up and I'd come to a flat in Salisbury, the home of a recently released prisoner. Jack Soames had served four years in Portland for armed robbery of a building society. Check your form runners first.

The chick at the door said he wasn't in.

"Any idea where he is?"

"Couldn't tell you."

"When did you last see him?"

"Yesterday morning. What's up?"

Bra-less and quivering under a thin T-shirt, she looked far too tasty to be shacking up with a middle-aged robber. But I kept my thoughts to myself.

"Are you a close friend of his, miss?"

She made a little sound of impatience. "What do you think?"

"What's your name?"

"Zara."

"And you spent last night alone, Zara?"

"That's my business."

"Jack wasn't here?"

She nodded.

"When he went out yesterday morning, did he say where he was going?"

"I'm his crumpet, not his ma."

I smiled at that. "He could still treat you like a human being."

"Jack's all right," said Zara. "I've got no complaints."

Don't count on it, I thought, sleeping with an ex-con.

Zara said anxiously, "He hasn't had an accident, has he?"

"Does he carry a gun?"

"What?"

"Don't act the innocent, love. We both know his form. Was he armed when he left here?"

"Course he wasn't. He's going straight since he got out."

It was time to get real. "There was an armed raid at a sub-post office yesterday and a man died."

"The postmaster?"

"No, the robber. It's just possible he was Jack Soames. We're checking on everyone we know."

"Oh, my God!"

"Would you be willing to come to the hospital and tell us if it's him?"

Zara looked, squeezed her eyes shut, and looked again. I watched her. She was easier to look at than the corpse.

"That's him, poor lamb."

"Jack Soames? You're certain?"

"Positive."

I nodded to the mortuary assistant, who covered the dead face again.

Outside, I thanked Zara and asked her where she wanted me to drive her.

She asked, "Will I have to move out of Jack's place?"

"Who paid the rent?"

"He did."

"Then I reckon you will."

"I can go to me Mum's place. What killed him?"

"We'll find out this afternoon, when they do the PM."

In her grief, she got a bit sentimental. "I used to call him Jack the Robber. Like ..." Her voice trailed off.

I nodded. "So you knew he was an ex-con?"

"That was only through the toffee-nosed bitch he married." Zara twisted her mouth into the shape of a cherry-stone. "Felicity. She claimed she didn't know she was married to a bank robber. Where did she think the folding stuff was coming from? She was supposed to give him an alibi and she ratted on him. He done four years through her."

"And when he came out he met you."

"Worse luck."

"I wouldn't say that," I tried to console her. "It's not your fault he went back to crime, is it?"

She didn't answer, so I decided not to go up that avenue.

She said, "What did he want to do a piddling post office for?"

I shrugged.

"Where did you say it was?"

"Five Lanes."

"Never heard of it. He told me he was going up the Benefits Office."

"It's a village three miles out. That's where he was at nine-fifteen yesterday."

"Get away," said Zara, pulling a face. "He was still in bed with me at nine-fifteen."

"That can't be true, Zara."

She was outraged. "You accusing me of lying?"

"Maybe you were asleep. You just thought he was beside you."

"Asleep? We was at it like knives. He was something else after a good night's sleep, was Jack." The gleam in her big blue eyes carried total conviction. "It must have been all of ten o'clock before he left the house."

"*Ten?* But he was dead by then."

"No way."

"How do you know?"

"Me watch."

"It must be wrong."

She looked down at her wrist. "How come it's showing the same time as the clock in your car?"

My boss was unimpressed. "Why is she lying?"

"I'm not sure she is," I told him.

"How can you believe her, dickhead, when you saw the body yourself shortly after nine-twenty-five?"

"She's got nothing to gain from telling lies."

"She's muddled about the time. She was in no state to check if they were humping each other."

"She's very clear about it, guv."

"Get this in your brain, will you? Jack Soames was dead by nine-twenty."

"Would you like to talk to her yourself?"

"No, I bloody wouldn't. You say she identified the body?"

"Yes."

"Well, then."

I had to agree. Something was wrong with Zara's memory.

Horgan made the first constructive suggestion I'd heard from him. "Find the wife. She's the next of kin. She'll need to identify him."

I didn't fancy visiting that mortuary again, but he was right. I traced Felicity Soames routinely through the register of electors, a slight, tired-looking woman in her fifties, who lived alone in a semi on the outskirts of Salisbury and worked as a civil servant. She was not much like the vindictive creature Zara had portrayed.

"I don't want any more to do with him," she said at first. "We separated."

"But you're not divorced?"

"Not yet."

"Then you're still the next of kin."

For the second time that morning, I stood well back while the mortuary assistant went through the formalities.

Felicity confirmed that the body was her husband's.

Zara's steamy sex with Jack that Monday morning was beginning to look like a fantasy, but I couldn't forget the sparkle in her eyes as she spoke of it.

"Right, son," said Johnny Horgan when I told him I had lingering doubts. "There's one final check you can make. The postmortem is at two. I'm not going to make it myself. Frankly, it's not high priority any more, one old robber who dropped dead."

My knees went weak. "You want me to ...?"

He grinned. "There's a first time for everything. Have an early lunch. I wouldn't eat too much, though."

"I'm sure the body is Jack Soames," I said. "I don't really need to be there."

"You do, lad. You're standing in for me. Oh, and make sure they take a set of fingerprints."

My hand shook as I held my mug of tea in the mortuary office, and that was *before*.

"So you're the police presence?" Dr Leggatt, the pathologist, said with a dubious look at me.

I nodded. This was a low-key autopsy. The man had died in furtherance of a crime, but there was nothing suspicious about the death, so instead of senior detectives, SOCOs, forensic scientists and photographers, there was just me to represent law and order.

Cosy.

173

"I'm supposed to go back with a set of fingerprints."

"No problem," said Dr Leggatt. "We'll start with that. You can help Norman if you like."

Norman was his assistant.

"I'd rather keep my distance."

"Fair enough. Shall we go in, then?"

I fixed my gaze on the wall opposite while the fingerprints were taken. Norman brought them over to me and said I could stand closer if I wished.

I nodded and stayed where I was. They were still examining the body for external signs when I started to feel wobbly. I found a chair.

"Can you see from there?" the pathologist called across.

"As much as I want to."

"Stand on the chair if you wish."

"Coronary," said Dr Leggatt when he finally removed his latex gloves.

"Natural causes, then?"

He smiled at the phrase. "Any middle-aged bloke who holds up post offices lays himself open to a fatal adrenaline response and sudden death. I'd call it an occupational hazard."

Some people call me cussed, others pig-headed. I don't particularly mind. These are qualities you need in police work. I refused to draw a line under the case.

Everything checked except Zara's statement. The fingerprints taken at the autopsy matched the prints we had from Soames's file at the National Identification Service. His mugshot was exactly like the man his wife and girlfriend had identified and the pathologist had dissected.

I tried discussing it with my boss, but Johnny was relentless. "Constable, you're making a horse's arse of yourself. Soames is dead. You attended the autopsy. What other proof do you want?"

"If he had a twin, or a double -"

"We'd have heard. Drop it, lad. Zara may be a charmer, but she's an unreliable witness."

"I know it sounds impossible -"

"So leave it out."

I was forced to press on without official back-up. I won't bore you with all the theories I concocted and dismissed. In the end it came down to whether Zara could be believed. And after hours of wrestling with the problem I thought of a way of checking her statement. She'd told me Soames had said he was going to the Benefits Office after he left her. If they had a record of his visit - *after he'd died* - Zara would be vindicated.

I called the Benefits people and got a helpful woman who offered to check their records of Monday's interviews.

She called back within the hour. Zilch.

I was down, down there with the Titanic.

Then something triggered in my brain. I asked the woman, "Do you have security cameras?"

"Sure."

"Inside the office?"

"Yes."

I drove down there and started watching videotapes.

"Guv, I'd like you to look at this."

"What is it?"

"Pretty sensational, I'd call it."

I ran the video. Two sergeants from CID who remembered Soames from before he went to prison came in to look. The screen showed tedious views of people waiting their turn to speak to the staff. I pressed Fast Forward, then slowed it to Play.

"Look behind the rows of seats."

A slight man with straight, silver-streaked hair came into shot and hesitated. He stared at one of the desks where a young woman was being interviewed, partially screened from the rest of the room. He took a step to the right, apparently to get a better view of what was going on.

I touched the Freeze Frame and held a mugshot of Soames against the screen. "How about that, guys?"

"My God, it could be him."

"No question," said one of the sergeants. "The face, the way he moves, everything."

"And look at the time."

The digits at the bottom right of the screen were frozen at 10:32.

"All right. Joke over," said Johnny. "How did you fix it?"

"I didn't. This is on the level."

"Run it again."

White-faced and muttering, my boss continued to stare at the screen until the figure of Soames turned away and walked out of shot.

"That man died at 9.20. It can't be."

"It must be."

We spent the next half-hour debating the matter. Johnny Horgan, desperate to make sense of the impossible, dredged up a theory involving false identification. Zara had lied when she came to view the body: Soames had put her up to it, seeing an opportunity to "die" and get a new name, and maybe plastic surgery, before resuming his criminal career. She, the dumb blonde, had stupidly blown his cover when I called on her.

It was a daft theory. How had he persuaded his wife Felicity, who had shopped him, to join in the deception? And why would he be so foolish as to parade in front of cameras in the Benefits Office?

"Any road," Johnny said when his theory was dead in the water, "we can't waste time on it. The post office job was the crime. Attempted robbery. There's no argument that the robber died of a coronary, whether he was Jack Soames or bloody Bill Sikes. The case is closed."

For me, it was still wide open. While the arguments were being tossed around, my mind was on a different tack. What had Soames been up to in the Benefits Office? He hadn't been interviewed, so he didn't collect a payout.

When the others had left the room, I ran the video again and made a stunning discovery. There *had* been a crime, and it was far more serious than a botched hold-up. Zara hadn't lied to me; hadn't even made a mistake. Impossible, it had seemed, because none of us made the connection. I slipped out of the building.

I found Felicity Soames in her place of work - at one of the desks in the Benefits Office. "It took a while for the penny to drop," I told her. "I was in here this morning to examine the security videos and I didn't spot you."

"Were you expecting me to be here?"

"To be honest, no. You told me you were a civil servant, but I didn't link it with this. You must have had a shock like a million volts when your husband walked in here on Monday."

She flinched at the memory. "I was terrified. He stood staring at me, putting the fear of God in me."

"We have it on tape. I watched it five times before I saw you behind your desk. We were all so gobsmacked at seeing him alive that we didn't give anyone else a look."

"He wasn't there for an interview. He just came in to check on me."

"To let you know he was out."

"Yes, I've lived in terror of him for four years. I put him away, you know. My evidence did it."

"And you're all alone in the world?"

"Yes."

"No, you're not, love. You've got a big brother. And you called him and poured out your troubles."

At the mortuary, I asked to see the body of the post office robber.

"I had the impression you'd seen enough of him already," said Dr Leggatt, smiling.

"Would you get him out, please?"

The pathologist sighed and called to his assistant. "Norman, fetch out number seven, the late Mr Soames, would you?"

I said mildly, "Jack Soames isn't the post office robber."

The doctor hesitated. "How do you work that out?"

"But I'd like to see his body, just the same."

Leggatt exchanged a world-weary look with Norman, who went to one of the chilled cabinets and pulled out the drawer.

It was empty.

Leggatt snapped his fingers. "Of course. He's gone."

"Not here?"

"Storage problems. I asked the undertaker to collect him."

"Along with the real post office robber, I suppose?"

Leggatt said, "You're way ahead of me."

"I don't think so, doctor. The man who held up the post office probably died of a heart attack triggered by stress, just as you suggested."

"What a relief!" Leggatt said with irony. But he wasn't looking as comfortable as he intended.

"You came out to Five Lanes and collected him. On the same day, Jack Soames, recently released from prison, decided to let his wife know he was at liberty. After a passionate lie-in with his girlfriend, he made his way to the Benefits Office where Felicity worked. She was terrified, just as he wished her to be. He had a four-year score to settle. When he'd gone, she phoned you."

"Me? Why me?" said Leggatt in high-pitched surprise that didn't throw me in the least.

"Because she's your sister, doctor. She's really suffered for blowing the whistle on her husband. Waking up screaming, night after night, all because she stood up to him. You told us about that after DI Horgan made his insensitive remark about the sub-postmistress."

"Idiot," said Leggatt, but he was talking about himself. "Yes, that comment angered me at the time. I'd forgotten. So much has happened since. And you made the connection?"

He'd virtually put up his hand to the crime. Elated, I held myself in check. "I think you saw an opportunity and seized it. You'd already taken in the body of the post office robber, a middle-aged man with greying hair, not totally unlike your brother-in-law. No one seemed to know who he was, so he was heaven-sent. You had a marvellous chance to kill Soames and end your sister's suffering without anyone knowing. You're a pathologist. You know enough to kill a man swiftly and without any obvious signs. An injection, perhaps? I think you believed your sister was in real danger."

"She was."

"Maybe," I said.

Leggatt shook his head. "There was no 'maybe' about it. He was waiting outside the Benefits Office for her. He wasn't there to make a scene. He intended violence."

"And you approached him, invited him into your car, killed him and drove him here. You chose a time when Norman was out of the mortuary - possibly at night - to unload the body into a drawer, the drawer supposedly holding the bank robber. You changed the tag on the toe."

"You watch too much television," Leggatt commented.

"When I came here with Zara, you wheeled Soames out. You knew I wasn't likely to take a close look at the face, seeing that I'd been so troubled by the sight of death. Anyway, I hadn't taken a proper look at the real robber."

"Your inspector did."

"Yes, but he delegated everything to me. He's new to our patch. He didn't know Soames, except from mugshots, so when he saw the security video from the Benefits Office he had Soames imprinted on his memory."

"You've got Soames on video? Thank God for that."

I nodded. "I expect your defence will make good use of it. Extenuating circumstances - is that the phrase?"

"Professional misconduct is another," said Leggatt. "Doctors who kill don't get much leniency from the courts."

"You carried out the autopsy on Soames, deciding, of course, that he died of a coronary, and it wouldn't be necessary to send any of the organs for forensic examination. But what did you plan to do with the other body - the poor old codger who dropped dead when the sub-postmistress looked him in the eye?"

"Not a serious problem," said Leggatt. "This is a teaching hospital and bodies are donated for medical research. We keep them here in the mortuary. It could all be fixed with paperwork."

"I wonder if we'll ever discover who he was," I said, little realising that it would become my job for the next six weeks. A DC who solves an impossible crime doesn't get much thanks from his superior. The reverse, I discovered. I'm still looking for promotion.

The Kiss of Death

The Diamonds were spending Christmas in New York. Steph's elder sister Ellie lived in Brooklyn. The sisters had years of family gossip to catch up on, so when the big detective tired of watching daytime TV, he slipped out of the apartment and took the subway into Manhattan and called on Johnny Flanagan, a detective with the NYPD who was once attached to Bath police for a short time. The two had got on well.

"You want action?" said Johnny, over coffee.

"I wouldn't want to get in the way."

"No problem. We have a case right now. It's been handled by a couple of rookies and I think I should take over. There's an outside chance it was murder."

"I want action, then."

The action in this case arose from the death of one Fletcher Merriman, aged seventy-eight, the senior partner in a small firm of accountants with an office in Canal Street. Old Mr Merriman had died in the Mount Sinai Hospital two weeks before, of heart failure.

"On the surface, straightforward," Johnny explained as they bumped along a street more potholed than Diamond had ever encountered in a large city. "The old guy was admitted with stomach pains. Mount Sinai treated him for gastroenteritis following an office party. The heart attack came later."

"Poison?"

"The autopsy report is in. They found a trace of betaphenylethylamine."

"Quite a mouthful."

"In more senses than one. It produces the symptoms of gastroenteritis. In a feeble individual - he had a heart condition - this can lead to a collapse of the cardiovascular system."

"You think someone popped him a dose of the stuff?"

Johnny took his hands off the wheel and spread them to show it was anyone's guess. "Peter, my friend, this is straight out of a whodunit. Merriman wasn't a nice old guy at all. Everyone at the party had good reason to want the son of a bitch dead."

"Everyone - how many is that?"

"Three."

"Small party."

"Makes our job easier."

"Absolutely."

"You don't mind spending Christmas Eve on this?"

Smiling, Diamond said, "It was either this or *White Christmas* on TV."

"Am I missing my favourite movie of all time? I hate this job."

The outer office of Merriman & Palmer was small, filled with desks and machinery. The surviving partner, Maurice Palmer, was there with a trainee, Sylvie Smith, tidying up for the Christmas break. Fiftyish, in the obligatory dark suit, Palmer had the look of a man who needed the holiday. "Actually, I'll be spending it in Key West," he said with more than a hint of self-congratulation. "Nicer weather."

Johnny didn't bother with introductions. So far as anyone here was concerned, Diamond was with the NYPD. "So this is where the party was held."

"No, the party was in here." Palmer swung open a door. "My office."

The crime scene.

A carpeted room dominated by a kidney-shaped desk with nothing on it except a phone. Shelving along two opposite walls stacked with account books and filing boxes. Palmer admitted his visitors, turned in the doorway and said to Miss Smith, "Why don't you finish off what we were doing?" Then he closed the door. "Fletcher worked from this office for many years before he retired in nineteen-ninety."

"So you invited him to your party?"

"His party. He brought it to us. He wheeled himself in - you know he used a wheelchair? - with three bottles of sherry, sweet, medium and dry, a box of mince-pies and a huge bunch of mistletoe, and told us it was party time. He liked to surprise people. His annual treat."

"If it's an annual treat how can it be a surprise?" said Johnny.

"We had no idea which day he would come in."

Diamond spoke for the first time. Johnny had told him to feel free to join in. "From what I hear, he was better off springing surprises than receiving them."

"His heart condition, you mean? Sure, he had to be careful. He'd had two coronaries since retiring. He withdrew entirely from the business. I've run it for years."

"But he was still the senior partner?"

"Right. He deserved some reward for all the years he put in."

"Meaning he had a big slice of the profits?"

"We're still a respected name around here."

"You'll keep the name?"

"Sure."

"And will his family get a share of future profits?"

"There is no family."

"So it all comes to you now?"

Maurice Palmer turned deep pink above his white collar. "Until I take another partner. I'll need to. Volume of work."

Diamond glanced at Johnny. "You don't mind if I carry on?"

"Be my guest."

"Let's get back to the party. What kind of bash was it?"

Palmer frowned. "What did you say? *Bash?* I wouldn't call it that."

"Did you have a mince-pie?"

"Two, actually."

"No ill effects?"

"I can eat anything."

"Did Mr Merriman have one?"

"He had two, like me. The ladies had one each."

"Did he eat his pies right away?"

"One of them. The other was here on the desk for some time. He had it eventually."

"Did you finish the sherry?"

"Not quite."

"Three bottles between four of you would have been good going. And was the mistletoe put to good use?"

Palmer lowered his voice. "You must understand that Fletcher belonged to a generation when political correctness was unknown."

"He was an old goat?"

"I wouldn't say that."

"Would the women?" asked Johnny.

"They wouldn't be so disrespectful."

"You didn't have to kiss him under the mistletoe. Let's speak to someone who did." As Diamond reached for the door, Johnny put a hand on his arm. "In here. Ask her to step inside, will you?" Then he told Palmer in the lofty tone he had used to his assistant, "Why don't you finish off what you were doing out there?"

Sylvie Smith looked nervous. She was as neat as a convent balance sheet, not much over twenty, with dark, intelligent eyes. Johnny invited her to sit down. The only chair without filing boxes on it was her boss's high-back executive job in black leather.

Johnny smiled at her. "Give yourself a treat. One day all this could be yours."

She perched uneasily on the edge of the chair.

"So how many of old Mr Merriman's surprise parties have you attended?"

"This was the first. I joined the firm in January."

"You must have wondered what was going on when he rolled through in his wheelchair waving a bunch of mistletoe. Did he insist on a kiss?"

Her mouth hardened into a thin line. "Not immediately. His word for it was a cuddle."

"And yours?"

"It makes me sick to think of it."

"If you'd complained, you'd have lost your job - and there aren't many openings for junior accountants?"

"That's for sure."

"Did you know the party was an annual event?"

"Dee said something about it, but I thought she was winding me up."

"Dee is the other woman who works here?"

She nodded. "She's been here six years. She'll be fully qualified next year."

"And she isn't in today?"

"Off for the holiday."

"Gone away?"

"I don't think so. She has an apartment in the Village."

"Lives alone?"

"Apparently."

"What age is Dee? All right, that's an indiscreet question. Is she under forty?"

"I don't know. She hasn't told me."

Diamond took over again. He'd been looking at the flat ceiling. The lighting was recessed. "I'm trying to picture this party. Presumably the old boy sat in his wheelchair under some mistletoe. I can't see where it was attached."

"We had to tie string across the room, from the top of one shelf to the other. Then the mistletoe was tied to the string."

"Got it. When you say 'we' ...?"

"Dee and myself."

"I'm getting the picture now. So whoever tied the mistletoe to the string must have stood on the desk to do it. Who was that?"

Sylvie sighed. "He told me to do it. Said I had longer limbs." She hesitated and reddened slightly. "I happened to be wearing a short skirt."

185

"The picture is even clearer. Did he hand you the mistletoe himself?"

"No. Dee did. He watched."

"So when he'd seen enough, and the mistletoe was in place, the party got under way. Drinks all round, no doubt. The food and drink was here on the table?"

"Yes."

"Sherry glasses?"

"Mr Palmer keeps some in his drawer."

"As every boss should. And who did the pouring?"

"Old Mr Merriman."

"Do you remember if the sherry was new? Were the bottles sealed at the neck?"

"Sure. He had to borrow scissors."

"You know why I'm interested? Something upset his stomach. What about those mince-pies?"

"They were fresh from Maisie's, he said."

Johnny said quietly, "Maisie's is one of the best bakers in New York."

Diamond asked Sylvie, "Were they open, these pies, or closed, in the traditional way?"

"They had lids, if that's what you mean."

"Closed, then. Did you have one?"

"Of course. I enjoyed it."

"And could anyone have slipped the old man a mince-pie from anywhere else?"

"I don't see how. We were all in here together."

"Making merry?"

"Going through the motions."

"I expect a few glasses of sherry helped."

"Not when he grabbed me and forced me onto his lap. That was disgusting. His bony old hands were everywhere." She shuddered. "It went on for over a minute. I could have strangled him."

"But you didn't," said Johnny. "Did Dee get the same treatment?"

"It wasn't quite the same. She was wearing a trouser suit."

"And did Mr Palmer kiss you?"

"That was no problem. Just a peck on the cheek. He doesn't fancy me, anyway."

Johnny thanked her and opened the door to the outer office. "We need Dee's address," he told Palmer.

"Dee? There's nothing she can add."

"How do you know? Maybe she saw something you and Sylvie missed." He got the address and they drove to Greenwich Village right away.

The apartment, just off Washington Square, was classily furnished. Dee was a classy lady, with a sexy drawl to her voice. She was not at all unfazed by their arrival. She offered them coffee and Johnny accepted, mainly to get a moment alone with her phone and check on the last call she'd received.

Quietly he passed on the news to Diamond. Dee's latest call was from the Merriman & Palmer office a few minutes after the detectives had left.

"I wouldn't get too excited about it," said Diamond. "Any colleague would tip her off that the cops were on their way." He took a book from the shelf by the door and flicked through the pages.

"Here's our problem," Johnny told Dee over the coffee. "Old Fletcher Merriman was taken ill on the day of the party. He may have been poisoned, triggering the heart attack. If so, we need to find out how he got the stuff into his system, and who did it. He brought his own food and drink to the party, right? Poured the drinks himself, in full view of everyone. Handed out the mince-pies fresh from Maisie's."

"Did they find poison inside him?" Dee asked as calmly as if she were enquiring about last night's rain.

"A trace."

"Why would anyone want to poison him?"

"Oh, come on," Johnny said. "Maurice Palmer stood to gain. The old man's death leaves him in control of the business."

Her eyes widened, obviously shocked. "Surely you don't suspect Maurice?"

Diamond looked up from the book and chipped in. "And Sylvie Smith was so disgusted by the groping she got that she felt like strangling him."

Sylvie as a suspect was more plausible to Dee. "She's got a lot to learn about men."

"His behaviour didn't bother you, then?"

"I've been six years with this firm. I know what to expect from Fletch the lech." She ran her fingertip thoughtfully around the rim of her cup. "Here's a theory for you, gentlemen. Is it possible during a kiss to pass a capsule into someone's mouth?"

"In theory," said Johnny.

"But nasty," said Diamond, thinking this had the reek of a red herring.

"Something like digitalis, that is taken by heart patients, but dangerous in an overdose?"

"What gave you this idea?" asked Diamond.

She shrugged. "In the absence of any other theory ..."

"Ah, but I do have another theory. A better one than yours." He replaced the book on the shelf. "Might I look into your bedroom?"

"What for?"

"To test my theory. This door?"

She was in no position to stop him.

A packed suitcase lay on the bed. "Going away for Christmas?"

"People do."

He stepped closer and checked the label. She was bound for Key West.

Johnny took a look. "Better cancel your plans, lady. You're not going any further than our precinct building."

"She's singing?" said Diamond.

"She will. Better than a choir of angels."

"You're sounding festive, Johnny."

"It is Christmas Eve. How did you crack it? What made you check the bedroom? Just a hunch?"

Diamond pulled a face at that. Hunches didn't feature in his philosophy. "Dee is a cool lady. Worked hard at her job, grinding through the columns, promising herself a promotion next year. She saw the younger woman, Sylvie, bright and ambitious, and decided she wasn't going to wait and be overtaken. Took her opportunity to send the senior partner to his final reckoning. Cozied up to Maurice Palmer and offered to spend Christmas in Key West with him. He was already thinking of taking on a new partner - professionally."

"You worked all this out from what we heard?"

"Don't kid me, Johnny. You were suspicious."

"So how exactly did she kill Fletcher Merriman?"

"With mistletoe berries."

Johnny was sceptical. "Peter, mistletoe is romantic, part of the magic of Christmas."

"Like Bing in a red and white cap? I checked her bookcase. There was one on the wild plants and flowers of America. Several deaths are credited to your romantic plant, through children swallowing berries at Christmas."

"Kids," said Johnny. "He was no kid."

"Adults don't usually make the mistake of eating the berries. He was tricked into eating them. In a tired old body susceptible to heart problems, as Merriman's was, the poison triggers stomach pains and nausea, like enteritis, and a failure of the cardiovascular system. It's in the book, Johnny. She knew. The poisonous principles in mistletoe are something called tyramine and ..."

"Go on."

Diamond smiled and shook his head. "You said it once. It began with 'beta'. The stuff they found in the body."

"How did Dee give it to him?"

"While everyone else was distracted. At the moment Sylvie - the young one - was climbing onto the desk in her

189

short skirt, Dee was holding the mistletoe, and she stripped some berries from the branches. She waited for her next opportunity, and it came when the old man was fondling Sylvie under the mistletoe. Nobody noticed Dee lift the lid of the mince-pie old Merriman had waiting on the desk, and press the berries into the mincemeat. After he'd finished mauling Sylvie, he ate the poisoned mince-pie."

"You don't think Palmer had a hand in it?"

"No. He wouldn't have told me about their trip to Key West. It was the first thing he mentioned. The perpetrator had to be one of the women."

"And it couldn't have been Sylvie."

"Right. She was under close surveillance from the old man. She didn't have the opportunity to remove the berries and add them to the pie."

"Good result." Johnny pulled out his desk drawer and took out a bottle of Scotch and two glasses. "Let's drink to a white Christmas."

"And not a mince-pie in sight," said Diamond.

The Stalker

As the senior detective on the Sharon Eakins case, I bear the responsibility for what happened. Only now, many months after my resignation from the police, can I face the task of setting down my version.

It started with one of those calls you dread, at 2.15 am, when you're in no state to pick up a phone. Ten minutes later DC Baker's car was at my door. Scarcely awake, I slumped into the passenger seat and we drove to 17 Dacre Street, Southsea. We arrived at 2.42. The door stood open. The victim, later identified as Sharon Eakins, aged twenty-four, was lying in the hallway.

Small, slim and dark-haired, she was dressed in lemon-coloured cotton pyjamas and a white dressing gown made of towelling. A young life ended. You'd have to be callous not to feel some pity.

The marks of her killer's hands were around her throat. I've seen several stranglings in my years with the murder squad. You get case-hardened, to a degree, but I was shocked by this one. The way I viewed it, anyone who crushes the last breath out of his victim with his bare hands is in a class of his own.

I interviewed the neighbour, Barry Campbell, from number 19, a single man, a bricklayer. He said he went to investigate after waking to the sound of thumps and screaming next door. He found the front door of number 17 had been forced inwards, the wood around the latch splintered. In the open hallway Miss Eakins was lying with her back to the door. After checking that she was dead, Mr Campbell returned to his house and called 999.

Dacre Street consists of small terraced houses with thin dividing walls. The family at number 15 confirmed that they, too, heard the screaming. They were a timid, retired couple, not the sort to do anything about it at that time of night.

Sharon Eakins was said by both sets of neighbours to have been independent and quiet in her way of life. Occasionally they heard her playing classical music. She had no regular visitors. She had lived in the house as a tenant for about eight months. She worked as a library assistant in Portsmouth.

We examined the rest of the house and found it in an orderly state. The curtains in the bedroom were closed and the edge of the quilt was pulled back, suggesting that Miss Eakins had gone to bed and been wakened by the sound of the front door being forced downstairs. Her handbag, containing her credit cards and thirty-five pounds, was still with her clothes on a chair in the bedroom. In the front room downstairs, the music centre and TV were still in place. Obviously theft was not the motive for the attack.

House-to-house inquiries next day gave us no significant information. Nobody had been seen entering or leaving 17, Dacre Street during the night.

Portsmouth Library spoke of Sharon Eakins as a reliable member of staff who joined the service eight months before with good references from her previous employer, Haldane Homes, the estate agents. Two of her librarian colleagues confirmed the neighbours' impression of a young woman leading a quiet life, with no obvious problems. She confided little about herself. They thought she was not dating anyone.

The post mortem was carried out on February 10th by Professor Jarvis of the Portsmouth Infirmary. His conclusion was that Sharon Eakins died of asphyxia caused by manual strangulation. She had not been sexually assaulted. In fact, she was still a virgin. Some particles of skin were recovered from the fingernails of her right hand, suggesting that she may have scratched her assailant. These were sent for DNA analysis.

The examination of the scene by forensic officers confirmed what I'd seen for myself, that the front door had been kicked in. Part of a heel mark was left on the surface, but all we could tell from it was that he was probably wearing boots or leather shoes. (I say "he" because I've never yet come across a case of manual strangulation by a woman, nor heard of a woman kicking in a door) The attack took place in the hall and fibres were collected and sent for examination.

So the murder investigation was launched. Our first line of enquiry centred on Miss Eakins's work at the library. It was suggested she may have attracted the attention of a stalker, a user of the library who had seen her there and become obsessive about her. A number of men known to visit the library frequently, either as book borrowers or newspaper readers, were questioned, without result.

The investigation then shifted back to Dacre Street. Two men in particular, residents of Dacre Street, were questioned about their contacts with her and their movements on the night of her murder. One had a record of violence and the second was a youth of sixteen who was receiving psychiatric counselling for depression and delusions. Both submitted to DNA testing and were swiftly eliminated from our enquiries.

The neighbour who reported the incident, Barry Campbell, was asked to provide samples, and co-operated. Some of the fibres found at the scene matched his dressing gown, but these were consistent with his stepping into the hall after the attack to check on the victim. The skin particles found in the victim's fingernails did not match his DNA.

For all the extensive enquiries and appeals for information, nothing more of significance emerged for six months. The "stalker" theory was still my best bet, but I had to concede that a sexual motive was unlikely, allowing that Sharon's pyjamas had been buttoned up and there were no indications of interference.

That's when the shrinks get a look in, when all other systems seem to have failed. The offender profilers deduced that the killer was not attracted to the victim, but deeply hostile to her. He had kicked down a pretty substantial front door to reach her. They gave us a picture of a man with a grudge against women in general, or Sharon in particular. The attack could have been triggered by something from his past, or something Sharon did, or said. He was likely to be obsessive and mentally unstable. Men in the Southsea and Portsmouth area known to have pestered or threatened women came under particular scrutiny, without result.

Personally, I've always treated offender profiling with scepticism.

The breakthrough came in September, 1998, out of routine inquiries. From the beginning, I had assigned a team of officers to assemble information about Miss Eakins's past. We succeeded in tracing a woman who had worked in the same Portsmouth office of Haldane Homes as Sharon for a spell of three months, July to September, 1996. She was Mrs Nicola Meagen.

This stable, dependable witness told us that in August, 1996, she noticed that Sharon was slow in sending out particulars of certain flats and houses on the agent's books. Descriptions of the properties were supposed to be routinely sent to all enquirers on the distribution list, but only a few were being sent out promptly. Sharon was late with the rest. Mrs Meagen suspected the delays were deliberate. When she was sure of her facts, and found that some clients she herself had dealt with were affected, she asked Sharon what was going on. Such behaviour is not unknown in the flat-letting business; usually it means back-handers are being paid to the agent to get priority, either for the vendor, or, more commonly, the purchaser.

Sharon was upset that any malpractice was suspected and denied it absolutely, blaming pressure of work for the delays. Soon after, Mrs Meagen left the job, and did no more about it.

This presented us at last with a new line of inquiry. What if the murderer was an aggrieved client who felt cheated by Sharon? Finding a place to live is one of the most stressful experiences people have to undergo. Competition is strong, and they expect a fair playing field. It was not impossible that someone blamed all his troubles on the young woman in Haldane Homes.

We took Mrs Meagen back to Haldane and asked her to pick out the files she knew had been affected by the delays. The names and addresses of people seeking properties in 1996 were still on file and we succeeded in tracing over ninety per cent of them. Nobody with an obvious grievance against Sharon was found. No one except Mrs Meagen seemed to know about the delays.

But an interesting pattern emerged. The details Sharon had been slow in sending out were all from properties in one area. She was being selective in sending out particulars of addresses close to her own, in Charity Avenue, Gosport. Some flat-seekers had been sent the details immediately, but the majority got them anything up to two weeks later.

At first, all our efforts were concentrated on the people who received the information late. I favoured the aggrieved client theory. Nothing helpful emerged, so I looked instead at the people who were the winners in Sharon's game.

Was she helping old friends she wanted living close to her? We ran a check on everyone had been found homes by Sharon. Four were still living close to Charity Avenue. One had moved again within six weeks of taking the flat. The four still in residence claimed not to have known Sharon prior to going to the Haldane Homes office. After questioning them we were satisfied that no favours had been asked and no bribes offered or accepted.

The fifth tenant - the one who didn't stay long - was a single man in his mid-twenties. He was eventually traced to an address in Southsea. He had changed his name, but he explained that he had changed it a number of times in his life, and we believed him. He was obviously a drifter. He described himself as a free spirit, unwilling to be labelled, or pigeon-holed. He played the guitar and at one time had made a number of recordings. Currently he was getting occasional work playing music in clubs and wine bars. Like the other tenants he denied receiving any favourable treatment from Sharon and said his dealings with Haldane Homes were perfectly in order. He had paid his rent for the short time he was there. He had moved to the new address simply because it was a better "drum". Something about his denials and his demeanour under questioning made the officers suspicious. He was asked to provide a DNA sample and refused. He was brought in for questioning.

I interviewed him myself. He was gaunt, long-haired, antagonistic towards the police - typical of many of the losers in the "baby-boomer" generation. We called him by the name he was currently using, Tom Hegarty. On the Haldane books he was Tom Hitchins. He said he couldn't even remember Sharon.

We had nothing to pin on him except his refusal to co-operate over the DNA, and he insisted it was his right to withhold a specimen. I couldn't guess what motive he might have for strangling Sharon. After all, he'd been one of the lucky ones who had got a flat.

We kept him almost the full twenty-four hours permitted. When the time was nearly up I hauled him back to the interview room and tried a piece of deception, simply fishing, and he took the bait. I let him believe we had picked up one of his hairs from the interviewing room and matched it to another found at the murder scene.

Hegarty rolled over and told all. It was an extraordinary story. He had first met Sharon when he called at Haldane Homes to enquire about flats. She gave him some particulars right away. She took him to see two he didn't like, but said she was confident one would soon come in that would suit him. He looked at several more before choosing the one in Gosport. Sharon was friendly and helpful, and he assumed she was good at her job and that was all.

After moving in, he received a number of phone calls from Sharon. There were queries over details and she asked him to come to the office to sign a form that could have been dealt with through the post. Later she phoned several more times to ask if he was satisfied with the flat. He could tell she was simply making excuses to talk. He said he wasn't hostile to women, but this one, so pushy and so humourless with it, didn't appeal to him at all. He tried to let her know he was not interested, but she persisted, as if he owed her some attention, stressing that she had gone to some trouble to find him the best flat on the agency's books.

How true the claim was, Hegarty didn't know at the time. He assumed she was just putting the best gloss on her work as a flat-finder. Thanks to Mrs Meagen, we knew better. Sharon had fiddled the system to make sure he was offered a place near hers.

It became obvious that she was infatuated. He met her on a couple of occasions near the flat and suspected she had been waiting for him. She remarked that she lived in the next street and if he ever wanted to borrow anything, he should-n't hesitate to call.

So it was a complete about-turn. Sharon had been the stalker.

As Hegarty described it, he first felt embarrassed by her behaviour, then impatient, then scared. Sharon took to phoning him whenever he was home, asking why he hadn't called yet. The more he made his anger obvious, the more persistent she got. Eventually she said she couldn't help doing it, and if it made him angry, she couldn't blame him. She said she was unable to stop herself. Even if he got violent with her, she would still want to be with him. He began to suspect that she *wanted* him to turn nasty. The calls came at all hours. She rang him at two in the morning saying she was sorry.

The next evening he returned early from the pub and to his amazement found her *inside* the flat. Apparently she had kept one of the keys. She admitted that she let herself into the place quite often just to be nearer to him and his things, and wasn't she a wicked girl? He said he would call her boss at

Haldane next day and see she was sacked if she didn't hand him the key and leave at once. She gave the key up so readily that he suspected she still had a spare one. A couple of evenings later when he went to bed he smelt her perfume on his pillow. The after-midnight calls started again. He disconnected the phone. But he knew he couldn't stay off line every evening. Most of his gigs came through phone calls.

Twice next day she approached him in the street. When he went to the pub, she came in with one of his drinking mates she had chatted up just to be one of the party.

As Hegarty explained it to us in the interview room, Sharon's arrival in the pub was a turning point. He was a man who had always found relationships difficult. At school, he had been a loner, an easy prey for the bullies. He felt he had let down his family. He had got no sympathy or understanding from his father. Before he was seventeen, he had left home for good. But lately, for the first time in his life, he had found a few friends he felt comfortable with. He was beginning to break out, talk a little in company, make jokes. Sharon was trampling on these tender shoots.

I believed him. But I ought to record that none of my colleagues did. They wouldn't accept the idea of a man driven to murder by a female stalker.

Hegarty decided the only remedy was to give up the flat and move out of Gosport altogether. He went to an estate agent in Southsea and deliberately used another name. A flat was available, not so nice as the one he was leaving, but he was glad to take it. Acting like a fugitive, he moved to the new address at six in the morning.

Sharon took about ten days to trace him.

The first he knew of it was a phone call about three in the morning. Sharon said as if it was the best news he would ever hear that she too had moved to Southsea and was living at 17, Dacre Street and wasn't she a naughty girl?

As Hegarty expressed it, "I was desperate. Couldn't sleep. Couldn't think straight. I got up and went to her place and kicked the door in and grabbed her. I knew she would give me no peace. Until you've been through it, you can't understand what that kind of torment does to you. I strangled her."

He signed a confession. He asked what kind of sentence he could expect and I said in view of his full and frank confession he might be treated leniently by a sympathetic judge, but he was still likely to get a custodial term of several years. He said he doubted if he could face being in jail. He valued his freedom above everything.

I'm sure he was speaking the truth. It was consistent with everything else he had told us.

As I mentioned at the beginning, I take full responsibility for what happened subsequently. I was at fault in letting him keep his belt in the cell.

I was the first in there after the alarm was raised. I cut him down myself, but he had been dead some time.

I resigned from the force the same day.

He was my son.

Ape

I blame my mother and father. Mother would insist on calling me Arthur. She played the tape of her all-time favourite musical while she was giving birth to me, and there was no question of her baby bearing any other first name than that of the King of Camelot. As for father, he thought Arthur was not a cool name for the twentieth century. He wanted me to have a fallback and his choice was Patrick. Not much cooler than Arthur, in my opinion, but I can live with it. I don't object to Arthur or Patrick. And I don't object to my surname. It's Egan. The one small matter neither Mr nor Mrs Egan noticed at the time was that their son's initials were APE.

You can imagine what I was called at school. Never mind Arthur, or Patrick. I was stuck with it for the rest of my life.

As boys do, I played up to the label, always monkeying around. I sometimes wonder if my character would have turned out differently if Dad had given me the second name Charles. As Ace, I would have had a different sense of self altogether. But the thing was done. I was the class fool, the kid who gave the teachers hell. I truanted, got into trouble on the streets and slipped easily into the life of a petty criminal. And I want to emphasise the "petty". Nothing I did was violent. You might argue that theft is a form of violence, but I don't agree. When I'd been caught a few times, I had no other choice but to steal.

I paid my debt to society several times over, in some tough institutions. It taught me to be more skillful. Inside, I learned from masters of the art. I can get through most security systems now. I don't leave prints or footmarks. I know how to fence the goods I liberate. I'm well respected in the business.

My last stretch was five years - just over three with good behaviour. I found it harder than ever. Prisons are getting no easier, believe me. On the day I was released, the Governor said, "You look ten years' older than the day you came in. Don't be a fool to yourself, Ape. Stay out of trouble this time. Get an honest job and stick at it."

Fat chance.

My skills are considerable, but not of much use to employers. I'm forced into self-employment.

But this time I did try going straight. Touch my heart and hope to die, I did.

The rehabilitation lady found me a place to doss. No, to be fair, it was better than a doss-house, a decent drum, my own bed-sit. I shared a kitchen with some others. Among them was Gerald.

You don't expect to find achievers in the kind of billet I was in. Most of the tenants are straight off the streets or fresh out of stir. A few, like Gerald, get there through some personality defect. His problem was a lack of confidence. Poor old duck, he was nodding his head, agreeing with me, before I even spoke to him. He must have been fifteen years younger than me, in the prime of his young life, not bad-looking and with a good physique as well, yet he took a step back and gestured to me to go ahead of him the moment I stepped into the kitchen. I don't know if he'd heard I was a jailbird.

"Carry on, squire," I told him. "I'll take my turn. What are you cooking? Smells terrific."

It was Spaghetti Bolognese. The meat was simmering nicely in one saucepan and the spaghetti in another. Anyone knows spaghetti doesn't take long. It's ruined if you leave it boiling too long, yet Gerald was proposing to step aside while I prepared my own meal. I had to close the kitchen door and stand with my back to it to keep him in there.

"Go on," I said. "I'm in no hurry."

He thanked me so effusively that my toes curled. The saucepan was about to boil over and I told him to watch out and he reacted as if I'd drawn a gun, thrusting both hands in the air. I don't know what he'd heard about me. I got to the gas just in time.

Gerald thanked me some more.

I got to know him reasonably well after that. You see, I'm not much of a cook myself. You don't get the chance in prison. All they ever let me do was peel potatoes and wash dishes. I persuaded Gerald to include me in his catering. He was only too willing to oblige, if I didn't mind eating really late, around midnight. It emerged that he had a part-time job in the kitchen of the Ritz Hotel. I think he did the basics there, loading plates into the dishwasher and so on. But he watched the chefs at work, and learned the culinary art. He could make anything taste delicious.

After a couple of weeks of this good living, Gerald and I were buddies. Sometimes he would bake something special in a single dish and we would share it in his room. He did amazing things with a few cheap ingredients like leeks, potatoes and cheese. Now I'd better make clear that these cosy suppers together were purely for convenience. I'm straight, always have been, and so was Gerald. I know, because we discussed women.

You're probably wondering how much experience the two of us had of the opposite sex - Gerald such a wimp, and me, a jailbird. The answer is less than we would have liked. I never asked him straight out, but I would guess he'd never had the pleasure. And mine was a distant memory. Yet that didn't stop us talking about it.

Of course, Gerald needed coaxing to talk about anything at all. A few cans of beer helped. They were my contribution to the supper. The subject of women just crept into our conversation. I was saying, "You cook so well, those chefs at the Ritz had better watch out. You'll have their job."

He smiled modestly at his plate. Gerald didn't go in for eye contact.

I said, "You can quote me for a reference any time."

"Thanks, Ape."

"Seriously, you're wasted stacking dishes. It must be so boring."

He shook his head.

"Not boring?"

"I don't get bored."

I waited, expecting him to add something, and eventually he did.

"I watch the chefs."

"You told me before."

"And when the chefs have finished, I look out the window."

Big deal, I thought. "What, to see what the weather is doing?"

"No. The window in the door."

I understood. Restaurants have those swing doors leading to the kitchens. For safety, there is usually a glass panel set into them. Gerald liked to peek through the door into the dining room.

He said, "Beautiful."

"I can believe it," I said. "I haven't seen the Ritz, but I can believe it. The gilding, the chandeliers, the mirrors, the painted ceiling."

"No."

"No?"

"The ladies in their dresses."

"Ah!" This was truly an insight. "The dishy diners."

Gerald had turned pepper-red.

"You fancy them, and I don't blame you," I said. "I would. I know the feeling. Many's the gorgeous bird I've clocked through glass during visiting. Unattainable. Breaks your heart sometimes."

"Only one."

"Who caught your eye?"

"She comes with her father and mother on Fridays, regular," he said. He was on a run now, actually putting more than three words together at a time. "Really dark hair fixed up high on her head like one of those goddesses. I watch out for her."

"A hot number?"

"Divine." Creases of tenderness spread over his face. "One of the waiters told me her name. Pippa. Pippa Coleridge. Her Dad owns one of the new railway companies."

"He'd have to be loaded to eat at the Ritz every week."

Gerald's mind was not on Pippa's father. "Her features are perfect. She doesn't wear much make-up. It's hard to think of her in the real world."

"She won't know much about the real world if her old man's that well off," I pointed out. "Probably swans around the family estate waiting for Prince Charming to arrive, if he hasn't already."

"Oh, no," Gerald said firmly. "She's untouched."

"Get away."

"I'm sure of it."

"How old would she be?"

"Nineteen, twenty ... I'm not sure."

"Gerald, old friend, if she's that good-looking, and rich, you can bet some Hooray Henry has bedded her by now."

"Don't say that." There was a threat in his voice, and I understood just how smitten he was. Dream on, I thought. No way will a misfit like you get a crack at Pippa. But I had some sympathy. Poor old beggar. I wished I could help.

Almost a year went by before the opportunity came. I was still in the same bedsit, getting my cordon bleu from Gerald, but starting to get a life again. It was neat, you have to agree. I was living up to my name. I became an ape. A great ape. A gorilla.

Let me explain. Since my last stretch in the slammer, a curious craze had developed: the gorillagram. Don't ask me to explain the appeal of it. The idea started, I think, with the stripagram. Typically, some old gent reaches retirement, throws a party for his workmates and they surprise him. Instead of a good-wish telegram, he gets a girl in black stockings, g-string, wasp-waisted corset and not much else who sits on his lap, plants lipstick all over his face and collar and provides

204

amusement all round. It adapts to almost any celebration from a birthday to a house-warming.

That's fine for blokes, but who do you hire to surprise a woman? A male stripper? In certain cases, yes, but most women find a fellow in a satin jockstrap more of a threat than a laugh. Gorillas are the number one choice for ladies. For one thing, they're anonymous. They're also furry, cuddly and a bit ridiculous.

One day a free paper was pushed through the door of our house. On the front was a picture of some smiling lady in the arms of a man in a gorilla suit. Eureka! I'd found the perfect job for an old con called Ape. I could work for myself with no fear of being recognized. I'd have all the fun of making whoopee at parties, cuddling the women, whisking them off their feet if they weren't too heavy and getting paid for it into the bargain.

I put a free ad in the same paper the next week:

THRILLER GORILLA
SURPRISE THAT LUCKY LADY WITH A GORILLA-GRAM. HE'S BIG AND BOISTEROUS AND FOR THE PRICE OF A FEW BANANAS HE'LL MAKE YOUR PARTY GO WITH A SWING. CONTACT APE. BOX NO. 129.

Two jobs came in the first week. I hired a gorilla suit from the costume shop in the high street and did my stuff. The clients loved it. I beat my chest like King Kong, chased the kids, stood on a car roof, played drums with the band and danced with the lady of the day. It was warm work, but wonderful fun. And I collected a fee for it.

After that, the work came in steadily. The word passed around that I was the greatest ape outside the zoo. I bought a mobile phone, took an ad in the Yellow Pages under Corporate Entertainment, and found myself listed with bouncy castles, murder weekends and hot-air balloons. For me, with my record, this was as good as being on a college honours board.

As a rising star, I got increasingly high-class work, and this was reflected in my fee. I demanded (and got) no less than two hundred pounds. By now I had two handsome gorilla suits of my own, a lifelike silverback and an extra woolly King Kong.

Out of the blue one June afternoon came the phone call that changed my life, and Gerald's:

"Mr Ape?" A woman's voice, young and beautifully articulated.

"Speaking."

"My name is Felicity Clacton-Hayes. You won't know me. I understand you do gorillagrams for parties and so forth."

"Sure."

"Super. Do you happen to be free on Saturday the nineteenth?"

I checked my personal organizer. "In the afternoon or evening?"

"This would be the evening. A friend of mine has a twenty-first birthday party at a country hotel - Cliveden, do you know it? - and some of us want to surprise her. If you could make an appearance at about eight, that would be absolutely brill."

"It's not impossible," I hedged, having taken note that Cliveden is about the swishest hotel in Britain, "but I'd need out-of-town expenses. I don't use a car in London."

"The expense is no problem at all," she delighted me by saying. "Just take a taxi and add the fare to your fee. I can arrange overnight accommodation if you like."

"No. I do the job and leave," I told her. "I'm a total professional. My fee for an event like this is three hundred. Travel expenses are extra."

She was unfazed. "Brill. Now I'm sure you're used to every kind of occasion, but I ought to tell you that some senior citizens will be at the party. Her grandparents. And her mother and father, too, come to that. We don't want anything they could object to, if you follow me. The hotel wouldn't want it,

206

either. I mean you can put your arm around Pippa's waist and give her a hug, but please no grabbing."

"Don't worry, miss. Grabbing isn't my style." I understood what she meant. I'd done every kind of party in my time and exhibited just about every facet of gorilla behaviour. At this stage I was more interested in Pippa's identity. It's a fairly uncommon name. "So the lady who receives the gorillagram is called Pippa?"

"Pippa, yes. Do you need a description? It will be fairly obvious who she is. She has dark, almost black hair, and she's very pretty indeed. And I'm Felicity. Short red hair. Passably good-looking, too, my friends tell me. I'll be in a black see-through dress and of course I'll look out for you at eight."

"Pippa who?"

"Coleridge."

I could hardly wait to tell my old chum Gerald when he got back from his evening at the Ritz. He was gobsmacked.

"Are you certain?"

"It's got to be her," I said. "There aren't that many people with her name who could afford to throw a party at Cliveden."

"Her twenty-first," he said wistfully. "Now I know how old she is."

"And I'll get to see this gorgeous woman you're always talking about."

He sighed. "You're so lucky."

"I'll give her a squeeze for you."

Now he looked pained.

"It's my job," I explained. "I've got to do my gorilla act. Give her a bit of a scare, chuck her over my shoulder and run around the room with her. They always scream, but they like it really."

He gaped. "You can't treat Pippa like that."

I spread my hands. "Do you think it gives me any pleasure? We all have to earn a living."

207

For the first time since he'd started cooking for me, he burnt the rice. After that, I shut up about the duties of a gorilla.

My brilliant idea dawned later, in the night. It was the neatest thing I ever thought of. It was beautiful. Perfect. Like the story of Cinderella. I was the Fairy Godmother, and Gerald would go to the ball.

I took him for a drink next morning and unfolded the plan. "Just because it means so much to you, I'm willing to make a sacrifice. You can go to Pippa's party instead of me."

He frowned. He didn't yet understand.

"You do the gorillagram."

"Dress up in a skin?" he said in horror. "I've never done such a thing."

"It's dead easy. I'll coach you. Just think of the benefits. You get to cuddle Pippa. You carry her around the room. She sits on your knee. You can say things to her, outrageous things, and she'll think it's fun. Play your cards right, and this could be the start of something you never even dared to imagine."

He said with a blush and a twitchy smile, "I'm not like you, Ape. I'm shy."

"When you get inside the skin, all that will go. You'll be supremely confident. Nobody will know who's under all that fur. Believe me, old friend, you'll have a ball."

I could see the conflict going on in him. His hands shook so much that he couldn't raise the beer to his lips. Part of him wanted desperately to take this heaven-sent chance.

"Look," I said. "Come back to the house and try on the suit. See what it feels like."

I knew he would be persuaded. Inside the suit, you feel amazingly secure. Strong. Assertive.

And it worked. The moment I fastened the Velcro and sealed him inside the silverback suit, he made an ape-like sound and shuffled across the room. He had the movement exactly, legs slightly bent, body stooping, arms swinging loose. Then he turned and beat his chest with his fists.

"Sensational," I said, and meant it.

You may think it strange that a man so introverted could transform himself in this way. It's not so remarkable. Many actors, for example, are shy people who only find confidence when they take on a role. Acting is their way of escaping from the prison of their personality.

In the next days, I taught Gerald the gorillagram routine. He had to learn how to make a big entrance, getting everyone's attention with as loud a roar as he could manage, and then loping over to the lady of the evening. That would be followed by a hug - "but not too vigorous," I stressed - and then conducting the guests as they sang "Happy Birthday". I told him he would probably get to dance with Pippa if he was gentle at the beginning. And if she seemed willing, he could carry her around the room. "Let her know you're not really a threat, and she'll be charmed," I promised him. "But there are also certain rules. No drinking, no disrobing and no groping."

When he was out of the costume he said, "I'm grateful, Ape. I'm really grateful."

I said it was a small return for all the suppers he had cooked. I didn't tell him I had an ulterior motive.

On the evening of Pippa's twenty-first, I rented a car and drove Gerald out to Buckinghamshire. Cliveden is an easy run, not far off the M4 motorway. It is approached along a grand drive, with a magnificent fountain playing in front of the house. Although I say all this as if I know the house intimately, I have never stepped inside. That was Gerald's privilege. Before entering the grounds, he changed into the gorilla suit. I drove up slowly, to get him there a few minutes before the scheduled time. It was still daylight, being so close to midsummer. I spent the last few minutes reminding him what Felicity Clacton-Hayes would be wearing. There was no need to tell him what Pippa looked like.

"Give it your best shot," I said as we pulled up at the entrance.

"Count on me," he said, so much more positive inside the suit.

"I'll pick you up here at ten sharp. Your duties will be well over by then."

He lifted one of his great pink hands and gave me a High Five. I drove off. I had things to do.

This, you see, was the neatest part of the plan. I had taken the trouble to look up Pippa's father in *Who's Who*. Sure enough, he was the railway magnate. Happily, his address was listed: a country home a mere half-hour's drive from Cliveden. Once a thief, always a thief. I couldn't pass up the opportunity of paying the place a visit and doing a little breaking and entering. I had a perfect alibi, didn't I? The Great Ape was wowing the guests at the party.

It should have been easy from then on. Unhappily for me, it was not. I found the Coleridge residence. I got close to it without anyone challenging me. No servants. No dogs. But what I hadn't anticipated were the videocameras mounted on each side of the house. Security technology had moved on since I last did a job. I only spotted them out of the corner of my eye when I detected a movement as I approached a window. Time to leave, I thought. Cursing, I abandoned the plan and drove slowly back to Cliveden.

Gerald was late coming out. I waited until twenty to eleven before he appeared, running across the gravel, still dressed in the suit, but with no semblance of a gorilla's movement.

I said, "Do you know what time it is?"

He just said, "Get me out of here," and I knew from his tone that something had gone wrong.

We drove for about a mile and he said, "Would you stop? I can't breathe."

I sympathised. After a couple of hours, a gorilla suit is pretty uncomfortable. We'd thought of this and brought a change of clothes in the car. I stopped in a quiet spot and waited while he peeled off the suit and changed.

210

"What was the problem?" I asked when he was sitting beside me again. "She was the right Pippa, wasn't she?"

Out of the suit, he reverted to his uncommunicative self. I barely got a nod in answer to the question.

"You did your stuff all right?"

Another perfunctory nod.

"She didn't faint, or anything?"

No answer at all. I gave up. At home, over a beer, he might be induced to talk.

But Gerald had other plans. As we approached central London, going through Hammersmith Broadway, he said with unusual clarity, "Let me out, please."

"What do you mean?" I said. "We're not home yet."

He said, "It's the only way."

"Gerald, what's up?"

"Stop. I want to get out."

He was so insistent that I braked and let him open the door. Before leaving me, he said, "Sorry." There was a moment's eye contact - so unusual with Gerald - and in that instant I felt I was staring into his soul. He was in torment.

I said, "See you later, then."

I never did.

When I got back to the house, there were two police cars outside. I stopped and got out. Lights were turned on me. An amplified voice told me to lie on the ground with my hands stretched out.

I said, "What for? I've done nothing wrong?" I hadn't even smashed a window of Coleridge's house.

"Do it!"

I obeyed. The only thanks I got for co-operating was two burly coppers throwing themselves on top of me, pinning me down.

After a bit, they drove me to West End Central Police Station and shoved me in a cell. They kept me there overnight. It was hours before I was interviewed.

"You are Arthur Patrick Egan, right?"

"Yes."

"You run a gorillagram service known as Ape?"

I nodded.

"Have you got a tongue in your head?"

"Yes, I do gorillagrams."

"You had a job at a party at Cliveden yesterday, is that correct?"

"It is. Look, would you let me in on the secret? What am I here for?"

"Save your breath, Egan. We've got you on video."

All this, for a failed burglary. "I did nothing. You can't stitch me up without evidence."

They listed their evidence. "A witness called Felicity, who hired you. A car rented in your name, the number noted by the hotel staff. A gorilla suit, found in the back. About two hundred guests who saw you dancing with the deceased."

"The what?"

"I was referring to one of the victims, Pippa Coleridge."

"Pippa is dead?" I could scarcely take this in.

"Don't act the innocent, Egan. You were caught on camera."

"Maybe, but not at Cliveden."

"Rushing down the fire escape in your gorilla suit after you strangled them. Pippa and her boyfriend Larry, in the bedroom where they'd gone for a few private moments. For crying out loud, it was her birthday. What did you have against those poor young people? You look sane enough sitting here, but this was a frenzied attack, as if you actually were a bloody great gorilla. Does something happen when you put on that suit?"

I pictured it. Gerald - meek Gerald - driven crazy by the discovery that Pippa had a lover and sneaked off to a hotel room with him. He must have found them in bed and gone berserk.

And they thought I was the killer.

I told them about Gerald. It took hours to persuade them to go looking for him. They didn't find him. And all the reports of Gerald described him as inadequate, immature, a timid, gentle man.

My last chance rested on the alibi. I'd been at the Coleridge mansion at the time Gerald was performing in the gorilla suit. I said I thought I was caught on the security video. They checked. I was not. I had no alibi.

They checked my DNA and found it matched samples from the gorilla suit. Was that any surprise when I'd worn it so often before? The jury thought it clinched my guilt.

A psychiatrist said in his psycho-babble that I was nuts. When I put on the gorilla suit my personality underwent a change. It was traceable to my childhood, when the kids called me Ape at school.

I was given two life sentences. I'm writing this in my cell in the special unit at a maximum security prison in the north of England. I don't expect anyone to believe me. The judge didn't, and nor did the jury.

I'm off the tranquillizers now. They know I'm docile.

Unless anyone calls me Ape.

The Usual Table

Two weeks after Ella and Gavin opened their restaurant on Bodmin Moor they heard someone say there would be shooting for the next three weeks on Harrowbridge Hill, just up the lane. Bad news. When they bought the business no one mentioned military exercises or field sports in the area. You can't serve relaxing meals to the sound of gunfire. Mercifully it turned out that the only sounds were a call for action followed by actors speaking lines. They were shooting a film. And even better news followed. The American film star Mikki Rivers spotted the restaurant sign and decided she would risk a meal there one evening. Danny Pitt, the director, made a reservation for two.

"Mikki Rivers! Brilliant!" said Gavin. "What a stroke of luck."

"It is *the* Mikki Rivers, is it?" said Ella, feeling both excited and terrified.

"We couldn't ask for a better endorsement," said Gavin. "Everyone for miles around is going to know she ate here."

"Please God she likes it," said Ella. "The menu is a bit thin."

"They'll know it isn't the Ritz. A limited choice, maybe, but what we serve is second to none."

Gavin didn't lack confidence. He was a trained chef, and a good one. The restaurant was tiny, just two rooms in a private house. You knocked at the front door, hung your coat in the hall and drank aperitifs in the small space in front of the bay window. But each item on the menu was *cordon bleu*.

Mikki Rivers came in on Wednesday evening with Danny Pitt. A photographer from the *Cornishman* got a shot of her stepping out of the Porsche in her mink. Ella was worried that Mikki would object to being photographed, but she gave her wide-screen smile and said she was used to far worse from the *paparazzi*.

They had the table closest to the log fire and everything was perfect. They ordered champagne and Gavin's special, the roast duck and black cherry sauce, and said it was the best meal they'd had since they arrived. At the end, Mikki Rivers said she wanted to come back Saturday.

She meant it. Danny Pitt made the booking before they left. Mikki's photo was on the front page of the *Cornishman* with the comment: "I'll be back Saturday. Try and keep me away!" By mid-morning on the day the paper appeared, every table was reserved. The phone rang through the day. Gavin and Ella could have filled their little restaurant five times over.

"We're made. It's a dream start," said Gavin.

"I hope they won't all gawp at her," said Ella.

"Not when they see the food you put in front of them. This is our chance, Ellie. Can you cope, or shall we hire an extra waitress for the evening?"

"If you can cook all by yourself, I'm sure I can manage my part."

They opened at seven on Saturday evening. Mikki Rivers didn't arrive until later, thank goodness, because there was a problem with some other customers, who had booked in the ominous name of Hellings.

"There must be a mistake."

"What's that, madam?" Ella asked with proper concern.

"Some people are sitting at our usual table in the conservatory."

Ella had never seen them before. She remembered with an effort that the restaurant had been in business for some years before she and Gavin took over.

"The con- which, madam?"

"Conservatory. Out there."

"Oh, the sun room."

"It's the conservatory. It's always been the conservatory."

"I didn't know that," Ella said humbly. "We haven't been here long."

"If you had," said the woman, a senior citizen with three rows of paste pearls that lent symmetry to the triple bags under her heavily made-up eyes, "you would know that we always have that table for our anniversary dinner."

"They'll have to move," said her companion in a combative voice. This burly man with a red bow-tie looked uncomfortable in his suit. His weatherbeaten face suggested he'd worked outdoors most of his life.

Desperate as Ella felt, she knew she must humour these people and get them settled before her star guest arrived. "Did you say it's your anniversary? Congratulations. Is it a special one?"

"They're all special to Wilf and me," said the woman. "Actually, this is the thirteenth. We come every year."

"And sit at our usual table," added Wilf. He wasn't to be sidetracked. "We're not sitting anywhere else."

"We asked for our usual table when we booked," said the woman. "That's the whole point of coming here, that table. There are better restaurants, with better food and better service, but that table has associations."

And Wilf chimed in, "So will you tell those people to move their arses, or shall I?"

Fortunately, he'd lowered his voice. Normally if you took the trouble to listen you could hear anything anyone said in the tiny rooms. How tempted Ella was to show the door to this obnoxious pair. On any other evening, she would have risked it.

She glanced across at the young couple sitting in the sun room. They were still looking at the menu. They might be persuaded to move. They appeared amenable.

"Listen," she said to Wilf Hellings and his lady, "I'm sure we can sort this out. Please have an aperitif with our compliments, while I speak to my husband."

"You can stuff your aperitif," Wilf told her. "We want action, not farting around."

Ella went into the kitchen and told Gavin about these appalling people. He was terribly busy cooking whitebait for starters. "Who took the booking? Did they mention a special table?"

"Does it matter who took the booking?" Ella said. "The point is, we'll have a riot if they don't get that table. Mikki Rivers could arrive any minute."

Gavin pulled the pan from the flame. "I'll speak to the people in the sun room, then." He moved off at speed.

Happily - and with the bribe of a bottle of Chablis, courtesy of the management - the young couple were willing to move.

So the Hellings, the customers from hell, took possession of their usual table. Ella handed them the menu just as Mikki Rivers and her companion Danny Pitt drove up.

"So pleased to be back in your wonderful restaurant," said Mikki as she slipped out of the mink. She was in a gorgeous glittery top and black skirt slashed to the hip.

"We're a little busier than last time," said Ella apologetically.

"No problem," said Danny Pitt. He winked. "Good to see fine cooking appreciated."

"If it is the cooking."

Ella showed them to their table by the fireplace and left them with the menu while she took other orders.

"Give me the wine-list," said Wilf Hellings, when she reached him. "The drinks are on Gus this evening."

"The whole meal's on Gus," said his companion, giggling.

"He's got no choice, has he?" said Wilf.

"Gus was my husband," the woman explained to Ella. "I still have his money in the bank."

"*Is* your husband," Wilf corrected her. "In theory, anyway."

Ella didn't show it, but her fury at these obnoxious people increased. They'd made a scene because they were supposed to be celebrating their thirteenth anniversary. And now it appeared they weren't even married.

"He disappeared one day," said the woman. "Gus, my so-called better half, vanished."

"Sank without trace," said Wilf, and for no obvious reason threw back his head and guffawed, and the woman joined in.

All of this was audible to anyone who cared to listen. The woman's piercing laughter must have got through to those with no interest in listening.

"He was a pig," she said of her husband. "You couldn't have brought him to a place like this."

"You wouldn't need to. He never left it," Wilf said in a cryptic aside, and earned another shriek.

"I wouldn't want him back," she said. "I don't mind spending his money, though."

Ella glanced nervously towards the table by the fire. Thankfully Mikki Rivers and her escort seemed to be oblivious of all this.

Wilf glanced at the wine-list. "Got anything unusual in your cellar?"

This won the customary hoot of amusement from his companion.

"Everything we stock is on the list, sir. Perhaps you'd like a little longer to make up your mind."

"What's on the menu?" the woman asked.

Ella went through the specials.

"Now tell us in plain English," Wilf said.

Ella knew he was winding her up, testing her, trying to find her breaking point. In her time as a waitress she'd never met anyone so unpleasant.

The woman said to Ella, "Come here, love. No, really close. I want to whisper something in your ear."

She wasn't sure if she wanted to get any closer, but she had to appear friendly, so she dipped her head and heard the woman say, "Play along with him and you'll get a socking great tip."

The tip was the last thing on her mind, but she gritted her teeth and explained what each dish consisted of.

"Right," said Wilf. "I'll have the pie."

"And would you care for a starter?"

"Just a big portion of fish pie and plenty of veg. I've had you for my starter, had you over a barrel, and very tasty it was. Might have some more before the evening's through."

The woman shook with mirth. "He's a wicked man. Don't take any notice. I'll have the pie as well."

In the kitchen, Ella told Gavin, "Two *saumon en croute*, and I feel like spitting in them. Those people in the sun room are horrible."

"Don't let them get to you."

"It's all right for you. You don't have to speak to them."

"Better change their knives and forks if they're having the salmon."

"Oh, God, yes."

Probably her state of mind had something to do with the fumble she made with the cutlery at the Hellings's table. A fish-knife slipped from her hand and dropped on the floor.

"Watch it!" said Wilf, at once. "Careful of my floor."

"Careful of your floor," his companion said, simpering at him. "It's not much of a floor if a fish-knife cracks it."

"Six inches of hardcore and six inches of concrete," said Wilf.

"Mostly hardcore anyway," she said, nudging him as if they had some private joke.

Ellie picked up the knife and said, "I'll get you another."

"And a bottle of house white," said Wilf.

"Mean bastard," said his lady.

When Ella returned with the knife and the wine, the woman said, "You must be wondering what Wilf was on about, talking about his floor as if he owned it. You see, he's a builder. He built this conservatory thirteen years back."

"You must have seen my name on the trucks in big red letters. Hellings," said Wilf with pride. He addressed this remark to the room in general, turning to see if anyone responded, and several nodded their heads to humour him. There was general interest in what was being said.

"He's very well known," said the woman, pitching her voice higher to involve more of the diners. "This building was my home, see, before it was a restaurant. I lived here with Gus, my lawful wedded pain in the arse. He always wanted a conservatory, and we weren't short of money, Gus being a garage owner, so we got the planning permission and hired the best builder in West Cornwall, and that was Wilf."

"That's why I called it my floor just now," said Wilf, looking around the room. "I built it, but it belongs to Pearl really."

"And Gus," said the woman now revealed as Pearl.

"Specially Gus," said Wilf, and got a giggle from Pearl.

Ella went to Mikki Rivers's table and took their order. The film star still seemed perfectly at ease, faintly amused by what she and everyone else had overheard in the last few minutes.

In the kitchen, Ella passed on the orders to Gavin and updated him on what had been said. "That woman with Hellings lived here, apparently," she told Gavin. "This was her house."

"If it is," said Gavin, "she's still the owner. We lease it through the agents, but it's owned by some company with a woman as managing director. Must be her."

"The husband left her, and I'm not surprised. He disappeared thirteen years ago, after Wilf Hellings built the sun room for them. She seems to have taken a fancy to her builder and moved in with him."

Gavin said, "Their salmon is ready. Got your tray?" He transferred the food to the plates. "Be nice to them, Ellie. I know it's difficult."

She carried the tray to the table with extreme care and set the plates in front of them.

"Right," said Wilf. "Let's see if the cooking is up to standard. The trouble with salmon is the bones."

"It's filleted," Ella assured him.

"Better be. There's nothing worse than finding bones when you don't expect them, eh, Pearl?"

"Shut up, you old fool," Pearl scolded him, half-smiling, and blushing, too.

"Relax," said Wilf. "I wouldn't embarrass you. We've been coming all these years and I've never said a word out of turn, have I?"

"He's not used to eating out," Pearl told Ella. "We have this anniversary meal once a year, and that's enough for him."

"The anniversary of the day her husband Gus disappeared," said Wilf, and once again he had the attention of just about everyone in the room, including Mikki Rivers. "He was a toe-rag, was Gus. Treated her like something the dog dragged in. I saw it at first hand when I got the job here, building the conservatory. How long was I working here, Pearl - six, seven, eight weeks? I say it myself, I'm a master builder. He knew he was hiring the top man around. It was purpose built, this conservatory, not one of those ready-made things that let in the damp. As I say, I saw him knock her around."

Pearl said, "You don't have to go into details, Wilf."

"He was a rich bastard and he thought that gave him the right to do as he liked," Wilf pressed on relentlessly, pouring himself more of the house wine. "She would have put up with it, wouldn't you, Pearl, if I hadn't come on the scene? She didn't know he was seeing other women."

While Wilf regaled the room with Gus's deplorable behaviour, Ella did her best to take the orders and serve the meals. It was difficult to get anyone's full attention. Even Gavin had the kitchen door open and was trying to listen. "Do you think they bumped off the husband?" he asked Ella when she came to collect some meals.

"They wouldn't talk like this if they had."

"It could be the wine talking. Maybe this anniversary of theirs is the anniversary of the murder."

"What a gruesome idea."

"They're a gruesome pair."

"That's true." She picked up her tray and took another order out.

In the sun room Wilf was saying in his carrying voice, "It all came to a head one Saturday morning thirteen years ago. I'd just finished digging the foundations, right here where I'm sitting. Back-breaking work. Pearl said she'd make me a coffee, and I don't turn down good offers from the ladies. We got talking, as you do, and I happened to mention I'd seen Gus the night before in the Jamaica Inn with a gorgeous red-head. Now, I swear I wasn't making trouble. I wouldn't have said a word about it - except I thought this girlie had to be his daughter. She was so much younger than old Gus, you see."

His story was interrupted by the doorbell, but like all good raconteurs, Wilf turned it to advantage.

"The front door opens, and in walks the man himself - Gus. He doesn't ring the bell, it's true, cause he's got a key, hasn't he? Just walks in. He's obviously been on the job all night. Looks a wreck. No prizes for guessing where he spent the night. They say it's really comfortable up there, and the cooked breakfasts are out of this world. Pearl asks the old stallion where he's been, and he tells her to shut up asking questions and get him a black coffee - and I decide it's time to get back to my foundations. I know when to make myself scarce. The trouble is, Pearl asks me to stay. She wants him in the dock, with me as witness for the prosecution. Isn't that a fact, Pearl? Am I telling it right?"

"You shouldn't be telling it at all," said Pearl, getting a word in at last. "People come here for a nice meal. They don't want to hear about my two-timing husband."

"They want to know what happened."

"It's no business of theirs."

"They're interested."

"Shut up and eat your dinner. And I don't think you should have any more of that wine. You're not used to it."

So for an interval, Wilf was gagged.

Back in the kitchen, Ella asked Gavin, "Did you go to the door just now?"

"Yes. Just some customer who came in at lunchtime and thought he left his umbrella."

"You let him look for it?"

"And missed part of the story. Where did Gus spend the night?"

"The Jamaica Inn, with a redhead half his age."

"I'm even more convinced they murdered him."

"What would they have done with the body?" asked Ella.

Occasionally two people who know each other intimately have the same thought at precisely the same time. In this instance, the shared thought was so horrific that neither spoke. Ella gasped and Gavin stared.

Finally Ella said, "The foundations."

Gavin, pulling himself together, said, "You'd better take the dessert trolley round."

Mikki Rivers opted for the raspberry mousse. She said the food had been delicious again.

Ella said, "I just hope you weren't disturbed by the loud-mouth in the sun room."

Mikki said, "We adored it. What a strange couple. We're dying to hear the end of the story."

Feeling slightly more relaxed, Ella pushed the dessert trolley into the sun-room.

Wilf Hellings put up two hands defensively. "Don't bring it over here. We're supposed to be dieting."

"It's tempting, though," said Pearl.

"If you fancy something, go ahead," said Wilf. "You won't get another crack at it till next time the anniversary comes around."

"I'd better not. Why don't you settle up now?"

"A coffee, perhaps?" Ella suggested.

They shook their heads.

From the other room, Danny Pitt spoke up. "Before you go, would you mind telling us what happened between you and Gus, the lady's husband?"

There were murmurs of support from all around the room.

Wilf looked at Pearl, who shrugged.

"There isn't much more I can tell you," said Wilf. "He called me a liar and I called him a rat and soon after that he disappeared. Who knows where he ended up? Someone suggested he may have gone down under, and there could be some truth in that." He paused and looked at the floor, milking the line for all it was worth.

Pearl began to giggle again.

"Anyway, it cemented our relationship."

Pearl found this uncontrollably funny.

"I don't think he'll surface now," added Wilf. "So we come here once a year and sit here at our usual table and have a meal on Gus, and, do you know, we feel quite close to him?"

Soon after, they paid their bill in cash and left. Ella got a ten pound tip. The money was unimportant. Her suspicions meant she would never feel comfortable in the house again.

Which didn't matter, as it turned out, because she and Gavin left soon after, even though the police convinced them that the story of the missing husband had been just a clever con. It was the bad publicity over the stolen mink coat that did for them.

The Problem of Stateroom 10

The conversation in the first class smoking room had taken a sinister turn.

"I once met a man who knew of a way to commit the perfect murder," said Jacques Futrelle, the American author. "He was offering to sell it to me - as a writer of detective stories - for the sum of fifty pounds. I declined. I explained that we story writers deal exclusively in murders that are imperfect. Our readers expect the killer to be caught."

"Now that you point it out, a perfect murder story would be unsatisfactory," said one of his drinking companions, W.T.Stead, the campaigning journalist and former editor of the *Pall Mall Gazette*, now white-bearded and past sixty, but still deeply interested in the power of the written word. "Good copy in a newspaper, however. In the press, you see, we need never come to a conclusion. Our readers cheerfully pay to be held in suspense. They enjoy uncertainty. They may look forward to a solution at some time in the future, but there's no obligation on me to provide one. If it turns up, I'll report it. But I'm perfectly content if a mystery is prolonged indefinitely and they keep buying the paper."

"The classic example of that would be the Whitechapel murders," said the third member of the party, a younger man called Finch who had first raised this gruesome subject. His striped blazer and ducks were a little loud for good taste, even at sea.

"Dear old Jack the Ripper?" said Stead. "I wouldn't want him unmasked. He's sold more papers than the King's funeral and the Coronation combined."

"Hardly the perfect murderer, however," commented Futrelle. "He left clues all over the place. Pieces of flesh, writing on walls, letters to the press. He only escaped through the incompetence of the police. My perfect murderer would be of a different order entirely."

"Ha! Now we come to it," said Stead, winking at Finch. "Professor S.F.X. Van Dusen. The Thinking Machine."

"Van Dusen isn't a murderer," Futrelle protested. "He solves murders."

"You know who we're talking about?" Stead said for the benefit of the young man. "Our friend Futrelle has a character in his stories who solves the most intractable mysteries. Perhaps you've read *The Problem of Cell 13*? No? Then you have a treat in store. It's the finest locked room puzzle ever devised. When was it published, Jacques?"

"Seven years ago - 1905 - in one of the Boston papers."

"And reprinted many times," added Stead.

"But The Thinking Machine would never commit a murder," Futrelle insisted. "He's on the side of law and order. I was on the point of saying just now that if I wanted to devise a perfect murder - in fiction, of course - I would have to invent a new character, a fiendishly clever killer who would leave no clues to his identity."

"Why don't you? It's a stunning idea."

"I doubt if the public are ready for it."

"Nonsense. Where's your sense of adventure? We have *Raffles, the Amateur Cracksman*, a burglar as hero. Why not a murderer who gets away with it?"

Futrelle sipped his wine in thoughtful silence.

Then young Finch put in his two-pennyworth. "I think you should do it. I'd want to read the story, and I'm sure thousands of others would."

"I can make sure it gets reviewed," offered Stead.

"You don't seem to understand the difficulty," said Futrelle. "I can't pluck a perfect murder story out of thin air."

"If we all put our minds to it," said Stead, "we could think up a plot before we dock at New York. There's a challenge! Are you on, gentlemen?"

Finch agreed at once.

Futrelle was less enthusiastic. "It's uncommonly generous of you both, but -"

"Something to while away the time, old sport. Let's all meet here before dinner on the last night at sea and compare notes."

"All right," said Futrelle, a little fired up at last. "It's better than staring at seagulls, I suppose. And now I'd better see what my wife is up to."

Stead confided to Finch as they watched the writer leave, "This will be good for him. He needs to get back to crime stories. He's only thirty-seven, you know, and toils away, but his writing has gone downhill since that first success. He's churning out light romances, horribly sweet and frothy. Marshmallows, I call them. The latest has the title *My Lady's Garter*, for God's sake. This is the man who wrote so brilliantly about the power of a logical brain."

"Is he too much under the influence of that wife?"

"The lovely May? I don't think so. She's a writer herself. There are far too many of us about. You're not another author, I hope?"

"No," said Finch. "I deal in *objets d'art*. I do a lot of business in New York."

"Plenty of travelling, then?"

"More than I care for. I would rather be at home, but my customers are in America, so I cross the ocean several times a year."

"Is that such a hardship?"

"I get bored."

"Can't you employ someone to make the trips?"

"My wife - my former business partner - used to make some of the crossings instead of me, but no longer. We parted."

"I see. An international art-dealer. How wrong I was! With your fascination for the subject of murder, I had you down for a writer of shilling shockers."

"Sorry. I'm guilty of many things, but nothing in print."

"Guilty of many things? Now you sound like the perfect murderer we were discussing a moment ago."

Secretly amused, Finch frowned and said, "That's a big assumption, sir."

"Not really. The topic obviously interests you. You raised it first."

"Did I?"

"I'm certain you did. Do you have a victim in mind?" Stead enquired, elaborating on his wit.

"Don't we all?"

"Then you also have a motive. All you require now are the means and the opportunity. Has it occurred to you - perhaps it has - that an ocean voyage offers exceptional conditions for the perfect murder?"

"Man overboard, you mean? An easy way to dispose of the body, which is always the biggest problem. The thought had not escaped me. But it needs more than that. There's one other element."

"What's that?"

"The ability to tell lies."

"How true." Stead's faint grin betrayed some unease.

"You can't simply push someone overboard and hope for the best."

"Good. You're rising to the challenge," said Stead, more to reassure himself than the young man. "If you can think of something special, dear boy, I'm sure Jacques Futrelle will be more than willing to turn your ideas into fiction. Wouldn't that be a fine reward?"

"A kind of immortality," said Finch.

"Well, yes. I often ask myself how a man would feel if he committed a murder and got away with it and was unable to tell anyone how clever he'd been. We all want recognition for our achievements. This is the answer. Get a well-known author to translate it into fiction."

"I'd better make a start, then."

The young man got up to leave, and Stead gazed after him, intrigued.

Jeremy Finch was confident he'd not given too much away. Stead had been right about all of us wanting recognition. That was why certain murderers repeated their crimes. They felt impelled to go on until they were caught and the world learned what they had done. Finch had no intention of being caught. But he still had that vain streak that wanted the world to know how brilliant he was. The idea of having his crime immortalised through the medium of a short story by a famous author was entirely his own, not Stead's. He'd deliberately approached the two eminent men of letters in the smoking room and steered the conversation around to the topic of murder.

He wanted his murder to be quoted as one of the great pieces of deception. In Futrelle's fine prose it would surely rank with Chesterton's *The Invisible Man* and Doyle's *The Speckled Band* as a masterpiece of ingenuity. Except that in his case, the crime would really have happened.

It was already several weeks in the planning. He had needed to make sure of his victim's movements. This crossing was a God-send, the ideal chance to do the deed. As Stead had pointed out, an ocean voyage affords unequalled opportunities for murder.

He had made a point of studying the routine on C Deck, where the first class staterooms were. His previous transatlantic voyages had been second class, luxurious enough for most tastes on the great liners. His wife Geraldine always travelled first class, arguing that an unaccompanied lady could only travel with total confidence in the best accommodation, her virtue safeguarded. This theory had proved to be totally misfounded. Another dealer, a rival, had taken cruel pleasure in informing Finch after Geraldine's latest trip to New York that he had seen her in another man's arms. The news had devastated him. When faced with it, she admitted everything. Finch shrank from the public humiliation of a divorce, preferring to deal with the infidelity in his own way.

So for the first days of the voyage he observed his prey with all the vigilance of Futrelle's creation, The Thinking Machine, getting to know his movements, which were necessarily circumscribed by the regularity of life aboard ship. He thought of himself as a lion watching the wretched wildebeeste he had singled out, infinitely patient, always hidden, biding his time. The man who was picked to die had not the faintest notion that Finch was a husband he had wronged. It wouldn't have crossed his lascivious mind. At the time of the seduction, six months before, he'd thought lightly of his conquest of Geraldine. He had since moved on to other lovers, just as young, pretty, impressionable and easily bedded.

He was due to die by strangulation on the fourth evening at sea.

The place picked for the crime, first class stateroom 10 on C Deck, was occupied by Colonel Mortimer Hatch, travelling alone. By a curious irony it was just across the corridor from the stateroom where Jacques Futrelle was pacing the floor for much of each day trying to devise a perfect murder story.

Mortimer Hatch was forty-one, twice divorced and slightly past his prime, with flecks of silver in his moustache and sideburns. His shipboard routine, meticulously noted by Finch, was well established by the second day. He would rise about eight and swim in the first-class pool before taking breakfast in his room. During the morning, he played squash or promenaded and took a Turkish bath before lunch. Then a short siesta. From about three to six, he played cards with a party of Americans. In the evening, after dinner, he took to the dance floor, and there was no shortage of winsome partners. He was a smooth dancer, light on his feet, dapper in his white tie and tails. Afterwards, he repaired to the bar, usually with a lady for company.

It was in the same first class bar, on the third evening out from Southampton, that Jeremy Finch had a second meeting with Stead and Futrelle. They were sharing a bottle of fine French wine, and Stead invited the young man to join them. "That is, if you're not too occupied planning your perfect crime."

"I'm past the planning stage," Finch informed them.

"I wish I was," said Futrelle. "I'm stumped for inspiration. It's not for want of trying. My wife is losing patience with me."

"*Nil desperandum*, old friend," said Stead. "We agreed to pool our ideas and give you a first-class plot to work on. I have a strong intimation that young Jeremy here is well advanced in his thinking."

"I'm practically ready," Finch confirmed.

"Tell us more," Futrelle said eagerly.

Stead put up a restraining hand. "Better not. We agreed to save the denouement for the night before we dock at New York. Let's keep to our arrangement, gentlemen."

"I'll say this much, and it won't offend the contract," said Finch. "Do you see the fellow on the far side of the bar, mustache, dark hair, in earnest conversation with the pretty young woman with Titian-red hair and the ostrich feather topknot?"

"Saw him dancing earlier," said Stead. "Fancies his chances with the ladies."

"That's Colonel Hatch."

"I know him," Futrelle said. "He's in the stateroom just across from mine. We share the same steward. And, yes, you could be right about the ladies. There was a certain amount of giggling when I passed the door of number 10 last evening."

"All I will say," said Finch, "is that I am keeping Colonel Hatch under observation. When he leaves the bar, I shall note the time."

"Being a military man, he probably keeps to set times in most things he does," said Stead.

"Even when working his charms on the fair sex?" said Futrelle.

"That's the pattern so far," said Finch, without smiling. "I predict that he'll move from here about half past eleven."

"With the lady on his arm?"

"Assuredly."

The conversation moved on to other matters. "Are you married?" Futrelle asked Finch.

"Separated, more's the pity."

"Not all marriages work out. Neither of you may be at fault."

"Unhappily, in this case one of us was, and it wasn't me," said Finch.

After an awkward pause, Stead said, "Another drink, anyone?"

At eleven twenty-eight, almost precisely as Finch had predicted, Colonel Hatch and his companion rose from their table and left the bar.

"I'm glad we didn't take a bet on it," said Stead.

"I think I'll turn in," said Futrelle. "My wife will be wondering where I am."

"Good idea," said Finch. "I'll do the same. I need to be sharp as a razor tomorrow."

Stead gave him a long look.

The next day, the fourth at sea, Colonel Hatch rose as usual at eight, blissfully unaware that it was to be his last day alive. He went for his swim, and the morning followed its invariable routine. Perkins, the steward for staterooms 10 to 14, brought him breakfast.

"Comfortable night, sir?"

"More than comfortable," said the colonel, who had spent much of it in the arms of the redheaded heiress in stateroom 27. "I almost overslept."

"Easy to do, sir," Perkins agreed, for he, too, had enjoyed an amorous night in one of the cabins on D deck. At the end of an evening of fine wine and fine food there are sometimes ladies ready for an adventure with a good-looking steward. "Shall you be attending the service this morning, or will you promenade?"

"The service? By jove, is it Sunday already?"

"Yes, sir."

"I've done more than my share of church parades. I shall promenade."

"Very good, sir."

The colonel felt better after his Turkish bath. For luncheon, he had the fillets of brill, followed by the grilled mutton chops and the apple meringue. He then retired for an hour. Perkins had thoughtfully folded back the counterpane.

The latter part of the afternoon was devoted to cards, afternoon tea and conversation. He returned to his staterooms at six to dress for dinner. His starched white shirt was arranged ready on the bed.

At ten to seven, the colonel went to dinner. The seven-course meal was the social highlight of the day. The first-class dining room seated five hundred and fifty, and there were numerous young women travelling alone, or with their parents. He was confident of another conquest.

Meanwhile, Jeremy Finch did not appear at dinner. His murder plan had reached a critical point. He was lurking behind a bulkhead in the area of the first class staterooms, aware that whilst the passengers were at dinner, the doors had to be unlocked for the stewards to tidy up and make everything ready for the night.

Finch waited for Perkins to open Colonel Hatch's staterooms. Methodical in everything, he knew what to expect. As each room was attended to, the steward left the door ajar, propped open with the bin used to collect all the rubbish.

Finch entered the cabin and stepped into the bathroom whilst Perkins was tidying the bed.

On Sunday evenings, there was no dancing after dinner. Colonel Hatch didn't let this cramp his style. He was as smooth at conversation as he was on the dance floor. He sparkled. But for once he experienced difficulty in persuading a lady to adjourn with him to the bar for champagne. The little blonde he'd targeted said the stuff gave her terrible headaches, and anyway Papa insisted she retired to her cabin by ten o'clock, and personally made sure she was there. The colonel offered to knock on her door at half-past and share a bottle of claret with her, but the offer was turned down. At half-past, she told him, she would be saying her prayers, and she always said extra on Sundays.

Hatch decided this was not to be his night. He returned to his own stateroom.

At eleven-forty that Sunday evening, Able Seaman Frederick Fleet, the lookout on the crow's nest, sounded three strokes on the bell, the signal that an object was dead ahead of the ship. It was too late. Nothing could prevent the *Titanic* from striking the iceberg in its path and having its under-belly torn open.

On C deck, high above the point of impact, there was a slight jarring sensation. Below, in steerage, it was obvious something dreadful had happened. At some time after midnight, the first lifeboats were uncovered and lowered. The confusion of the next two hours, the heart-rending scenes at the lifeboats, are well documented elsewhere. The women and children were given priority. It is on record that May Futrelle, the wife of the writer, had to be forced into one of the boats after refusing to be parted from her husband. Futrelle was heard to tell her, "It's your last chance: go!" It was then one-twenty in the morning.

Futrelle would go down with the ship, one of about fifteen hundred victims of the sinking. The precise figure was never known. W.T.Stead also perished.

Between one and two in the morning there were pockets of calm. Many expected to be rescued by other vessels that must have picked up the distress signals. In the first-class lounge, the eight musicians played ragtime numbers to keep up the spirits. Some passengers got up a game of cards. Well-bred Englishman don't panic.

Stead, Futrelle and Finch sat together with a bottle of wine.

"Whether we get out of this, or not," said Stead, "I fear it's our last evening together. If you remember, we had an agreement."

"Did we?" said Futrelle, still distracted.

"The murder plot."

"That?"

"It would do no harm to put our minds to it, as we promised we would."

"I thought of nothing worth putting on paper," said Futrelle, as if that was the end of it.

"Yes," said Stead. "It defeated me, too. My brain can't cope with the intricacies of a fictional crime. But I fancy Mr Finch may have interesting news for us."

"What makes you think so?" Finch asked without giving away a thing.

"I believe you had a plan in mind before you ever joined the ship," said Stead, "and I think you were tickled pink at the prospect of disclosing it to us and thus providing Mr Jacques Futrelle with a perfect plot. Is that correct?"

"In broad terms," Finch conceded.

"Capital. And tonight you put it to the test."

"You mean he actually killed someone?" said Futrelle in horror.

"That is my strong belief," said Stead. "Am I right, Mr Finch? Come on, the ship is sinking. We may all perish. We deserve to be told."

Finch sat back in his chair, vibrating his lips, deciding. Finally he said, "If you're so well informed, why don't you tell it?"

"As you wish. On the evening we met, you were a shade too eager to raise the topic of murder. You must have known of Futrelle's ingenious books - the stories of The Thinking Machine. You wanted your perfect murder enshrined in fine prose by a great writer."

"The theory, you mean?"

"No, sir. More than a theory. I first had my suspicions when you spoke to me of the great shock you suffered at the news of your wife's infidelity on some transatlantic crossing. A real motive for murder."

Finch shrugged.

Stead went on, "Yesterday evening in this very bar you drew our attention to Colonel Hatch in intimate conversation with a young lady. You told us precisely when they would leave together, and you were right. It was obvious you had made a study of his movements."

"True. I didn't hide it."

"His routine was central to your plan."

"Indeed."

"Tonight you didn't appear for dinner."

"How do you know? I may have come late."

Futrelle spoke. "Actually, I saw you. I was late going to dinner. I spotted you hiding in the corridor near my staterooms. It was clear you weren't bothered about missing the meal. You had something else on your mind."

"And that," added Stead, "was the murder of Mortimer Hatch, your wife's seducer. Cunningly you waited for an opportunity to gain admittance to his staterooms. The steward went in to tidy up and prepare the bed, put out the pyjamas, and so forth. You crept through the open door and hid in one of the rooms, probably the bathroom, which happens to be closest to the door. How am I doing?"

"Tolerably well."

"You waited for the Colonel to return, and as it happened, it wasn't such a long wait. He came back early, having failed to sweet-talk tonight's young lady into the bar, let alone into bed. You killed him cleanly in his own staterooms, either with a blow to the head with some heavy object, or strangulation. Opened the porthole and pushed the body through. By then it was dark, and nobody saw. You left, unseen. I raise my glass to you. Perfect revenge. A near perfect murder."

"Why do you say 'near perfect'?"

"Because we rumbled you, old man. A perfect murder goes undetected. And isn't it ironical that you chose tonight of all nights?"

"You mean it may not have been necessary?"

"We shall see."

"Is this true?" Futrelle demanded of Finch. "Did you really murder the Colonel?"

Finch smiled and spread his hands like a conjurer. "Judge for yourselves. Look who's just got up to dance."

They stared across the room. In the open space in front of the band, a couple were doing a cake-walk: Colonel Mortimer Hatch, reunited with his flame-haired partner of the previous night. Some of the women had refused to leave the ship, preferring to take their chances with the men.

Stead, piqued, gave a sharp tug at his beard and said, "I'll be jiggered!"

"Caught us, well and truly," said Futrelle.

Finch chuckled and poured himself more wine.

"What an anticlimax," said Stead.

"On the contrary," said Finch. "Do you want to hear my version? I might as well tell it now, and if either of you survives you must put it into writing because it was an undetected murder. I killed a man tonight in the Colonel's staterooms, just as you said. Strangled him and pushed his body out of the porthole. Nobody found out. Nobody would have found out."

"Who the devil was he?"

"The degenerate who seduced my wife. They're notorious, these stewards."

"A steward?"

"Perkins?" said Futrelle.

"They're in a position of trust, and they abuse it. Well, Perkins did, at any rate, aboard the *Mauritania*, and I suffered the humiliation of being told about it by an acquaintance. So I took it as a point of honour to take my revenge. I made it my business to learn where he'd signed on. Discovered he'd been hired as a first-class steward for the maiden voyage of the *Titanic*."

The two older men were stunned into silence.

Eventually, Stead said, "You've certainly surprised me. But was it perfect, this murder? Would you have got away with it? Surely, his absence would have been noted, not least by the passengers he attended."

"The method was foolproof. Of course there would be concern. The Chief Steward would be informed he was missing. It might even reach the Captain's ears. But the possibility of murder wouldn't cross their minds. Even if it did, can you imagine White Star conducting a murder inquiry in the first class accommodation on the maiden voyage of the *Titanic*? Never. They would cover it up. The passengers Perkins attended would be told he was unwell. And after we docked at New York it would be too late to investigate."

"He's right," said Futrelle. "He was always going to get away with it."

"What do you think?" asked Finch, leaning forward in anticipation. "Worthy of The Thinking Machine?"

"More a matter of low cunning than the power of logic, in my opinion," said Stead, "but it might make an interesting story. What say you, Jacques?"

But Futrelle was listening to something else. "What are they playing? Isn't that '*Nearer, My God, to Thee*'?"

"If it is," said Stead, "I doubt if your story will ever be told, Mr Finch."

At two-eighteen, the lights dimmed and went out. In two minutes the ship was gone.

Murdering Max

In 1989 I wrote the first youdunnit. A small accomplishment, you may think, not to be compared with the first manned flight or walking on the moon. To me, a humble crime writer, it brought satisfaction. For in 1983, Umberto Eco, the celebrated author of *The Name of the Rose*, had observed:

"It seems that the Parisian OULIPO group has recently constructed a matrix of all possible murder-story situations and has found that there has still to be written a book in which the murderer is the reader."

Pardon my vanity. *Youdunnit* is my claim to stand in the Pantheon with the Wright brothers and Neil Armstrong.

Do you doubt the importance of the achievement?

Am I guilty of self-aggrandisement?

Reflect on this. In the long history of the crime story, no one else had succeeded in writing a youdunnit. From Edgar Allan Poe to Umberto Eco himself, no mystery writer found a way to resolve the problem. Conan Doyle, Agatha Christie, Dorothy L.Sayers, John Dickson Carr, Hammett, Chandler, Simenon, brilliant and ingenious as they were, couldn't crack it.

I did, in 1989. I pulled it off. And for ten years I stood alone. No other writer matched me. I believed I would see out the century as the one writer to succeed in devising a youdunnit.

And I almost did.

In November, 1999, Francois Gallix, Professor at the Sorbonne, in Paris, wrote to tell me he had prepared a paper on "Twists and Turns in Crime Fiction - Peter Lovesey's *Youdunnit*." It was to be delivered at the Sorbonne before an international audience.

I turned cartwheels of joy.

After ten years my achievement was to get recognition from the academic establishment. You see, for some reason I don't understand, my story had not (till then) received its due acclaim. In fact it had passed most people by.

Now, however, my reputation would soar. My life was to be transformed. I decided forthwith to go to Paris.

Ladies and gentlemen of the French Academy, meet Peter Lovesey, trail-blazer, pioneer, writer of the first youdunnit.

Bravo!

Then I read the rest of the professor's letter and received a body blow. "There is a French author, Max Dorra, who also wrote a short story - *Vous permettez que je vous dise tué?* - in which the reader is the murderer."

Unthinkable.

To say that I was appalled is an understatement. With just a few weeks left, this man Dorra had ruined the twentieth century for me. My claim to be the only man in the century, in the millennium, to write a youdunnit, was dashed.

I hated him.

The professor's letter went on to state that Dr Dorra was invited to the lecture. In my hour of triumph, this upstart would be there to undermine me, devalue my currency, smirk behind my back. It was insufferable.

For a week, I scarcely slept. Dorra was with me day and night, deep in my psyche, irritating, immovable, the grain of sand in the oyster. I pictured him sitting in the lecture room smiling arrogantly, confident that his youdunnit was superior to mine.

Reader, you will have divined by now that I don't like competition. Once or twice I've been told I'm a monomaniac. I don't accept that at all. Why should I believe the nonsense fools say about me? But when I am attacked from behind, I fight back.

I would devise a plot even more brilliant, even more ingenious than *Youdunnit*.

First, it would be necessary to find out more about Dorra. More knowledge of the man would be painful, but necessary. I have a French friend I shall call Gerard. For the purpose of this, I must disguise his identity. Gerard once translated one of my stories (not *Youdunnit*) and took the trouble to call me about some ironies in the text. That's unusual in a translator, such care over detail. We became the best of friends.

I phoned Gerard and asked what he could tell me about my rival. He knew very little, but offered to find out, promising to be discreet in his enquiries. In the heart of Paris (Gerard informed me) there is a marvellous library known as the BILIPO (*La Bibliothèque des Littératures Policières*), a superb research facility for scholars of crime fiction. Every crime story published in France is stored there.

Gerard happened to know a Ph.D student, Delphine Kresge, who regularly used the BILIPO and was remarkably well informed about crime writers. This young lady was brilliant at ferreting out information, and could be trusted not to speak to a soul. She was ideally placed to act for us. In a couple of hours studying the cuttings library at the BILIPO, she compiled a dossier. Gerard faxed it to me. Thanks to Delphine, I was informed about Max Dorra's literary output, career, family, education, daily routine, the papers he read, the way he voted, the glasses he wore, the blend of coffee he preferred. More than enough.

Without going into detail, Dorra was a medical doctor living in Paris who wrote fiction as a second career. The staff at the BILIPO didn't know him personally. They hoped he might call in when he came to the Sorbonne for the lecture on November 27th. They were also hoping for a visit from me.

They would get one.

I travelled to France by Eurostar on November 25th and took a room in the Hotel des Grandes Ecoles in the rue du Cardinal Lemoine, the same street as the BILIPO. That afternoon I visited the place and announced who I was. My reputation as the writer of *Youdunnit* must have gone before me. The director of the library, Catherine Chauchard, came specially from her office to greet me. She and one of her colleagues, Michèle Witta, showed me round. And I discovered that my translator friend Gerard had not exaggerated in the least. Truly, the BILIPO is a house of treasures. Thousands of books, magazines and documents are kept in ideal conditions, the air maintained at fifty per cent humidity, the temperature at a constant seventeen degrees Celsius.

Happily, this location was perfect for my plan, as I realised when I was shown upstairs, where the books by foreign writers are stored. The upper floor is not usually open to the public; you reach it by elevator, operated by a secret digital code. I watched my host tapping the numbers on the panel, and memorised the sequence.

"Would you like to see your own book?" they asked.

I was taken into a room with tall metal bookshelves with winding-handles or cranks mounted on the ends, and it was explained to me that the shelves were on tracks and could be moved aside with ease by turning the handles. Michèle Witta demonstrated and three shelves slid to the left and closed against each other.

"Dangerous, if someone is between the shelves," I commented.

"Yes, we have to be careful. That's why the public aren't normally allowed up here."

"But if I wanted to study books in translation ...?"

"We would make an exception for you."

"I see. May I turn the handle?"

They allowed me to try the mechanism. The shelves moved the other way and made a metallic boom as they slid together. Anyone caught between them would have been trapped, squeezed and possibly crushed.

"And nobody except the staff comes up here?"

"Only certain people we trust."

"Such as writers?"

"And some researchers."

I was shown other things, including the strong-room containing rare and valuable items, but my thoughts were still on the sliding shelf-system.

That evening, I finalised my plans. I knew exactly what to do about Max Dorra. I went shopping in the rue Descartes, where there are some fine food shops.

The lecture on *Youdunnit* took place as scheduled in the Salle Louis Liard at the Sorbonne. It was an appropriate setting, a magnificent gilded room with an allegorical painting on the ceiling and portraits of the elite of French literature on the walls. I positioned myself to one side of the tiered seats and waited for Professor Gallix to begin. I knew he must be a man of exquisite taste, and I was pleased to find that he also spoke eloquently and in perfect English, his eyes sparkling in the light of the great chandelier above us.

"I was hoping," he said almost at once, "that Peter Lovesey would be present this morning."

I declared myself with a modest wave.

"Ah! Welcome." He smiled. "... and we also have Max Dorra with us, the writer of a second story in which the reader is the culprit."

In the centre of the room a slim man in glasses gave a nod and then swung around to stare at me, as if challenging me to do something about it.

I glared back, and then turned to listen to the lecture. I didn't give him a second glance. I didn't allow anything to spoil my enjoyment of the occasion.

It was, I have to say, a brilliant, witty and authoritative lecture touching on many obscure manipulations of the genre. The OULIPO, I learned, was a group of intellectuals dedicated to the study of crime literature and its potential manifestations. They had analysed every permutation of sleuth, victim and murderer from Edgar Allan Poe onwards. It was gratifying to have it confirmed that my story was truly original, a first of its kind. Dorra's was mentioned, but not, I felt, in the same glowing terms.

By a curious quirk of fate, Professor Gallix concluded his lecture with a speculation. "Perhaps we may look forward to a story which is yet another innovation, one in which the author himself is the murderer and the victim is another author who has written a similar story."

The hairs rose on the back of my neck. I said nothing.

At the end, I demonstrated that I was a decent Englishman and a good sportsman by crossing the room to shake hands with the man masquerading as my equal. Just as I expected, he professed not to have read my story. "Has it gone out of print?" he said offensively and in quite a carrying voice.

"You can read it in the BILIPO," I informed him. "They have it upstairs, with the other books by distinguished foreign authors."

"I shall go there at once," he announced. "Where is this place?"

I offered to show him. Together, we walked the short distance to the rue du Cardinal Lemoine. Little was said until we reached the BILIPO. We went in together.

I returned to England the same evening, quietly satisfied.

A full week passed, and I was beginning to wonder when I would hear from France. At last came a fax message from Professor Gallix:

"I am not sure if you have heard that that there is some concern here about your fellow-author, Max Dorra. He has not been seen since the day of my lecture. There are fears for his safety and the police are investigating. Some people say he left the Sorbonne in your company, and it is possible that French detectives may wish to interview you. I thought in courtesy I should let you know. Perhaps you can throw some light on the matter."

Of course I threw no light on the matter. I was interviewed next day by a British detective who said he was making inquiries on behalf of Interpol. I signed a short statement confirming that I had escorted Dorra to the BILIPO where he proposed to read my story.

I was not troubled again.

In Paris, however, strange things were happening. The staff on the upper floor at the BILIPO became conscious of an unpleasant smell invading their refined atmosphere of constant temperature and humidity. The odour seemed to come from the area of the sliding shelves where the foreign books were stored. They moved one of the shelves and noticed some fragments of glass and wire that turned out to be a pair of broken spectacles. Alarmed at what they might find behind the next shelf, they called the police.

It was necessarily a slow process. The forensic team had to recover all the bits of broken glass and test all the shelving for DNA traces and fingerprints before rolling aside the next stack to see what lay behind. They fully expected to find a corpse.

When, eventually, they had all their "evidence" and moved the stack of shelves aside, they found only a plastic bag containing an over-ripe Roquefort cheese.

"You're the victim of a hoax," the senior detective told Catherine Chauchard, the BILIPO director, as if the police themselves had not been fooled at all.

"This Dr Dorra," said another of the police team. "Is he a practical joker?"

"I couldn't tell you. We only saw him once. He's a writer."

"Was he wearing glasses?"

"Yes."

"What kind of thing does he write?"

"Crime stories."

"Devious, ingenious, tricky?"

"All of those."

"Ha." This discovery seemed to have a discouraging effect on the police. They started losing interest in Max Dorra. From that point on, they listed him as a missing person, but they scaled down the investigation into his disappearance.

Late the following year, I had a phone call from Professor Gallix:

"I thought you'd be interested in a new development in the Max Dorra disappearance."

My stomach gave a lurch, but I made sure my voice was steady. "What's happened?"

"He's still missing."

Thank God for that, I thought.

"But they published a picture of him in one of those magazines that list missing persons. When I saw it, I was thrown into confusion. The picture isn't anything like the man who came to my lecture."

"I expect they got the captions mixed."

"No. I checked with his publisher. I can only conclude that the man you and I met - the man claiming to be Dorra - was an impostor."

"How extraordinary."

"Why anyone should wish to pose as a writer and attend a rather esoteric lecture is a mystery."

"It defies explanation," I said convincingly.

"It makes me wonder if something happened to Dorra before the lecture took place."

He was getting too close to the truth for my peace of mind. "I shouldn't think so."

I didn't enlighten the professor. I didn't tell him I had arranged to meet Max Dorra the evening before the lecture, and that his body now lay deep in the Seine, weighted down with scaffolding bolts. Nor did I tell him that my translator-friend Gerard had been only too willing to play the part of Dorra. Pity the poor translators. They are starved of the attention they deserve. Gerard had savoured the admiring glances of the BILIPO staff when he arrived with the cheese and took the elevator to the upper floor and planted it there with the spectacles. Knowing the secret combination, he left without drawing attention to himself, a nonentity once more.

"I doubt if we'll ever know the truth," said the professor.

"If there were no mysteries, you and I would be out of a job," I said.

"One other thing," he added, "and quite unconnected with this. Did you give any consideration to my suggestion?"

"What was that?"

"The story in which one author kills another."

"Impossible," I said. "It will never be written."